MICHELLE DE BRUIN

Follow His Call ~
Michelle De Bruin

MANTLE ROCK
PUBLISHING LLC

Published by Mantle Rock Publishing LLC
2879 Palma Road
Benton, KY 42025
http://mantlerockpublishingllc.com

Printed in the United States of America

ISBN Print Book 978-1-945094-58-3

Ebook 978-1-845094-59-0

Cover by Diane Turpin at dianeturpindesigns.com

All scripture quoted is from the King James Version of the Bible.

To the memory of my grandparents, Elmer and Elizabeth Van Zante. Thank you for teaching me how to discover God in the every day.

ACKNOWLEDGMENTS

The creation of a book is truly a team effort, and I have wonderful people on my team that I wish to thank.

Thank you to my husband, Tom. You've supported me and been proud of me from the beginning, even before we knew my book would find a publisher. I'm grateful for your love and faithful encouragement.

Thank you to my sons, my parents and family, and to my husband's family for cheering me on. I appreciate your interest and support.

Thank you to Christian Opportunity Center and Third Reformed Church for allowing me the flexibility I needed in my schedule to get this book ready for publication. I am grateful to serve with you in doing the Lord's work. Thank you, Pastor Kevin, for your prayers as I journey through the publishing process. Your support and encouragement mean so much.

Thank you, Liz Tolsma, for all the editing work you did on my manuscript. I learned and grew so much under your guidance. I'm grateful for your willingness to go the extra mile by helping me in so many ways.

Thank you to the staff at Mantle Rock Publishing. You are all very good at what you do. Thank you for applying your expertise to my manuscript to make it better than ever. You are a blessing to me.

Thank you to the Lord for inviting me into this creative kingdom work. It is truly a pleasure to partner with Him in advancing the gospel message. This book has come about because of His miraculous power that conquers the impossible.

Praise the Lord.
Praise God in His sanctuary.
Praise Him in His mighty heavens.
Praise Him for His acts of power.
Praise Him for His surpassing greatness.
Let everything that has breath praise the Lord.
—Psalm 150:1-2, 6

CHAPTER ONE

Oswell City, Iowa
August, 1910

"The Lord bless you and keep you." A tremor shook Reverend Logan De Witt's outstretched hand as Walter Brinks entered the church.

The teenage son of the family who managed the hotel carried a white slip of paper and paced the back of the sanctuary. The Oswell City Hotel was the only place in town with a telephone. Someone in Logan's care was about to receive bad news.

He swallowed and attempted to finish the blessing. "The Lord make his face to shine upon you—" A drop of water from above splattered his sermon notes. He wrestled with the longing to move them out of harm's way, but a full sanctuary waited on him to finish the benediction. "—and be gracious to you."

A second fat drop fell, headed not for all those well-chosen words from hours of study, but for his nose. It rolled off the tip and spilled onto his Bible.

His chest tightened at the audacity of these shameless drips. A little water damage to his sermon he could deal with, but spoiling his Bible was another matter entirely. He lifted his gaze to the vaulted ceiling above just in time to watch a third drop plummet from the heights. More followed. Splat. Splat. Splat. All over the eighth chapter of Romans.

Pews creaked. Someone in the front row coughed. The time had come to wrap up the service, but Walt chose that moment to stride down the aisle and join him at the pulpit. Two more drops splashed his nose. He snatched up his Bible.

Walt nudged him. "Pastor Logan, I've got a message for ya."

Bad news had no place in the benediction.

"This is for you." Walt laid his slip of paper on the pulpit and ran out as quickly as he'd appeared.

A sour taste filled Logan's mouth, making speech even more difficult. "The Lord lift his countenance upon you . . . and . . . and give you p . . . p . . . peace." He'd come so close to getting through the service without a stutter. He fled the pulpit to read the note while everyone sang the *Doxology*.

Reverend De Witt,

A man named Vern Patterson called here. He says your mother wants you to come home as soon as possible. Your sister found your father on the floor of the barn at milking time this morning. The doctor said he suffered a heart attack. I'm sorry you have to find out about your father's death like this. Let me know if there's anything I can do.

George

A heavy weight sank in his stomach. His tall, strong father was dead. Tears gathered in the corners of his eyes while the truth pierced his heart.

A line of people eager to make weekly contact with their pastor formed. Logan stuffed the paper in his pocket and met the task of shaking hands.

The line shortened until Paul Ellenbroek, mayor of Oswell City, stood before him. "Wonderful sermon, Logan, but it looks like the rain from last night's storm felt the need to attend church today."

"Yeah, and determined to find a way in." Logan rubbed his forehead. "I didn't know the roof had any holes."

Paul studied him. "Is something wrong? Why was Walt here?"

He wished to reply, but his tongue had stiffened again. He depended on Dad for the support his prayers and encouragement brought to his ministry. Who would pray for Logan now? Whose eyes would shine with love for Logan and pride in his sense of call?

Logan's thoughts returned to the note. "My father died of a heart attack. I have to return to the farm."

"I'm sorry to hear that. You have my sympathies."

Lorraine, Paul's beautiful, dark-haired daughter, left her group of friends and joined their conversation. "Pastor Logan, you will be happy to hear that Mother intends to start coming back to church next week. Isn't that great news?"

"Yeah. Wonderful." Logan's voice went flat. He should celebrate with her, but if Mrs. Ellenbroek felt well enough to attend church again, that meant she'd no longer need Logan to call on her. And if that happened, his pattern of spending Sunday afternoon with Lorraine would end.

A question lingered in Lorraine's large brown eyes. "Aren't you happy for Mother?"

"I . . . uh . . . well." Logan's tongue stiffened. Good grief. Whenever the beautiful Lorraine Ellenbroek turned her attention on him, he couldn't force a word out to save his life. He cleared his throat. "Of course I am. You and . . . and your father must feel . . . relieved."

Lorraine's features relaxed. "Yes, we are. She wants to get out again. See her friends. Attend social functions with Father. He's had to go so many places alone. It's hard to see her ill." She grasped his hand for a short moment. "Keep praying for Mother."

"I will." Paul walked over to a group of businessmen, leaving

Logan alone with Lorraine. "You probably saw Walt come in earlier."

Lorraine nodded. A concerned expression claimed her face.

"He brought news that my father died. I must return home as soon as possible."

"I'm so sorry."

"This means our dinner date for Friday won't work out." Logan ran a hand through his hair. After gathering every last bit of his courage to ask her to dinner, now he must cancel.

"Perhaps another time." She offered him a faint smile.

He tried to return the smile, but the fear that he'd lost his chance drowned it out. His shyness around beautiful women interfered too often with his ability to secure dinner dates. In his handful of past attempts to spit out the invitation, a polite "no" had been the response. At least Lorraine had accepted. He didn't want to let such an astonishing opportunity pass him by. But now he was the one saying "no." His gaze shifted to the floor. Maybe he should give up and resign to living the single life.

Paul returned and held his timepiece out. "I found out that a train is departing in an hour. Take as much time as you need on the farm. We'll manage here."

Logan wanted to believe him, but so many things crowded the schedule. How would they ever get along without their pastor? "The men's Bible study breakfast is tomorrow morning. The pie social is Tuesday night. The banker's wife is in the hospital. And now we've got this leak in the roof."

Paul shook his hand. "I'll take care of it. Don't worry. I'll even find someone to preach for you next Sunday. You have our sympathy and our prayers."

"Plan on my return in time for Katie Wegman's wedding. She asked me months ago to perform the ceremony."

"I'll let the board know."

Reality cloaked him like the black robe he wore over his suit. He loved his life, his work, and the people in Oswell City. But he loved Silver Grove too. His mother and sister stayed on his mind. He must get home to see them. Their hearts were surely as broken as his.

Silver Grove, Iowa

AN EVENING BREEZE tousled Logan's hair as he walked the familiar road to the farm. A windmill creaked on the neighbor's land. Crickets whirred in the grass, cows lowed in the distance, but it was the ache to see Mama again that propelled him down the lane. He crossed the porch where the paint had worn away, exposing the boards. Bursting through the door, he called out. "Mama."

The lace-trimmed hanky she held to her face fell away. Her eyes grew wide as she rested her hand on her chest. "Logan." His name came out like a blend of a relieved gasp and a desperate cry as she got up from the table to embrace him. "I'm so glad you could get here today."

"I came as soon as I heard." He swallowed the thickness in his throat.

Tears spilled over her cheeks. "I've needed you."

She sagged against him and clung to him. His heart broke all over again. Footsteps sounded from the parlor. Wiping her eyes, she pulled away to set out cups and a coffeepot.

"Logan. Good to see you. My sympathies." Peter Betten, his best friend from seminary, entered the kitchen and shook his hand.

"Thanks." He should say more, but no words could describe his pain. Pete nodded and joined him at the table where they each took a coffee cup.

He'd rather talk about anything except his raw feelings, so he changed the subject to his friend's wife. "How's Anna?"

"Wonderful." Pete's mustache twitched above a smile. He pushed up his wire-rimmed spectacles and smoothed his dark red hair. His features sobered. "She helped your mother prepare the body for burial. The coffin was delivered an hour ago."

"Have you made any plans yet?" Logan choked out the words.

"Dad is laid out in the parlor," Mama whispered, wiping her eyes with a corner of her apron. "All the neighbors will be stopping in tomorrow afternoon."

Logan managed nothing more than a nod. Words lodged in his throat. Maybe later he'd thank everyone for all they'd done.

"The funeral is Tuesday morning at the church," Pete said between sips of coffee.

Mama joined the men at the table and drank her coffee in silence.

Usually he was the person with the words that brought comfort to others, and now he was the one in need of consolation. He sipped from his cup, glad that neither one of the people in the room expected an answer. He had none to give. Not this time. Logan gulped the rest of his coffee in a vain attempt to clear his throat of the emotion that clogged it. He calculated the distance to the stairway. Maybe he could escape before anyone noticed the tears ready to flow.

Pete walked by and patted his shoulder. "See you tomorrow."

Logan nodded.

Mama disappeared upstairs after Pete left. Logan went to the parlor where he ventured close to the open coffin, his gaze traveling over the still form. Dad's hands were folded over the dark blue suit and white shirt. A small cut near the hairline gave witness to a hard fall against the barn floor. The blond hair so closely resembling Logan's was combed away from the face. The mouth held a serene smile. His eyes were closed.

Those eyes would no longer shine with love. The mouth's task of smiling at him and the heart's job of beating in prayer for him were completed. Dad's life was over. Logan wiped his eyes, trying to get himself to believe it.

"Logan?" A quiet, familiar voice spoke his name.

He glanced up and scanned the parlor. "Tillie." His kid sister occupied one end of the settee, her eyes stained red.

A sob choked her. "You're home again. You're really here. I can't believe it."

He caught her in a solid hug. "I came as soon as I could."

She responded with more tears.

Logan held her tightly while they leaned on each other. After several moments, he turned towards the coffin, still embracing her. "You remember his excitement about going to Heaven someday." Dad was there now, alive in a city sparkling with the light of his Lord. "He loved us, Tillie. Very much."

"I loved him too."

Dad was gone. Dad was gone. The words pounded through his head. *Oh, Lord, I need You. It's hard to think of the future without my father in it. He should've lived much longer.*

Wiping her eyes, Tillie released him. "I'm exhausted. Good night." She headed for the stairs, leaving him alone in the darkened parlor.

He should follow her example and get some rest so he could survive tomorrow. The days ahead asked of him stamina he couldn't produce on his own. He'd welcome all the support and encouragement he could get right now, but the person he counted on to offer it was gone.

CHAPTER TWO

"*T*hanks for stopping in." Logan shook hands with his best friend as they stood in the kitchen.

"I wanted to check up on you." Pete replaced his hat on his head. "Your family has had a rough couple of days."

He pulled the door open for Pete to pass through, but someone blocked the way. Tom Hinkley stood on the porch with his fist raised to knock on the door Logan had just opened.

Logan blinked away his surprise. "Well, good afternoon, Tom. Can we help you with something?"

"I came over to remind you that the new teacher is comin' in on the afternoon train." He stepped into the kitchen.

"The teacher?" Logan studied his neighbor.

"Oh, no!" Mama covered her mouth.

"Are you all right?" Logan turned to Mama.

"Your father offered to board the teacher for this school year. The Hixsons usually provide accommodations for the teacher. But Sally's father is coming to live with them, so Tom asked us if we'd do it instead." Mama sucked in a couple deep breaths. "With everything that's happened, I completely forgot." She stepped away from Logan and grasped the back of a chair. "I find it difficult to welcome a stranger into our home so soon after John's death. It was his idea. I'm not sure I want to do it anymore."

"She'll pay ya room and board." School board chairman Tom still stood near the door with his straw hat in his hands.

"She? Who is it?" Logan asked.

"We don't know much about her except that her name is Karen Millerson. The superintendent usually sends us a young lady aged seventeen or eighteen, hardly through high school."

Logan chewed his lip as he considered Tom's description.

"You've got the room, don't ya?"

They had the spare bedroom at the top of the stairs. It was kind of small and used whenever Mama's relatives from Bridgewater Springs paid them visits, but they could give it up to a permanent occupant if necessary.

"Ya gotta understand that country school teachers don't make a whole lot, but she'd at least pay ya enough to buy the groceries."

Maybe the extra income would buy the supplies to paint the porch floor, or a new pane of glass for the horse barn, or wire to repair the fence. Logan turned to Mama. "What do you think?"

A sigh whispered across Mama's lips. "I guess we should do it."

"How about you, Tillie?" Logan studied her.

She shook her head. "I don't want to. It's a bad idea. We don't need anyone else around. Just you."

Logan's heart twitched. What would happen to Tillie after he left for Oswell City? She needed a friend. A young lady Tillie's age would make the perfect companion in his absence. Tom's request took root in his mind. "Let's do it."

Tillie sent him a look that said he'd slapped her across the face.

"Look, Tillie. She'll be gone to school during the day and busy checking papers or planning lessons in the evenings. You'll hardly notice another person in the house at all. But give yourself time to adjust. You might find her to be a good friend. Before you know it, the two of you will be spending all your Saturdays and Sundays together."

He turned to Tom and shook his hand. "We'll give her the spare bedroom upstairs."

"I knew I could count on you." A broad smile claimed Tom's face but soon disappeared. He cleared his throat. "Logan, you need to look out for the teacher just like you would any other member of the family. She'll need your help. Take her places. Assist her at school until she can find her way around and anything else you see she might need. Are you comfortable with this arrangement?"

"Yes." By the end of the week, he'd have the teacher settled and comfortable, giving him plenty of time to return to Oswell City.

"All right. Glad we got that covered." Tom wiped his brow. "School was scheduled to start tomorrow, but I've decided to push it back one more day to give you folks a chance to adjust."

"Sandy, why don't you and Tillie come with me to the church? If I remember correctly, there's a picnic tonight so that all the families of students who attend the Silver Grove School can meet the new teacher." Pete extended his hand to Mama. "I sure could use your help with the preparation."

Mama moved to the cupboard where she pulled out a basket and began filling it with utensils. "Tillie, get that apple pie you baked last night."

Tom replaced his hat on his head. "The teacher should be in town by now. I'll go pick her up and bring her out here for ya."

"Thanks. I appreciate it." Spared a trip to town, Logan could use the saved time to get a head start on the milking.

"Can I count on you to bring the new teacher to the picnic?" Tom asked Logan.

"Definitely."

Standing at the window in the vacated kitchen, watching everyone depart, Logan might as well have been the lucky survivor of a cyclone. But the feeling didn't last long. Tom and their new occupant would arrive before he completed the evening milking. He'd better get to the barn and work as fast as possible if he planned to get to a picnic tonight.

Karen Millerson leaned forward for another look out the coach's window. This trip had taken hours. Surely she hadn't missed her stop when she dozed earlier that afternoon.

Cornfields blocked the horizon. She slumped back against her seat. It was the same monotonous landscape. Nothing about this trip had changed since the rickety bridge spanning the Mississippi.

She reached into her satchel to retrieve the letter with information about her new position. She unfolded it and read:

Dear Miss Millerson:

I am happy to inform you of your position with the Bridgewater Springs Community High School as teacher of English and reading. Classes begin August 16, so please make plans to travel by train as far as Silver Grove.

Karen wanted to jump up and show the letter to everyone in the surrounding seats. Teacher of English and reading in a high school. Reading. Her specialty. She unfolded the second letter that had arrived in the mail just last week. Scanning past the congratulations written in the first paragraph, she read the next one.

You will reside with Mr. and Mrs. De Witt for the upcoming school year. They will meet you at the station and provide you with a ride to Bridgewater Springs.

Mr. and Mrs. De Witt. They sounded like a sedate, middle-aged couple who would remind her of Uncle Henry and Aunt Fran back in Chicago. Living with a couple like that would ease the homesickness threatening to settle in. Maybe they possessed a large, comfortable home of the kind to which she was accustomed, or at least one with a water closet and electricity. She might adjust to her role as a teacher in a small Midwestern town much easier than she first thought.

"Next stop, Silver Grove."

The words jarred Karen. She jerked upright to find a blue-suited conductor passing her. He wandered the narrow aisle of the coach and repeated the announcement.

Karen reached for the spotless white gloves on the seat next to her. She slipped them over her hands, thankful her sister Julia allowed her to borrow them. The hat she wore belonged to Mother. The dark green made a perfect match to her traveling suit. Karen reached to check the pin holding the hat in place. Parting with Julia and Mother hurt less thanks to these accessories from their own spacious closets.

A quick smoothing of the twisted hair below the hat brim assured her no wisps of hair had escaped during her nap. Karen smoothed her skirt to rid it of any wrinkles. A first-time appearance in a new town with wrinkled clothing and loose strands of hair would never do.

Grinding iron wheels announced her arrival in Silver Grove. Karen turned her attention to the scene beyond the window. The whole length of the main street and the crude little buildings lining it fit into the one pane of window glass.

She hardly knew how people survived life in primitive places like this. Maybe the day was coming when they would have running water. Bridgewater Springs would offer much more refinement. Karen expected nothing less from a town boasting a brand new high school.

The door to the coach opened. Karen crept down the aisle behind other travelers and stepped onto the platform of the Silver Grove depot.

She scanned the crowd for anyone matching her image of Mr. and Mrs. De Witt.

Two businessmen and one older lady emerged from the coach and scurried away. Down the platform, a cluster of family members embraced. A group of men in cowboy hats shook hands with a balding man in coat and tie. She turned in the other direction. The platform emptied as people scattered to find bags and trunks.

"You Miss Karen Millerson?" A voice with a relaxed drawl asked from behind.

Karen turned around to find a large-framed man in bib overalls. "Yes. Yes, I am." She frowned. "Surely you aren't—"

"Logan De Witt?" The man slapped his knee and chuckled. "Shucks, no. Logan's waitin' for ya at home." He held out his right hand. "I'm Tom Hinkley. School board chairman here in Silver Grove. Right pleased to meet ya, ma'am."

Karen shook his offered hand.

"Come this way. I'll get your things loaded up in my wagon. Then I'll drive ya on out to the De Witt place." Mr. Hinkley strode towards the station.

Karen commanded her stiff legs to follow him.

Mr. Hinkley loaded her hatboxes, two trunks of clothes, and three crates of books into a high wagon. He assisted her climb over the steel wheel and waited until she was settled on the wooden seat.

"Ready?" he called up to her, shielding his eyes from the sun.

"Yes." Karen straightened her skirt and steadied her hat. Checking her gloves for dirt, she smiled to find them still clean.

Mr. Hinkley climbed into the wagon. He took up the reins and started the horses down the street.

"How far must we travel to reach Bridgewater Springs?" Glad to finally be able to see above the cornfields, Karen scanned the horizon. No buildings indicated the location of another town. Only the silhouettes of silos, hip roof barns, and a few windmills broke up the landscape.

"We ain't goin' to Bridgewater Springs."

"What do you mean?" Karen's middle stretched tight.

"Didn't anyone tell ya?" He turned to her. Crows' feet etched deep lines in the sun-browned skin around his eyes.

"I received a letter that said I am to teach English and reading at the Bridgewater Springs High School."

Mr. Hinkley shook his head and clicked his tongue. "Oh, the sad communication in our school systems these days." Slapping a horse with the reins, he cleared his throat. "The school in Bridgewater Springs combined subjects. The community got worried about how many students might actually decide to go on to high school. They wanna hold off before hiring too many teachers. Don't wanna get too carried away with offering a lot of subjects if no one comes to school to take 'em. You know how that goes." He transferred both reins to one hand, reached in his front pocket, pulled out a toothpick, and stuck it in a corner of his mouth.

The toothpick wagged a bit before he continued speaking. "At the last minute, the superintendent told me that the girl who taught our school last year got engaged over the summer. So, since you were a teacher without a school, and we were a school without a teacher, he made the decision to send ya here." He chewed on the toothpick for a moment before looking over at her once again. "Sorry ya have to find out this way. I thought maybe someone already told ya."

"You mean to tell me, to tell me that I . . ." She gave up in a sigh that collapsed all the air from her lungs.

"Now I know we ain't the most educated folks you'll run across, but our kids deserve a chance. Just like any in the big city."

"But I . . . I still need to . . . to . . ." Karen groaned about the sputtering that betrayed her chaotic mind. She drew in a deep breath and tried again. "I traveled all this way to begin my career."

"Well, now, I think we can work somethin' out." Mr. Hinkley drove on a road that crested a small hill and dipped to a stone bridge spanning a brook.

"You're overqualified by a long shot for our small country school. I sure don't want to hold ya to a place that can't utilize all your skills. How about if you stay for a couple of weeks, long enough to help us get the school year started. That will buy me some time to try and find a teacher better suited to our school and a position more appropriate for you. Fair?"

Her cheeks heated at the sound of his gracious words. Those overalls concealed a big heart. "Yes. Quite fair. Thank you. I'm honored to teach in your school, Mr. Hinkley. Honestly." Karen's heart twitched. These people might not have any modern conveniences to make life easier, but they had families. Families made up of children who deserved an education.

Mr. Hinkley guided the horses up a slope and into a long lane. After the wagon rolled to a halt, he came around to her side and assisted her to the ground. She followed him through a gate in the picket fence, up the steps, across the porch and into a kitchen. The pump with its skinny handle and the large metal basin at the sink told Karen this household had never known the concept of running water.

"I'll start bringin' in your trunks and crates." He turned and left the house.

Karen shifted her weight from one foot to the other. Mr. and Mrs. De Witt must not mind the intrusion if they left the house empty and accessible to whomever may stop in at any given moment.

Mr. Hinkley entered with one of her trunks. He lugged it into the kitchen and shoved it against the wall.

"Let me help you. I can at least carry the hatboxes."

She joined him on the way to his wagon. They worked together until all of her belongings were stacked in the kitchen.

Mr. Hinkley pulled a red bandana from his pocket and wiped his brow. "The De Witts are givin' ya their spare bedroom. Up the stairs, first door on the right."

Karen stored the information away, ready to claim the new room and start unpacking.

"Oh, and one more thing. There's a picnic at the church tonight so that our local families can meet you. It starts at six. Logan's plannin' on bringin' ya." He reached to shake her hand. "Welcome to Silver Grove, Miss Millerson. See ya at the picnic." He turned and strode out of the house.

Karen allowed her gaze to wander about the room, curious where the residents of this home were hiding. Spotting no one, she opened a trunk and retrieved a lighter weight skirt and blouse. Then she took the stairs to prepare for the evening ahead.

CHAPTER THREE

*S*ix chimes from a grandfather clock rang through the empty house. Karen stole yet another glimpse out of the kitchen windows looking for her ride. No one else occupied the premises. The picnic had started without her. She wrinkled her nose. Tardiness would never do. She must try to get to the picnic on her own. Mr. Hinkley had driven past a small church on the way to her new home. That must be the location of the evening's gathering. Retrieving her hat from the table, she secured it with a pin and reached for the doorknob.

Another door slammed. Karen spun around and studied the opposite end of the kitchen that led to a small covered porch. Two heavy objects clumped onto the floor. A male voice hummed the melody to *Now the Day is Over,* one of Karen's favorite hymns. A young man in a white undershirt, bib overalls, and stocking feet came into view on his sprint to the washstand. The day's growth of whiskers glistened along his jaw line. A blond wave of hair fell over one eye giving him a boyish, mischievous charm.

Through the drying off, he continued to hum like spending a hot afternoon on a smelly farm was the most fun he'd ever had. He returned the towel to a slim wooden bar of the wash stand and then whisked across the room to the stove. A large metal basin rested against the side. He picked it up and ladled water into it from a copper boiler.

Karen released the breath she'd been holding.

The humming cut off mid-phrase, and his motions froze. Water splashed over the side of the long-handled dipper from the sudden halt. Surprise flickered in the bluest, sincerest eyes she'd ever seen. Little butterflies tickled the insides of her stomach as he approached.

"You must be Miss Millerson," he said, offering to shake her hand.

She nodded.

"Welcome to Silver Grove, and to the De Witt farm." He flashed a smile that rivaled the sun for warmth and radiance. "I'm Logan De Witt."

"Pleased to meet you, Mr. De Witt." Karen shook his hand.

"Just call me Logan. No need to be so formal." He grinned and turned away. "You'll meet the rest of my family at the picnic." He finished filling the metal basin. "Sorry I'm running late. After a quick bath and a shave, I'll be ready in twenty minutes." He disappeared up the stairs.

Karen's gaze took in the kitchen as well as the part of the dining room visible through the doorway. A family meant high chairs and toys scattered about. But no evidence of children met her curiosity.

Mr. De Witt was young. Mrs. De Witt probably was too. Perhaps they were newlyweds and no children had yet joined the family. He might as well be married. She wasn't looking for a man anyway. She had a school to teach. Even if she did wish to marry, the only man that had the slightest chance of securing her attention would be someone who would replace the trust she'd lost in her reverend father.

This sort of man would naturally live up to her family's expectations for her. In Uncle Henry's eyes, anyone was better for

Margaret's girls than a preacher. Julia had chosen to marry a lawyer. A professor would do very well for Karen. Oh, yes. Someone who shared her love for history, religion, or some other lofty topic.

But this tiny, out of the way place, was a long way from any of those dreams. Even if she found him, he still might die like Father did, leaving her to support herself. Karen was better off pursuing a career in the first place. If she followed that course for her life, she wouldn't need to depend on anyone to support her. Mother had lost her husband at a young age. Uncle Henry had offered her a place to live, but Karen didn't want to take the risk. She'd do everything in her power to make sure the heartache Mother endured during Father's lifetime and the grief after his death never happened to her.

She claimed a chair at the table to wait for the ride. A picnic would be fun. So would be meeting the other members of the De Witt family, whomever it might include. She did her best through more chimes from the grandfather clock to contain her excitement.

"MAY I HELP YOU?"

Karen stood beside Logan, who was ready to assist her climb into the black buggy's seat. The late afternoon sunlight filtered through the large oak leaves overhead, speckling everything beneath with dappled shade.

"Thank you." Karen held his hand and climbed into the buggy.

Logan strolled to the other side and claimed the narrow space of seat next to her. He took up the reins. "Did you find room for everything?"

"I haven't started unpacking yet. Mr. Hinkley brought me to your farm with just enough time to prepare for this evening." She tucked her skirt in to protect it from the dust.

"I'll carry your trunks upstairs when we come home." Logan kept his gaze on the road.

"I would appreciate that very much."

Silence grew between them while they traveled. Grasshoppers whirred in the tall grasses at the side of the road. Yellow butterflies chased invisible fragrances in and out of the bouquet of golden black-eyed-Susans, blue cornflowers, and Queen Anne's lace. The wind rose and fell in warm puffs, bringing the scent of the flowers to Karen's nostrils. She inhaled and scanned the open fields of lush corn stretching away to the far horizon. Although tiny and insignificant, Silver Grove was a beautiful place. She might get used to living here.

"Oh, no." Logan groaned. "Cows are out." He pointed to the road ahead where cattle munched on roadside grass. Some of them raised their heads and gazed at the horse and buggy as though Karen and Logan were the intruders. "The road is the worst place for Vern's herd to look for supper."

Karen scanned the fence line. A large section of boards was broken and jabbed into the ground, allowing easy passage for curious and discontented cows.

"With everyone at the picnic, we're the only ones to herd them back to pasture. Vern's been so helpful this past week, I'd sure like to return the favor." His brow furrowed when he glanced at her. "Will you help me?"

Her lace blouse, blue skirt, and white leather heels were hardly cowgirl attire. "I don't know a thing about cattle." Placing herself within arm's reach of a cow was a risk any sensible woman avoided.

"I'll give you an easy job."

Nothing could possibly be easy about convincing large beasts that the grass they'd deserted was just as tasty as any along the road.

Logan guided the horse near the broken fence, jumped out of the buggy, and tied the reins to one of the few remaining posts. He turned and waited to help her to the ground. "If you could stand on the road so they can't go any farther, I'll herd them through the gap in the fence."

Remaining seated in the buggy was the most prudent course of action. Did Logan really need her? Those old cows weren't in any hurry. Couldn't he tell Vern and let the farmer take care of his own problems?

"Please? We're running out of time."

The rumbling in her stomach prompted her. "Oh. All right." She removed her sister's gloves, heaved her frame off the seat, and allowed Logan to help her over the wheel.

Logan handed her a long stick he retrieved from the leftovers of the broken boards. "Use this to make them turn around." He swung the stick in a wide arc. "Stand here until I return."

Karen swallowed, the impatient words pressing against her tongue. Of course she'd stand here. The sooner she could return to the buggy, the quicker she'd recover safety. Besides, she was no match for those bloated, staring monsters Logan felt the need to coerce.

With practiced ease, Logan swung his arms and yelled out some choppy syllables that sounded as if they were borrowed from another language. He nodded at her as a cue that she should wave the stick.

She did, but with far less zest than he showed.

The herd lost interest in eating and turned to watch the commotion. Somehow, he got them all turned in the same direction and headed through the broken fence. Throwing one last encouraging grin over his shoulder, he disappeared down the hill.

Karen stood in the road, swatting insects and watching for oncoming wagons or buggies. A stranger visiting from another country would feel more at home here than she did at this moment. Life as she knew it no longer existed. She'd traded Uncle Henry's large Chicago home for a dusty country road, a farmer with no sense of punctuality, and stray cattle. Maybe she should still attempt to walk to this picnic. The dusty road stretched to the horizon. She'd better stay put. Logan might worry if he returned and found her missing. Moaning under her breath, she dropped the stick and wandered to the side of the road to pick flowers.

A bouquet had begun to take shape when warm breath blew over her backside. A rumbling bellow filled the air.

Karen whipped around. She stood face to face with the largest beast she'd ever seen.

Resembling a buffalo, the beast possessed horns that curled away from its ears. Rust tinted fur covered the top and sides of its hide. Meaty legs ended in rock-solid hooves. One pawed the ground.

Her stick lay out of reach, not that it offered much protection against this wooly mammoth. The buggy, on the opposite side of the road, stood too far away to provide any shelter. Karen's heart rate accelerated with an uncontrollable speed.

She screamed. "Logaaaaaaaaaan!"

The beast bellowed again and lumbered forward, head low to the ground. Long horns boasting dangerous pointed ends were aimed straight at her.

Breaking into a run, she descended the hill. The beast followed. Her chest burned, causing her to take in short gasps.

An animal weighing at least a ton should not be able to move so quickly.

At the foot of the hill, a stream appeared, escape awaiting on the other side. She strained forward but failed to move any faster. She tumbled head over heels, landing in cold, slimy mud. The ground rumbled with pounding hooves. That beast would soon reach her. She tried to scream, but her lungs held no more air. After one last feeble try, the world went black.

"KAREN." Someone shook her shoulder. "Karen, are you hurt?"

She didn't know. Her tangled arms and legs might as well have belonged to a rag doll. Her eyes fluttered open to find Logan's worried face hovering above her own.

"Logan." His name came out as a groan.

"I'm right here."

"This . . . huge cow . . ." Her voice trembled. She gave her head a brief shake to clear it. "A huge cow chased me."

"Vern's bull."

"I don't know where he came from."

The lines creased deeper on Logan's brow. "I'm so sorry for leaving you alone on the road. I never would have done it if I'd known the danger."

His voice led her to believe he was remorseful. "You did nothing wrong."

"He charged you."

"Yes. I got scared so I ran but fell in the mud."

"I saw it happen."

"You did?"

"I heard your scream but got slowed down crossing the creek. I reached you just as you went down."

For a moment, she gazed at the tree branches far overhead. A thicket of underbrush surrounded her. "How did I get here?"

"I picked you up and moved you so the bull couldn't find you." His features relaxed.

Dirt smudges all over the front of his white dress shirt caught her attention. Brushing at them, she assessed the damage. "Sorry about your shirt. I hope Mrs. De Witt can find a way to remove the stain."

He watched her movements but offered no reply.

"Where's the bull now?"

Logan glanced over his shoulder in the direction of the creek. "He probably found the rest of the herd. You won't have any more trouble."

"We missed the picnic."

23

"Yes. I made us late and with this delay the meal will be finished by now." He glanced at the mud on her blouse. "Are you hurt?"

"No. Just filthy." She touched the top of her head and found it uncovered. "I lost my hat."

"You weren't wearing it when I picked you up. Maybe it blew off while you ran."

"Could we look for it on the way up the hill?"

"Sure. Can you stand?" He pushed to his feet.

"I'll try."

"Let me help you." He took her by one hand and assisted her to a seated position.

Karen got her first look at her skirt. More brown than blue, it clung to her legs in a sopping wet mess. She gasped at the sight of her stockings and shoes. Brown and dripping with muck. Ruined. Her eyes filled with tears. She'd much rather deal with tardiness than dirt and filth. Julia's white gloves remained in the buggy. At least they were spared this initiation into country life.

Swiping at the tears on her cheek only smeared mud from her hand across her face. She sniffed and wiggled her right foot. Her sodden skirt blocked all movement. Still, she must try to stand.

As soon as she pushed to her feet, a sharp pain shot through her left ankle. She plopped back into the mud with a little cry. "I guess I'm hurt after all."

"Your ankle?" Logan asked.

She nodded.

He lifted her and cradled her close against his broad chest.

"No. Please." Karen pressed her hand to his shirt adding to the smudges. "I can walk."

"It's a long way to the top."

The hill's horizon sloped away from the distant road. He was right. She slumped in surrender to the truth.

The uphill climb with her weight in his arms cost him no slow pace or labored breathing. When they arrived at the road, he transferred her to the buggy seat. "I'll make a quick search of the ditch for your hat." He crossed the road and wandered around for a few minutes. "Didn't see it," he called on his way to untie the reins.

Logan turned the buggy in the direction of his farm and put the horses into a quick trot. After settling the team in the barn, he came to her side of the buggy where he assisted her descent, not to the ground, but into his arms.

Karen failed to consider how she'd get into the house. She wanted to push him away again, but the weight of her skirt and the pain up her leg made walking impossible. "I'm afraid I'll make a terrible mess of your house."

"Don't worry about it." Logan's chin bumped the top of her head as he crossed the lawn. "I'm more concerned about your injury." He pulled the door open one-handed and deposited her on the love seat in the parlor.

Karen held her breath. The stylish parlor furniture shouldn't have to sustain this sort of abuse.

"Which ankle did you sprain?"

"The left one."

"Anything else hurt?" His scrutiny shifted from her muddy shoes to her lace-covered arms.

"No. I'm more in need of a change of clothes than medical attention." Her unpacked trunks reposed in the kitchen, full of clean garments. If she could just get to them.

He puffed out his cheeks. "Not much I can do about that. But I can at least wash your face. I'll be right back." A moment later, he returned with the wash basin, a stack of towels, and a tin case with a medical cross symbol on it.

He bent to his knees and dipped one of the cloths in the water of the basin.

If she could only go back and change the recent events, none of this would've happened. Her stomach twisted. "I'll do it." She reached for the cloth, but Logan pulled it back.

"You've got some sand on your forehead that might get in your eyes. Since you can't get to the mirror, maybe you'd better let me do it." He pointed to the ornate-framed mirror on the opposite wall.

Her ankle would never get that far against the resistance of her mud-soaked skirts. She gave a silent nod as yet another surrender of her so-called venture into independence.

After cleaning her face, Logan stood and lifted the basin, splashing water onto the rolled-up sleeves of his shirt. "Maybe you'd like to tend to your ankle while I fix supper." With the toe of his shoe, he pushed the tin closer before leaving the room.

The clink of a metal spoon in a cooking pot and the thump of jars on a wooden counter stirred her hunger. She didn't know what to do about her muddy skirt. She really should take it off, but the process would leave a larger mess in the parlor than if she left it on. Plus, she had no privacy. Taking the steps in the heavy mass was out of the question. Karen shifted her position until she could reach her soggy shoe to pull it off her foot.

When she had her foot bandaged, the result didn't look the smoothest, but it would at least help with the swelling.

Logan returned, delicious aromas of garlic and onion preceding him. He set a tray down on a small table nearby and pulled a footstool up to the side of the sofa, using it as a seat. "Stew made with vegetables from the garden." He handed her a bowl filled with a brown broth.

She took a bite. "Wonderful."

"Mama baked bread this morning, so I cut us a couple of slices. Please, help yourself." He reached for small white cubes on the corner of the tray. "Here's some ice if you think it might help your ankle."

"Thank you." Karen took the ice and settled it on her bandage. Even if the coolness of the ice failed to change the swelling, it would still offer relief from the hot summer evening.

The kitchen door creaked open and pounded shut. "Logan, are you here?" An older woman's voice echoed through the house.

"In the parlor," he called back around a bite of bread.

"Why weren't you at the picnic?" A woman in a floral dress bustled into the parlor. "We waited and waited, but the children needed fed, so we started without you." She gazed at Karen.

Logan stood. "Mama, please meet the new teacher, Miss Karen Millerson."

Karen's cheeks heated. She'd much prefer an introduction wearing her traveling suit instead of a bandage or at least standing up instead of smearing mud all over this lady's furniture.

"Nice to meet you, Miss Millerson." She smiled. "It looks like you had a bit of an accident."

"Yes. I sprained my ankle helping Logan."

She turned to her son, a question present in her eyes.

"Cows were out, so we herded them back to pasture." Logan looked down at her. "I mean, I herded them and Karen . . . well, she guarded the road."

Karen sent him a grateful smile for sparing the details of her undignified sprawl into the mud.

He rewarded it with a wink.

Any more of those and she'd forget all about teaching.

"I see." The woman rubbed her chin while she glanced between her son and Karen.

A dark-haired young lady entered the room.

"Karen, please meet my sister, Matilda. We all call her Tillie." He gestured to her and then at his mother. "And of course, you've already met my mother, Cassandra, known to friends and family as Sandy."

Tillie smiled with her lips, but her eyes remained untouched.

"Welcome to Silver Grove, Karen. We're pleased to have you." Sandy squeezed her shoulder.

The gesture warmed her with its mother-like touch. Tears blurred Karen's vision.

Sandy turned her attention to Logan. "We wondered if you had trouble of some sort. Pete thought something might have come up during the milking, but when you never arrived, we guessed it was more serious. He sent Wade Patterson to look for you, but he came back without any news."

"We were probably at the farm and just missed him." Logan gulped some water from his cup.

Sandy blew out a breath which teased a strand of gray hair that had worked loose from the full bun on the back of her head. "I'm glad you're both unharmed. Well, mostly."

"So am I." Logan nodded.

"I need to help Tillie put things away. May I get you some bath water, Karen?" Sandy gestured toward the kitchen.

"Yes, thank you." She'd rather run from the room. The doting, middle-aged couple with a large home in town didn't exist. Karen would live on a farm with a mother, her daughter, and her handsome and quite unattached son.

Logan De Witt didn't match her perceptions of an ordinary farmer, the country bumpkin type with terrible grammar and horrific manners. He possessed education and intelligence along with a finesse that undermined his bib overalls and work-calloused hands. And that voice. Her insides turned as soft as caramel candy when he spoke her name. So smooth and warm.

She could care for him quite easily. He was the sort of man she could fall for. Kind. Thoughtful. Not to mention all his charm and ease with words. Already, she knew the safety found in his arms and the tenderness of his touch.

She shook her head to clear it. Thinking of what to tell Mother in a letter was a much safer train of thought. She must write all about her travels, the change in her location, and the news of her new position. But the truth of how small her room really was or her injured ankle would only cause worry. Neither would she mention the facts about Logan's single status or the fall covering her in mud that landed her in his arms in the first place. Karen groaned under her breath. Her first day in a new town should not be ending in this way.

CHAPTER FOUR

*L*ogan crouched on the milking stool with the top of his head pressed into the side of a Holstein, his gut wrapped in a tight knot. Squeezing his eyes shut, he failed to block from his mind the sight of Karen crumpled in the creek, her scream replaying through his memory. What may have happened to her if that horned bull had reached her before he did?

The fact that the bull had left Karen in peace didn't stop the flood of regret that followed. Boy, he'd done a few dumb things in his life, but leaving a seventeen-year-old city girl alone on a country road topped the list. None of their troubles would've happened if his common sense had kicked in.

Mama stood at the sink washing dishes when he entered the house. "Your shirt is in the dining room, dear." She pointed to the table visible through the doorway.

He picked up the garment and held it out in front of him. Once the spotless companion to his suit, his shirt was now tinted a new shade of off-white dinge. Mama had washed it for him, but the poor thing was forever stained. Tan splotches marked the areas where Karen had smeared mud all over him. He tucked the shirt under an arm. When he returned to Oswell City, he'd have to go shopping. At least here in Silver Grove he could hide in the crowd instead of standing up front with a roomful of people focused on him. His suit coat should provide adequate cover. Not even the splotches around the button placket would show if he kept his coat buttoned.

A paper lying on the table caught his attention. "What's this?"

Mama approached and looked over his shoulder. "An application form Tom brought on Thursday when he stopped in to tell us the first day of school was changed to Monday. Karen has been working on it while her ankle heals. She plans to give it to him at church today." Mama returned to the kitchen and her sink of dishes.

Logan picked up the application and studied it. Karen's name and his address were written in the appropriate spaces along with her date of birth. June 15, 1885. His mouth fell open. 1885? Why, that meant she was twenty-five. Only three years younger than he was. Two-and-a-half to be exact. He peered at the paper again. His eyes were playing tricks on him. He was boarding a girl Tillie's age, not a young woman in her mid-twenties. Wasn't he?

Written in plain sight in Karen's own handwriting was her birthday. No mistake about that. His boarder wasn't a kid-sister type in need of a guardian. Rather, she was a woman in need of what? The question dominated his mind as he climbed the stairs to his room.

A place to live. Of course. He was providing her with a place to live. That was easy. Plus, he made some money as a result. He removed his bibs, tugged on his black trousers, and slipped his arms into the sleeves of his Sunday shirt.

His strength. The thought blew through his mind like a summer breeze. His fingers paused in fastening the buttons. Karen had needed his strength. She'd been as limp and fragile in his arms as a wilted flower. Carrying her was effortless. Her head had leaned on his shoulder in full trust he would keep her safe. Strength and safety. Yes, he could offer those.

Logan returned to the kitchen for a quick breakfast of scrambled eggs and toast. Mama, also dressed for church, joined him at the table.

Tillie's empty chair drew his attention. "Did she already eat?"

"I haven't seen her yet."

After a gulp of coffee, Logan left his seat and took the stairs. "Tillie?" He knocked on her bedroom door.

Silence answered him.

A brief conference with Mama turned up no further information on Tillie's whereabouts, so Logan left the house. When they were kids, a certain small pool under an oak in the pasture made the perfect getaway to think over childhood sorrows. On this first Sunday morning without Dad, she would be there.

The wide stump of an old tree still occupied the creek bank. Seated on it was Tillie, a family portrait in her grasp. He lowered himself into the grass at her side and studied the picture. Logan, sixteen, stood behind his parents with his hand on Mama's shoulder. Five-year-old Tillie sat on Dad's lap.

"It's time for church," Tillie said.

"Mama's waiting."

"I can't go without him, Logan. I just can't. Not today. Not ever." Tears streamed down her face.

"It gets easier."

"Don't you miss him?"

"Of course. I think about Dad all the time."

"When will I ever stop thinking about him?"

"Maybe never. Memories of Dad will keep him alive in your thoughts and in your heart."

"I'm thankful to have memories, but they hurt so much."

"The pain goes away as time passes. Your memories will turn sweet and strengthen instead of hurt you." He'd watched it happen many times with his Oswell City parishioners.

"How could God just take him away from me like that?" She jerked free from his caress.

31

"Tell me what happened." Logan offered her his white hand-kerchief.

"We were working together in the barn. I carried a pail of milk to the house. I was gone only a few minutes. I returned to the barn to tell him breakfast was ready, but by the time I got there. . ." A sob caught in her throat.

"He was gone."

"I didn't have time to tell him I loved him." She leaned against Logan's shoulder. "How can I face all the neighbors asking how I'm doing? Their sympathetic looks and pats on my arm. Like any of it will bring him back. He's gone, Logan. Gone. I can't sing or pray or listen to Pete. It hurts too much. God's so unfair." Sobs overtook her. She clutched the portrait against her breast.

Pain swelled in Logan's heart. He'd wrestled with the same thoughts. Could he still sing or praise or believe?

He was doing his best. Dad's sudden death might be a mystery to all of them, but Logan hung on to the promise of who God said He was, a loving and faithful heavenly father.

The grass rustled behind him, and the morning breeze carried the faint scent of lilac cologne. Mama had found them.

"What's wrong?" Mama grasped the tree trunk.

"How can you even think of going to church?" Tillie swiveled and threw an accusing glance at Mama.

"My friends are there. They'll help me through this time. So will the comfort I find in the songs and the preaching." Mama gazed at her daughter. "It won't be the same without your father. I miss him every minute. But we have to remember that Dad is in Heaven. He's free, and he's perfect. I wouldn't want to change that." Tears glistened in Mama's eyes. "Are you ready to come to the house and prepare for church?"

Tillie shook her head and stared at the still waters of the little pool. "I'm not going. Especially since today is his birthday." Tillie wiped her eyes and turned to Mama again. "Don't you even care?"

"Of course I care." Mama squeezed Tillie's shoulder while

tears dampened her own cheeks. "But Dad would want us to go anyway. It might help us feel closer to him." She pressed Logan's arm. "And closer to each other."

He prayed that Mama's words would come to pass.

"The reception for Karen was moved to today, so I would like to be there, but I don't want to leave you home alone." Mama's gaze rested on the top of Tillie's head where morning sunlight glistened on her dark hair.

"I'll be fine." Tillie wiped a sleeve across her face.

"We'll be home by dinner." Logan reached for Mama's arm. "If we're going, then we need to leave. Church will start soon."

Mama nodded and allowed Logan to guide her to the house.

A vision of elegance and sophistication obstructed his thoughts when he and Mama entered the kitchen. Her dress was the color of the June sweet peas that bloomed in Mama's garden. Golden curls of hair framed her face under a wide hat with a cluster of flowers on the brim the same color as the dress. Her other outfits had looked nice on her too, but they didn't hug her waist or show off her fair skin above a scooped neckline. Logan's heart pounded.

"You look lovely, Karen." Mama's eyes shined.

Logan wanted to agree, but the words caught in his throat. All he could manage was a nod.

"Glad to see that your ankle is better." Mama reached for the black gloves lying on the table.

"A complete recovery." Karen slid her foot in a dainty slipper away from the hem of her skirt. Her trim ankle emerged.

This young woman was no kid sister.

Mama went out the door. With all his might, Logan tried to move a leg to follow, but he remained stuck as though sturdy bolts fastened his feet to the floor.

Karen crossed the room ahead of him.

"Wait." A gentleman didn't stand around like a statue while a woman looked out for herself. The thought put enough starch in his stride to carry him to the door. "Allow me." He held the door open so Karen could pass through.

"Ready, Mama?" In the lane, Logan stood ready to assist her climb into the buggy.

"Help Karen first, dear. She's our guest."

"But, Sandy, you should go first."

Mama shook her head. "Today, you get to receive our best hospitality." She raised her brows at Logan as a prompt to heed her commands.

That was the gentlemanly thing to do, to look out for the guest. But if Karen got in the buggy first, that meant she would sit in the middle. And if she sat in the middle, that meant he'd have to sit next to her. And if he sat next to her, those pink skirts would brush against his side for the entire ride. And if he had to put up with all that, he'd shrivel faster than an earthworm in the sun.

"We're running late." Impatience edged Mama's voice. "Help Karen into the buggy so we can get to church on time, for pity's sake."

Seldom did Mama get after him. But when she did, he knew the time had come to endure all suffering and appease her.

Holding his breath in and his hand out, he helped Karen into the buggy. After Mama found space on the seat, he got in on his side, squeezed in next to Karen in spite of her efforts to make more room for him, and sweated his way to church.

CHAPTER FIVE

*L*ogan reclined at the head of the breakfast table and sipped coffee. The empty stairs lured his attention. Karen had yet to make an appearance on this, her first day as teacher of the Silver Grove School.

"Eggs, dear."

"Hmm?"

"Please pass the eggs." Mama's voice interrupted his vigil over the stairway.

He set his cup down, picked up the dish, and stretched across the table in one swift motion.

"Good morning." Karen breezed into the kitchen before the dish hit the table at Mama's end.

Logan leaned forward and pulled out her usual chair.

"Oh, I don't have time to eat. Thank you, though, but I must get to the school."

"Logan is driving you, Karen. He hasn't finished his breakfast yet, so you have a few minutes." Mama spooned scrambled eggs onto her plate. She held the dish of eggs out to Karen. "You might as well join us."

"Well, I suppose." Karen accepted the empty chair.

He resumed his comfortable posture and refilled his coffee cup. Leaning back in his chair, he found the perfect vantage point from which to steal glimpses of Karen.

Gone were all the flowers and pink lace of yesterday's outfit. In their place Karen wore a loose white shirt waist with high collar and long sleeves. A black skirt void of any decoration flowed to the floor. Her hair twisted into a tight bun at the base of her neck with no curls anywhere.

He took long slow sips of coffee enjoying the relief that seeped deep into his bones. Whatever nerves had bothered him yesterday dissipated. He could handle this Karen. The schoolmarm Karen rid of tailored bodices that hugged her figure and showed off the fact that she was a grown woman too close to his own age. The boarder Karen who would be gone all day and not hanging around the house or seated at the table like she was now, close enough to brush arms whenever either of them reached for silverware.

Life began to look like what he'd expected the day he agreed to board the teacher. Confidence straightened his spine. He'd survived the worst. All he had to do now was get her to school on time. Sounded easy, but the past few days had proven this a more difficult task than he first thought.

"Oh, my, it's getting late." Karen hastened away from the kitchen table into the dining room. She returned with a stack of books and waited at the door.

"Ready?" Logan moved to hold the door open for Karen to pass through.

Mama approached with a slip of paper in her hand. "Could you please stop in town, dear? I need a few groceries. They're written down on this note. Don't lose it."

He planned to stop in town anyway and take a look at wire to repair a length of fence. He wanted to get that project completed this afternoon, but the hayfield in need of another cutting loomed more important on his list of things to do.

Logan reached for Karen's books and settled them on the seat of the buggy he'd parked in the lane before breakfast. Holding her hand, he assisted her climb over the wheel.

"I'm glad for the rain that fell last night. The temperature should feel cooler than it did the past few days." Karen looked at the low clouds overhead. "But if the sun should come out, the school could get quite hot by afternoon."

"I'll open the windows. A few might stick," Logan answered as the buggy rolled down the lane.

Once they arrived, Logan unlocked the door and worked at opening the windows. "Anything else you need?" He turned around to find Karen standing behind her desk, a stack of books arranged neatly on one corner.

Her gaze traveled over the desks and open windows before returning to him. "Someone to listen to my stories when I come home."

He grinned. "It's what I do best." Hours spent with Oswell City parishioners had honed his skills well. "Have a good day. I'll pick you up at three." Her smile stayed with him as he guided the horse out of the yard.

As he drove, relief at having the teacher healed of her injury and settled into the first day of class rolled over him. But the pleasure didn't last long. Concerns about Mama and Tillie crowded in. They struggled just to get up in the morning and start each new day. How would they ever run a farm on their own?

He guided the horse around the corner that outlined the Hixson farm a half-mile to the north. They couldn't. The answer emerged too obvious. Logan must figure out a solution. Maybe they could hire someone to do the milking and the fieldwork. One of the Patterson boys was in his last year of school. He might have the desire to start farming on his own. Maybe he could start out by looking after his widowed neighbor.

Logan's heart soared as the buggy rolled into town. Mama had options. The sooner he helped her make a decision, the quicker he could return to the Lord's chosen path for his life.

He brought the horse and buggy to a halt outside Carter's Mercantile and strode down to the post office. "Any mail for the De Witts?"

The postman made a brief check of the boxes on the wall behind him and handed an envelope to Logan before moving to help another customer.

The address, 225 Edgewood Lane, Oswell City, belonged to Paul Ellenbroek. With eagerness, Logan tore it open and read.

Pastor Logan,

Oswell City Community Church isn't the same without you. We are counting the days until you return. You'll be happy to know the roof is repaired. Harley and the boys from down at the lumberyard got it done in one day. Some rain moved through here yesterday, but the church stayed dry. A seminary student is preaching on Sunday, so please don't worry about us.

My wife is recovering quickly. A sixtieth birthday celebration is planned for her next Friday night. Since you'll be in town anyway for Katie's wedding, I thought you might like to attend. Hope you can make it.

Take care,

Paul

Another paragraph followed written in Lorraine's fine script.

Hi, Logan,

So sorry about your father. We understand why you left so suddenly, but we still miss you. I'm sorry you had to cancel our dinner date on Friday.

Friday night should have been spent with Lorraine enjoying himself and beginning a courtship. Instead, he'd spent it tossing and turning trying to forget Karen's scream from her encounter with the raging bull.

Are you coming to Mother's party? Could we talk when you get back to town?

Sincerely,

Lorraine

His heart twitched. Lorraine wanted to talk. It was a good sign she was still interested in having dinner with him. A smile spread across his face as he tucked the letter in his pocket and headed to the mercantile.

Nora, the owner's wife, helped him find all the items on Mama's list. He paid her, stashed the purchases in the buggy, and made his way down the street to Jake's Hardware.

"Be there in a minute." Jake's voice boomed through the building when Logan entered.

Strong smells of wood varnish assaulted Logan's nostrils, making him lightheaded.

Wiping his hands on a rag from the pocket of his denim apron, Jake appeared from the room where he built furniture and reached to shake Logan's hand. "Sorry about your dad. Glad my wife and I could get to the funeral. John was in here just last week lookin' at fence wire." Jake wagged his head back and forth. "Who woulda believed it'd be the last time I'd see him." Jake met Logan's gaze. "Your dad was a good man, Logan. It was an honor to help you folks out with the coffin."

"We appreciate it."

Jake stuffed the rag back in his pocket. "Anything I can help ya with this morning?"

"I'd like to take a look at that fence wire."

"Come on over this way and we'll get ya fixed right up." Jake led the way to a corner near the rear of the store. All sizes of wire were coiled and hanging from nails in the wall. Jake suggested the tools he thought Logan should have and then left when the bells on the door announced the arrival of another customer.

While down on one knee examining the handles of a wire cutter, shiny patent leather shoes halted near the faded knee of Logan's overalls. His gaze traveled over the black shoes, up the sharp crease of the pressed pants, across the stiff white shirt, and onto the face belonging to one of Logan's least favorite people in the whole world.

Some things about Silver Grove never changed. Eldon Kent was one of them. Son of the town banker, Eldon had been an expert at placing demands on people and getting his own way for as long as Logan could remember.

He stood to his feet where he towered over Eldon by a good eight inches. Drawing in a deep breath, Logan prayed he'd say nothing he'd regret later. "Good morning, Eldon. Nice to see you again." Toleration flattened any hint of enthusiasm from his voice.

"Likewise." Eldon extended the obligatory hand shake, his response as stiff as his clothing.

"Are you looking for wire cutters too?" One look at Eldon's hands told Logan the guy hadn't cut wire a day in his life.

"No. Actually, I'm looking for you."

Logan's eyes widened.

Eldon shifted his weight to one foot and ran a finger over the thin mustache on his upper lip. "I want you to come to the bank so I can show you your father's account."

Why would Eldon seek him out his first day in town and invite him to the bank? "When I finish up here, I'll be right over."

Eldon almost smiled, but his mouth failed to stretch across his face like it had never learned how to express friendship. "I'll be waiting."

After finding everything on his list, Logan paid Jake and took his new supplies to the buggy. The rain had quit, but the street, if the lane through town lived up to the description, was rutted and muddy. Logan picked his way across to the brick bank.

A teller spotted him and ushered him to Eldon's office. He left muddy tracks on the floor behind him, but there was no place to remove his shoes. Since the staff appeared unconcerned about dirty floors, Logan ventured down the hall behind the teller.

"Good of you to come so promptly." Eldon stood behind a desk with a black ledger lying open on its surface. "Please, sit down." He motioned to a chair covered in dark red leather.

Eldon pushed the black book in his direction. "This is your

father's financial record. As you can see, he owes the bank a considerable amount of money." Two dollar amounts were written in black at the top of the page, each in their own column.

Logan gulped. On the day Dad died, he owed the bank two thousand dollars.

Eldon pointed to the second column where another amount appeared. The sum written there said three hundred dollars. "This is the accrued interest. As you can see, no payments have been made against it." He sat down, folded his hands, and looked at Logan. "This is where I need your help."

Logan peered back at him, doubtful Eldon would prove as cooperative as he sounded.

"Your father agreed to pay the entire loan by April with a promise to pay the interest off by the end of this year."

Logan's whole body went numb. Words wouldn't come. He shot out of the chair and paced.

"I told him the bank refused to help him further unless that interest was taken care of." Eldon's voice hardened. "The loan will get called in the first of the year if I don't see this interest money on my desk by December 31."

Logan turned toward the desk in time to see Eldon jab the ledger with his index finger. He approached the desk and studied the figures. The sight of the severe black script on the innocent white page thawed him out until his insides simmered. "And how do you expect a man who couldn't pay the interest to come up with all that money by the first of January?"

"He'd have to sell the farm." Eldon's voice carried the calm tone of a guy with everything under his control. "Whatever profit he made would come to the bank until that loan was paid."

Logan groaned. Boy, he hated asking Eldon's opinion, but he had to know what sort of expectations Eldon had imposed on his father. He stared Eldon down with the expression he used on neighborhood dogs that trespassed on the Oswell City church lawn. "What do you suggest?"

Again, Eldon almost smiled. "Harvest season is coming. That's a good time to make a payment. Of course, you have the income from the milk. You could apply some of that against the interest."

"But wasn't Dad already doing those things?"

"All his payments were applied to the loan."

"And he still fell behind."

"Unfortunately."

"That means the farm isn't making enough money on its own to pay you back."

Eldon's eyebrows rose.

Logan clenched a fist in his lap. The self-satisfied expression on Eldon's face dared him to escape. No way would he allow Eldon to have the last word. This unexpected inheritance could not lock an invisible chain around him. He had a church to lead, sermons to preach, and a girl back in Oswell City he wanted to court. Logan blew out a breath. "Mama and I need to talk things through. Make some decisions."

"By all means." Eldon gathered up the book from Logan's hands.

Logan trudged out of Eldon's office with a glum satisfaction about the mud he'd smeared all over Eldon's floor. Too bad a little manure hadn't been mixed in with it. Even if it had, Eldon still held the prize for making the worst messes.

KAREN SMOOTHED her dark skirt as she scanned the room. Children of all ages and sizes filled every last available seat. In the front row, five-year-old Ben Hixson swung his feet as he reached for a long braid of his seat mate, Lizzie Kent. Behind them, three boys, all wearing overalls and expressions on their faces that told her they'd rather be anywhere but here, crowded into a desk. One of them leaned over and whispered into his buddy's ear.

Across from them on the other side of the stove, Tom Hinkley's daughters occupied a desk. The only children in the room sitting still, they looked like they might actually enjoy learning. Behind them, the older students filled the back row. One boy, who had announced his name earlier that morning as Emmett, caught her eye just as he darted a wad of paper at a comrade across the aisle. His black hair stuck out every which way, and he wore no shirt under his overalls. One word came to Karen's mind as she watched him. Trouble. She'd need to keep her eye on him in the days to come.

"All right class," Karen called out as she took her seat behind the desk. "Direct your attention to the front, please." She waited while the smaller children followed her instruction. Emmett and the recipient of his paper wad grinned and pointed at each other. She cleared her throat. "Emmett, look here, please."

He grimaced but followed directions.

Karen smiled at him. "Thank you. The first rule you will learn is that throwing articles of any sort is not allowed. Since this is the first day of school, you are not in trouble because we are all still trying to get used to each other. But in the future, you will miss recess if you throw in class."

Emmett crossed his arms.

"Understood?" She scanned the room.

"Yes, Miss Millerson," the students responded in unison.

"Good." Karen reached for her attendance list. "Now, I have discovered that many of you are brothers and sisters. So, to help me learn your names, could you please stand when I say your last names?"

A few of the students nodded.

Karen proceeded through the list of names, Patterson, Hixson, Jones, Hinkley. Most families sent three or four children to school. She called out the next name. "Sanders."

Six children stood. She moved on. "Kent."

Four more children stood.

She drew in a deep breath. The Kent family wasn't any larger than most of the others represented in her classroom. But they resembled closely the members of the Sanders family. All the way down to the dark unruly hair and the defiant set to their mouths. Cousins. "Thank you. Please sit down."

She looked out over the assembly once more. Those three bib-clad boys were from the Kent family. Emmett's last name was Sanders. The buddy across the aisle was a brother. Ten children, all from the same family. And none of them wanted to be there. Her stomach rolled. Oh, she would have her hands full.

CHAPTER SIX

"Find everything you wanted in town?" Mama asked while Logan spooned green beans onto his plate for the noon meal.

"Uh, yeah." And more. Eldon's disclosure of information filled his simple list of barn repairs with so much that needed fixed. He stole a glimpse of Mama seated at the other end of the table, her focus on him. What would she say if he blurted out that she and Tillie were on the brink of losing their home with nowhere else to go?

Logan didn't want to lose the farm either. It was his home too. Even though he lived in a distant town, busy with his own career, he liked knowing the farm belonged to them, and it never changed. Dad stayed here working the land, planting or harvesting according to the seasons.

But that was gone now.

And Logan was the one who had to figure out what to do next.

"You're quiet, dear."

He dropped his fork. It clattered against the side of his plate.

"Something on your mind?"

He wished he could protect her from the awful truth. He picked up the fork. "I, uh, well." After taking a deep breath, he cleared his throat. "The morning in town proved more difficult than I expected." Logan gulped the water in his glass wrestling with how much to tell her and Tillie. They needed to know the desperation of the situation, but he didn't want the news to spoil their memories. Or scare them.

He must help her make a plan that would ensure her security without telling her the whole story. "I was thinking that a hired man might be the best solution for you after I leave for Oswell City. Maybe you could get Wade Patterson to come over after school until he graduates from eighth grade. The profit from milk sales would cover the salary." He preferred for Mama to use the milk money in this way instead of as interest payments like Eldon suggested. Maybe she could sell some crop after harvest to satisfy the bank.

"I don't think so, dear." Mama's voice came out raspy.

"What's wrong with a hired man?" Logan leaned forward to press his case. "He'd do the milking and work the fields."

Mama shook her head.

Logan set his glass down with impatience in his movements. "Mama, you and Tillie can't run the place on your own. I don't see any other way for the work to get done."

Tears shone in Mama's eyes. "Please don't hire anyone."

"Why?" The request sounded ridiculous to Logan's ears. Mama needed help. She'd lose her home without it.

She picked up the corner of her apron and brushed it under her eye. "Your father tried that once. It didn't work out."

"What happened?" Lots of area farmers relied on outside help from time to time. Rarely did the arrangement fail.

"Oh, Logan." Mama broke down and wept for several moments.

Tillie patted her arm. She sent Logan a look that held him responsible for Mama's pain.

What did he say? All he tried to do was provide for her future.

Now she cried and Tillie blamed him. "You can tell me what's wrong."

Mama still wept.

"I'm a preacher, Mama. People tell me their problems all the time. I'd really love to hear yours."

She heaved a deep breath in a way that made her sound one hundred years old. "Like I said, your father hired someone to help him in the fields. We thought it a good plan at the time, but it set us back." Mama drank from her glass. "You see, John couldn't afford to pay for the extra help. He had to use the milk sales for the salary."

"Wise choice," Logan said, pleased his plan echoed his father's.

Mama shook her head. "Not at all. Since your father spent all his profit on hired help, he had no way to pay for repairs on machinery."

"Why didn't he sell some of the crop after harvest to cover the debt?"

"He didn't have any to sell. The livestock ate most of it over the winter. Your father saved back enough seed to plant the next spring, but one year the weather was dry, so he had to buy seed." Mama looked into Logan's eyes. "He borrowed money from the bank. Over two thousand dollars, if I remember correctly."

Mama knew about the loan. Her explanation filled in enough of the gaps for this puzzle to fall into place. The complete picture it made revealed to him an awful truth. He didn't want to believe it. One fact from Mama would confirm his worst fear. He swallowed it away. "How long ago did Dad borrow this money?"

Tears filled Mama's eyes again. "When you left for seminary five years ago."

Logan's stomach plummeted. The family was in this situation because of him. He'd known leaving the farm would add to Dad's work load, but he had no idea of the financial burden his absence had caused.

"Why didn't Dad say anything to me?"

Mama sniffed. "He wanted to spare you the details so that you wouldn't quit seminary and return to the farm."

"But, Mama, I would have helped him any way I could. You know that."

"Sure I do, but your father didn't want you to worry about him and what was going on here at home." She wiped her eyes again. "He knew you needed to get an education in order to preach, and he didn't want to hold you back."

Logan's heart swelled. He'd had the best father in the world. What sacrifices Dad had made for him. His vision blurred.

"Nothing has been the same since you left."

The morning Walt Brinks found him in church, he never dreamed his life would get so complicated this fast. He struggled with the longing to recover the simple plan of helping Mama with the funeral, finding someone to take over the milking, and returning to life as he knew it. He must find a way to right his world before he left, but only a few days remained. He might run out of time.

"YOU'VE DONE WELL TODAY, children. Adjusting to a new school year is hard, so I won't assign any homework."

All of the boys cheered.

"Remember to put your readers away over here on the shelf by the window." Karen pointed to the empty ledge awaiting its store of books. "Nick and Kelvin, it's your job to fill the water bucket at the pump in the morning."

Nick's red head bobbed, and so did Kelvin's blond one.

"Class dismissed."

Students scampered out of the building.

In the flurry, Logan entered, tall and lightly tanned, his blond hair tousled from the breeze. His appearance matched that of a man who'd spent the summer afternoon outdoors. Since he was a farmer, that was probably what he'd done.

Karen's stomach twisted. Men who spent all of their time outside fell prey to accidents, or at least that's what Ella's brother had taught her. His foolish operation of a threshing machine proved his lack of concern for the wife and family he left behind to mourn his death. If Karen wanted to avoid the heartache that over-whelmed Mother after losing Father, she'd do well to stifle any more feelings that threatened to develop for this man who stood in her classroom.

At least he wasn't a preacher. That occupation was ten times worse than farming. A farmer might put himself in danger, leaving his family to suffer, but a preacher possessed the power to endanger many people. The misery extended beyond any one family and affected an entire congregation, a neighborhood, and whole sections of the city. Karen knew. Her family was still trying to forget this terrible truth.

She dropped her gaze to the open books on her desk.

"Ready to go home?" Logan's footsteps thumped down the aisle.

"Yes." She turned around to apply the eraser to the chalk board. "I'll take these."

Karen replaced the eraser on her desk as Logan picked up her stack of books. He strolled with her to the waiting buggy.

A good way to curb those feelings would be to spend less time with him. Karen kept her focus on the road in front of them, her voice firm. "I appreciate you driving me back and forth to school, but I'll walk from now on."

"Why? I can easily take you."

"But the school is only half a mile away. There's no reason why I shouldn't go on my own. Walking will also save you time in the mornings. I'm sure you have jobs that get put off so you can drive me to school."

"I do, but it's important to me to see you delivered safely."

She paid him for room and board, not for extra rides to places she could reach on her own. This fact strengthened her resolve. She turned to him. "Thanks, but I want to walk."

Logan nodded. The brief smile he gave her said he accepted her decision although he disagreed.

Another concern occupied her thoughts. "Do you know the Kent family?"

Logan flinched. "I do. Eldon Kent, along with his father and brother Evan, own the bank."

"I see. Do Eldon or Evan have any children?"

"Evan has four, I believe."

His answer aligned with the information she'd received that morning. "And the Sanders children?"

"Their mother is a sister to the Kent brothers. Eldon lives in town, but the rest of the family farms a huge piece of land south of here."

They were cousins. She'd guessed correctly.

"Were all of these kids at school today?"

"Yes."

Logan slapped the horse with the reins. "Well, I hope they cooperate instead of following in Uncle Eldon's footsteps."

AT NOON ON THURSDAY, Logan stood in line behind Tom Hinkley waiting for his turn at the wash basin.

"Fried chicken is ready. Come find your seats," Mama called while she hustled around the kitchen.

Logan sloshed water over his hands and forearms, relieved to get rid of the dusty bits of straw that clung to him. How he'd love to pour the whole bowlful over his head to cool and soothe his skin. He held back for the sake of Mama's clean kitchen.

After drying off, he moved to the table where Tom, Vern Patterson, and Clyde Hixson were seated. Tillie brought a large platter heaped with chicken to the table. Mama followed with bowls of corn, mashed potatoes, and gravy.

"You've got a nice hay crop." Tom spooned man-size portions of food onto his plate.

"Thanks. I appreciate you helping me get it in the barn today."

"The least I could do after all the help you boys gave me yesterday."

As discussed at church on Sunday, all of them had mowed their hay fields on Monday and raked the cut hay on Tuesday. Tom's hay was dry the quickest, so the crew of four had started at Tom's farm yesterday and moved to Logan's today. Since he was leaving tomorrow, the crew of three would continue on to Vern's and Clyde's farms throughout the week until the job was finished.

The bowls of food made their way around the table until reaching him last. After filling his plate, Logan ate in silence, unable to concentrate on the conversation around him. Haying gave him entirely too much time alone with his problems. Hour after hour, seated on the mower behind the horse, back and forth in long straight lines through the field, Logan started to think. The conclusions he drew left him fighting with a truth that made him sick.

If Mama didn't want to hire anyone, then the only other choice available to any of them was for Logan to do the work. This would mean staying on the farm instead of returning to Oswell City where the life and work he loved waited for him.

But Mama needed him. She looked to him for advice and support. If he left the farm, no one would provide this for her.

And Tillie. She needed him too. She'd finally returned to the house Sunday afternoon. What if the scene repeated in the weeks and months to come? Someone must help Tillie through the pain. But if he chose to stay in Silver Grove, no one would see to those same cares for the Oswell City congregation. He couldn't leave them without a pastor. He just couldn't. Logan ate a spoonful of corn without really tasting it.

He couldn't leave Mama and Tillie swallowed in debt either. What was a man to do? If only there were two of him. That's what he needed. A replication of himself to stay here in Silver Grove while the real Logan returned to preaching and to Lorraine. He'd nearly forgotten about her in his quandary. If he stayed, pursuing a relationship with her would grow much more difficult.

His gut clenched as he listened to the men at the table share local news with Mama and Tillie. The whole situation was so unfair. Why did he have to be the one to pay the price? God had a claim on his life. He needed to obey the call. Follow where God led him. His family or a demanding banker shouldn't have the right to pressure him into roles that didn't fit this plan.

Logan spooned another helping of mashed potatoes onto his plate. He was heading back to Oswell City. Mama would just have to take the risk on a hired man. With a little encouragement, she'd go along with his plan. Logan's life headed in another direction, one that had pulled him off of the farm years ago. God had complete control of Logan's life, and nothing would interfere.

CHAPTER SEVEN

Oswell City, Iowa

*A*t six o'clock he left for the party at the Ellenbroeks'. Horses and buggies lined the circle drive. Men in dark suits clustered in wicker furniture on the manicured lawn. Their laughter floated to Logan's ears. A group of youngsters played croquet nearby.

Large stone steps led to a broad porch. Young women in white dresses and wide-brimmed hats sipped punch from cut glass cups. The windows of the grand, brick house pulsated with light, inviting Logan to join the festivities. He jogged across the drive and waved at the men in wicker chairs. Taking the steps two at a time, he bid a good evening to the women on the porch.

Paul welcomed him and gestured to the swarm of activity behind him. "Please come in. You are just in time. We are getting ready to cut the cake." Paul turned and led him through the crowd gathered in the spacious parlor.

Logan followed, shaking hands while greeting parishioners along the way.

In the dining room, an imposing, layered cake covered in white and pink frosting rose buds stood on the table.

Mrs. Ellenbroek stood near the table, looking perfectly healthy and as regal as a queen. Her silver hair was coiled on top of her head, and her purple gown shimmered in the chandelier's light.

Paul lit the candles on the top layer of the birthday cake while the entire gathering sang "Happy Birthday." When the song ended, Mrs. Ellenbroek closed her eyes and blew out the flames. Everyone cheered.

Logan waited his turn for a slice. After filling his plate with snacks from the hutch, he moved to the parlor and found a seat. Wanting to know everything that had happened in town over the past two weeks, he listened to the conversation that buzzed around him as he savored his dessert.

Once all the guests were served, Mrs. Ellenbroek entered the parlor. Logan approached her and took her hand. "You look well tonight, Mrs. Ellenbroek. Happy birthday."

"Thank you, Pastor Logan." Her cheeks flushed. She smiled. "I'm so glad you could be here."

"How are you feeling?"

"Fine. I might get a little tired from all the activity, but nothing rest won't fix."

"I will pray that your health continues to improve."

She nodded and moved on to talk to her other guests.

Logan handed his empty plate and cup to one of the Ellenbroeks' household staff. He scanned the room in search of Lorraine but didn't find her. Perhaps she ate her cake outdoors. She wasn't among the young ladies gathered on the porch. After a wave at them, he wandered around the corner of the house.

Lorraine strolled in the rose garden.

His pulse quickened. What a perfect place to discuss courtship. No other house in town possessed a more romantic setting. Well-tended roses in varying shades of pinks thrived under the spreading branches of ancient maples. He hastened across the lawn. "Lorraine."

She glanced up. Surprise flickered across her face. "Good evening."

"Hi." He drank in the peach glow of her skin. "Enjoying the party?"

"Yes."

"I'm glad to see your mother recovered. It must be a great relief to you."

"She looks wonderful tonight."

"Certainly." He agreed, but he wasn't referring only to her mother.

Pink stained her cheeks. "This is the mother I know. That pneumonia gave Father and me quite a scare."

"I can understand why."

She fingered the blossom of a rose. "Thanks for coming to the party."

"My pleasure."

"Your attendance tonight means so much. Town isn't the same without you. We've all come to depend on you." She sat down on the white bench at the base of a tree.

"Thanks." Logan eased in next to her. "I want to have a talk with your father tomorrow. I need to ask his advice on some changes that have come about in my life."

"What kind of changes?"

"Since my father died, my mother and sister are left with a farm they can't manage alone. I'm concerned that I might have to stay on the farm indefinitely, but I hope it doesn't happen."

Lorraine gave him an empathetic smile.

He clutched the back of his neck. "I wanted you to know because . . . well because I had hoped." Oh, no. His tongue refused to cooperate. Of all the times for his courage to abandon him. He took a deep breath. "I hoped to . . . to ask, well, to ask if I could court you when I took you to dinner, but that didn't work out." He rubbed his forehead. Perspiration dampened his fingers. "We can write and keep in touch. Maybe I can visit you at Christmas." He dragged in a deep breath.

Lorraine bit her lip. Her long lashes brushed her cheeks.

Logan gathered his shredded courage. "Will you wait for me, Lorraine?"

"I can't." The words came out as a moan.

"What?"

Her pleading gaze rested on his face. "I'm sorry, Logan. I admire you so much, but I don't think we could ever have a future together."

"Why?"

"Because you're a preacher."

"That shouldn't matter."

"But it does." Lorraine twisted her lace handkerchief around in her hands. "Preachers come and go. They move from town to town. I don't want to leave Oswell City. I want to stay here, close to Mother."

"God may never call me to leave Oswell City."

"He already has. You left town in a rush when you received the news of your father's death. Now you might have to leave again."

"But I'll come back. Someday, I hope, I'll come back." He resisted the impulse to hold her hand so he might reassure her of the truth behind his words.

Lorraine fingered the edge of her handkerchief, now wrinkled from the previous twisting. "What if God asks you to leave again? Not for the farm, but for another town? You know you would go where He sent you. But I wouldn't, and that's not fair to you."

"Maybe you'd change your mind."

She shook her head.

"But, Lorraine—"

"No, Logan."

He leaned against the back of the bench. His persuasive skills worked so well on Sundays. Now they deserted him at a time when he needed them most.

Lorraine smoothed her skirt. "There's another reason why you cannot court me."

He turned to her. What other faults might she name?

"I don't know how to tell you, but, um, Brandt Koelman is already courting me. We're even talking about getting engaged."

Her words tore through him like shrapnel from an explosion.

"We courted all summer. Even before Mother got sick. This is what I wanted to talk to you about when I wrote to you in Father's letter."

His chest tightened. He rubbed his forehead again. Perspiration dripped from his fingers. Pain throbbed down the side of his head. He must be having a heart attack. Is this how Dad felt in those last moments of his life? "Why did you agree to go to dinner with me?"

Lorraine chewed her lip for a moment. "I wanted to tell you about Brandt. When you visited Mother on Sundays, I could see your interest in me. You deserved the truth. The dinner invitation seemed like a good opportunity to explain."

"Let me get this straight." He sucked in a breath. On top of all his other symptoms, his blood simmered in his veins. "You accepted my invitation to dinner for the one reason of talking about Brandt?"

She nodded.

Lorraine had no feelings for him at all. He'd spent week after week building himself up for the moment when he could finally ask to court her. His dreams plummeted, shattering like the glass chimney of a lantern on a rocky barn floor.

Tears glistened in the corners of Lorraine's eyes. "I'm sorry. I believe I could love you very easily. I already do a little." She leaned over and pecked his cheek with a light kiss. "Best wishes, Logan." Standing, she offered one last smile tinted with sadness and walked to the house.

He stayed behind, catching his breath. She wanted to talk about courtship, he had that part right. But she wanted to talk about someone else courting her, and that was where he went wrong. Another rejection. Good grief. He was fast becoming an expert on every line a young lady could possibly dream up to prevent a romantic relationship from forming with him.

He scowled at the festivities going on in the dining room. Muted laughter filtered from the house. Paul crossed in front of the window, a plate of cake in his hands and a broad smile on his face. Brandt's father slapped him on the back as though the two of them shared a terribly funny joke. Maybe they were both happy their offspring made a match. Music from the piano tinkled on the night air. The melodic phrase belonged in the song *All I Ask of You is Love*. He choked. Lorraine was probably the one playing the song, and with Brandt in mind. Not him.

He kicked at a rock protruding from the bark mulch around the roses. Shoving his hands in his pockets, he hiked across the lawn. He might as well return to the church. The extra evening hours would give him a head start on Sunday's sermon. The celebration going on in the house suddenly lost all appeal.

IDEAS TUMBLED from Logan's mind and onto the paper in his notepad. Except for the scratch of the pencil, the steady tick-ticking of the clock on the wall was the only other sound in the room.

Memories of last night's party cut into his thoughts. Brandt Koelman. If anyone knew how to woo and flatter the women, it was Brandt. Any young lady would fall for him. Dark, perfectly controlled hair. Wealthy partner in his father's law firm. Possessor of the smartest little Model T Ford along with ample time to entertain the ladies with rides.

Everything Logan wasn't.

Why did he struggle? He could preach to a full sanctuary Sunday after Sunday and even write articles for the newspaper's religion section the entire town would read. But uttering his interest in a young woman terrified all the courage right out of him. Courtship shouldn't be so hard. But maybe he couldn't find a girl to court because there wasn't one. What if God wanted him to serve unattached to any other?

The apostle Paul commented on it in Corinthians. Logan knew the passage, but he turned there in his Bible anyway. The Scripture said that it was well to remain unmarried. The letter to the Corinthians also said that the unmarried man is anxious about the affairs of the Lord and how to please him.

Footsteps thumped on the stone floor of the hall. Logan flipped back to the place where he'd been taking notes. He looked up as Paul Ellenbroek entered. "Good attendance at your party last night."

"My wife was pleased. She had a great time and wasn't even too tired afterward." Paul settled into a chair. "You seem down about something. I first noticed it when I met you at the door last night."

Logan rubbed his forehead. He had Lorraine on his mind, but his problems from home would've been his biggest concern at the time he arrived at the party. "My mother and sister are in a desperate financial situation now that my father is gone. They need someone to work the farm for them. Mama doesn't want to hire anyone, so our only other option is for me to do it."

Paul said nothing. He leaned back in his chair and stroked his mustache.

"I don't want to because my absence from Oswell City would leave the congregation without a pastor."

Paul nodded.

Logan exhaled. "I'm not sure what to do. I wanted to ask your advice and see what you suggest."

"You've got a tough situation on your hands." Paul straightened. "But I'd advise you to go home to your mother and sister."

"You would?"

"Yes. We shouldn't expect to receive all of your time and attention." Paul smiled. "It's easy to do when the pastor is single but unfair all the same."

Logan worked to prevent a frown. Paul's own daughter was the one Logan hoped would help change his single status. "I feel God calling me to ministry, not farming. That means I should stay here."

"Why don't you test it out? If we end up finding a replacement for you, then you can trust that's God's plan for you, to take some time off to spend with your mother and sister. If we can't find a replacement, then maybe that's God's way of telling you to return." Paul crossed his legs and studied him.

Logan returned the solemn gaze. Paul just proved he was one of the wisest people Logan had ever known. He understood why the town voted for him as their mayor and why he'd chosen Paul as a friend. "So, I have permission to leave town tomorrow."

Paul nodded, a small smile on his lips.

"All right. This is somewhat unexpected. Thank you." The weight of struggle with this impossible dilemma fell from his shoulders. The situation remained far from resolved, but Logan believed answers would come. He reached his hand out to Paul.

He accepted it in a firm shake. "Everything will work out."

CHAPTER EIGHT

"*C*lass, please open your math books." Karen surveyed her students. Each one, from Ben Hixson in the primary grade to Carrie Kent in eighth grade, lifted the tops of their desks and produced a book from within.

During this first week together, she'd managed to instill the simple lesson in each child to wait until she finished talking before carrying out an instruction. Only after every child had completed the task could the group move on. If they remembered nothing else, at least they had learned how to behave in a multi-graded classroom. If Tom Hinkley didn't find her another position, a whole year of country school stretched before her. She may not survive to the end.

"Sixth and seventh graders, please turn to page three." Karen picked up the teacher's copy. "Do the ten problems you see on the page for tomorrow."

Groans accompanied shuffled paper as the assignment got written down.

Karen switched the book in her hands for the elementary version. "Third, fourth, and fifth graders, please do the problems on page four in your books." She paused until the directions were followed.

"Yes, Miss Millerson," echoed around the room.

She turned back a page. "Becky, Mary Ellen, and Jessie, please do the problems on pages two and three in the book." Taking a step toward the smallest desk in the front, she said, "Ben and Lizzie, you may work with me at the blackboard tomorrow. At that time, I will begin your math lesson."

"Yeth, Mith Millerthon." Lizzie Kent, five years old, lisped due to a missing front tooth.

Karen smothered a chuckle. She turned to her desk and opened the reader. "For the last few minutes of class, please finish the reading assignment I gave you this morning."

Desks squeaked open and thumped closed until all the math books were put away. The room quieted as each student bent their heads over their reading books, deep in concentration.

Karen sat at her desk and organized both her thoughts and her teaching materials. The day really had passed quickly, considering she was still learning nineteen new names, and considering the school room had heated up as though a fire roared in the stove all day. She'd taken the risk of holding afternoon classes in the shade. The students had perked up a bit in the breeze. Everyone, teacher included, returned inside revived and ready to finish the day's class schedule. All in all, the day had gone well, but teaching the varied range of grades and abilities drained her. Would she always be this tired after every day of school, either at this job or in high school? For a year? The thought alone exhausted her. Somewhere, she was going to need to get a hold on a large dose of endurance.

The door creaked open and pounded shut. The young man who entered was a stranger, a well-dressed one, but a stranger none-theless.

Students twisted their necks for a glimpse of the visitor. Members of the Kent and Sanders families greeted him. "Hi, Uncle Eldon."

He offered a stiff nod and thin smile. His gaze rested on Karen. "Miss Millerson?"

"Yes." She eased out of her chair.

He made his way to the front of the room. "I'm Eldon Kent, Loan Officer at the Silver Grove State Bank."

"Nice to meet you, Mr. Kent. Are you here in regard to one of your nieces or nephews?"

He shook his head. "No. I'm here to see you." He reached in his suit coat and pulled out a small box which he handed to her.

Karen's eyes widened. Candy. He'd brought her a box of candy. In Chicago, when young men offered candy in this fashion, it signaled their interest in courtship. Is that what Mr. Kent wanted? Today, on their first meeting?

"Thank you, but I can't accept." She pushed the box away.

"I'll take that off your hands, Mr. Kent." Tim Hixson leaned forward from his desk in the back row, his hand outstretched over the top of Evie Patterson's head. Laughter ran through the other boys in the neighboring desks.

Evie smoothed her hair back into place and scowled at Tim.

Karen tried to scowl too, but heat radiated from her cheeks. Mr. Kent should acquaint himself with the rules of decorum for her classroom. Suitors didn't belong.

Marty Kent slapped Tim on the back, and the boys shared a grin. Once again Tim succeeded as the accomplice to mischief.

She should reprimand him for not raising his hand to speak in class. But she may have called on him. That would've done nothing but help Mr. Kent along, now that she caught on his own nephew had put Tim up to the offer. The heat on her cheeks deepened. Karen drew in a deep breath both to cool off and to calm down.

"I brought my buggy. It would be an honor to escort you to the De Witt farm at the close of the school day." He still held the candy out between them like he relied on it as bait to entice her to ride with him.

"Ith he going to give you a ride?" Lizzy Kent raised wide eyes to Karen's face.

"No. He will not." Karen accentuated the "t" to give her voice authority.

Mr. Kent still held out the box of candy. He must put the thing away before it stirred up any more trouble from the older boys.

"I already have a ride. He'll be arriving soon." Karen's conscience pricked. She'd lied. No one was coming to pick her up. If Logan hadn't left, he might have gone against her wishes to walk and come to get her. But she'd never see him again. At the breakfast table on Friday, he'd informed her of his plans to attend the birthday party of a friend in a town where he intended to return to a previous job. She'd wanted to ask questions about the town's name and what kind of work he did, but she ran out of time before she needed to leave for school.

Mr. Kent's eyes narrowed with a coldness that chilled Karen's bones, even on this hot summer day. After a moment, the cold disappeared and his cordial manner returned. "Well then, I'll just wait." He turned and strode to a back corner.

Karen drew in a ragged breath. She may have told a falsehood, but at least it made the box of candy disappear. "All right, class," she said to the stares coming her way. "Pick up in your readers where you left off before recess. You may read until I dismiss you."

Mr. Kent wasted his time waiting around on her. If he thought he'd try again when her so-called ride appeared, his plan would fail. She'd come up with some way to outlast him. He hadn't exactly said he accepted her refusal, but he hadn't pressed her either.

The ticking of the clock drew her attention. Five more minutes and class would be over for the day. Karen held her breath. She didn't want to get left alone with this man, but neither did she want to extend the school day for the selfish reason of detaining the students until he gave up and went home. She stole a glance at him. His straight posture and gaze fixed on her said that he'd wait on her as long as necessary.

"Teacher?"

"Yes?" Karen replied, thankful for an interruption however small, to Mr. Kent's scrutiny.

Mary Ellen sat at a desk in the second row with her hand up. "I don't know this word."

Karen moved to look over the eight-year-old's shoulder.

Mary Ellen's chubby finger pointed to the page in her book.

Karen pronounced it for her and when Mary Ellen asked its meaning, supplied her with the definition.

Mary Ellen smiled. "Thanks, Teacher."

Karen returned to stand near her desk to keep watch on the students, but also on the clock. If she possessed the power to stop time, she'd do it now.

Mr. Kent shuffled his feet, his attention returned to her.

The slam of the school door brought everyone's attention to the rear of the room. There stood Logan, a deep furrow in his brow.

Karen's head throbbed. Logan left town on Friday. A one-way trip, he'd said. So how could he possibly be in her classroom today, this very minute?

"Everything all right?" He peered at Mr. Kent.

"Yes." Karen released the breath she'd been holding.

"Good." In his casual way, Logan leaned against the doorjamb. "I think I'll stick around and give the teacher a ride home, if she's willing."

"Quite. Thank you." Karen gathered her wits as a smile broke out on her face. She hadn't told Mr. Kent a falsehood after all. "You may put your books away now," she said to the class. "Remember your math homework tomorrow. I'll have each grade come to the front and recite the answers to the problems. Any questions?" Karen scanned the room. "See you tomorrow. Class dismissed." She turned and gathered books and papers from her desk.

The room exploded with activity. Desktops thumped closed. Feet pounded on the wood floor. Metal lunch pails clanked. Young voices hollered. The school emptied, leaving Karen alone with the two men.

"Afternoon, Eldon." Logan shook his hand.

Mr. Kent's eyes narrowed. This time, he didn't smile.

"Anything I can help you with?"

"No. I came to offer Miss Millerson a ride, but I see it isn't necessary." He turned to Karen. "Perhaps another time. Good day." A smile stretched his mouth but failed to reach his eyes. The smile faded, and a glare replaced it when he passed Logan on the way out the door.

Logan turned to her.

"I can't believe you're here. I thought you planned to stay away."

"Yeah, well." Logan thrust his hands in his pockets. "My plans got changed." A tiny frown pulled at his mouth.

"Care to talk about it?"

A shadow crossed his clear blue eyes, and he quickly attempted a grin. "Boring details." Logan leaned against the doorframe once again. "Maybe you want to talk about what's going on with Eldon Kent."

"He arrived just as I was about to dismiss. He offered me candy and a ride home." Karen hugged herself. "There's something about him that makes me uncomfortable."

"I feel that way about him sometimes, too." Logan straightened. "May I?" He made a grand bow and held his arm out to her.

The dapper Eldon Kent couldn't have done better. Karen laughed and placed her hand on his arm like they were a couple dressed in their finest and headed to a concert of the Chicago Symphony instead of a school teacher and bibs-wearing dairy farmer at the end of a hot day in the country. She'd much rather accept this sort of escort. Mr. Kent had better be smart enough to remember the lesson he'd learned in her classroom this afternoon.

CHAPTER NINE

*A*nother encounter with Eldon was the last thing Logan needed, but his first payment was due. He'd saved only a meager amount, but it was enough to start making a difference at the bank. He took the long way to town, the way that took him past the school. Safe delivery of money to the bank topped his list, but the safe arrival of Karen at the school ranked just as high. If he could spy her through the window and ease his mind that the school day got off to a normal start, then he might tolerate Eldon a little easier. At least he couldn't bother Karen while Logan took up his time at the bank.

He stopped in front of the square, brick building, tied the reins, and went inside. "Eldon Kent, please," he said to one of the tellers.

The man nodded and led him down the hall.

"Ah, Logan, here to make your first payment." Eldon gestured to one of the leather chairs near the desk. "Please sit down."

Logan reached into his pocket and retrieved the slim stack of bills. He slid them across the polished surface of Eldon's desk.

Eldon flipped through the money while he counted out loud. A sober expression covered his face. "This is all you brought?"

"Yeah."

He arched his brow. "It's not very much."

Logan didn't need Eldon's help in recalling that fact.

"When do you plan to make your next payment?"

"The end of the month." He would collect Karen's room and board payment at that time, giving him more funds to work with.

"I see your family is boarding the teacher this year." Eldon folded his hands on the desk. "Good. You'll need the income. Each day that passes adds more interest to your debt."

Logan leaned forward. "If you remember, I still have oats to harvest. Maybe as soon as next week. All the money from the sale is designated for payment to the bank. Added to the milk sales, profit from the teacher's room and board should cover our living expenses." His mouth stretched into a smile. "I've got it all worked out."

From the bank, Logan crossed the street and entered the mercantile.

Andrew Carter jumped off the ladder propped in the display window. "Hey, Logan."

"Mama sent a list." He dug around in his overall pocket for Mama's grocery list. He handed it off to Andrew who glanced over the items written on the paper.

"Come on over to the counter." He jerked his head to the rear of the store and led the way down the pots and pans aisle.

"Your mama not working today?"

Andrew handled the paperwork while his father supervised the shipping and unloading of freight. Seldom did Andrew take over Nora's place behind the counter.

"She is, but ah, I wanted to talk to you." Andrew licked his lips and tied a linen apron around his waist. "I saw ya go in the bank earlier so knew you were in town."

"What's on your mind?"

Andrew leaned over the counter and whispered. "I want to ask if I could start courting your sister."

"Tillie?" Her name shot out of his mouth with the explosion of a canon ball. She was his responsibility. And only seventeen. Besides, she wasn't interested. He'd witnessed no show of admiration for the mild-mannered, brown-haired Andrew Carter.

"Shh." Red stained Andrew's cheeks.

Logan glanced around as shoppers pulled their attention off of him and back to the items on the shelves.

Andrew resumed scooping flour into a cloth bag. "I don't need permission from the whole town. Just you."

Logan cleared his throat. "Sorry. You surprised me."

"Why?"

He propped an arm on the counter and slouched down on it. "How do you know Tillie would welcome this new relationship?"

"Isn't new. She came to town with John on every trip. She'd deliver your mother's grocery list and stay to talk with me until he finished his errands. Then he'd pick her up and take her home." A smile curved his lips. "I looked forward to an hour every week spent with Tillie."

Logan's ears rang with this news. "How long has this gone on?"

Andrew shrugged. "Since March."

"March?"

Andrew met his gaze. "Tillie turned seventeen in March."

"She wasn't allowed to see anyone until then?"

"Sort of."

"What do you mean? Did my parents make her wait?"

"No. I did."

Logan stood to his full height and smiled big-brother approval on this honorable young man. "How long have you wanted to court her?"

Red returned to Andrew's cheeks in full force. "Since eighth grade."

"Eighth grade?"

"Shh. Keep your voice down." Andrew batted the air in front of Logan's face like he could control the volume.

"Sorry."

A few moments of silence passed before Andrew spoke again. "I planned to ask your father, but he's gone. I figured the respectable thing to do was to ask you." He tied up the flour bag and went in search of the rest of the items on Mama's long list. "So, what do you think?"

A grin tugged at Logan's mouth as he took inventory. "I think I owe you a pile of money for all these groceries."

Andrew crossed his arms and fought a smile. "You know what I mean."

Logan turned serious. "Tillie is struggling. Losing Dad has been hard, but you might be the best thing that ever happened to her." At the sight of Andrew's beaming face, he continued. "You have my blessing. I wish you all the best." He shook Andrew's hand.

"When should I come?"

"Saturday night."

"I'll take Tillie to supper at the hotel and bring her home afterward."

"I'll tell Tillie to have the parlor ready." Logan winked again at the red-faced Andrew and left the store.

On a warm Wednesday morning, Karen instructed the students to find their lunch pails and take the one-hour break for the noon meal and recess.

The last child left the room as Eldon Kent walked in. Heart pounding, Karen dropped her pencil. He'd better not offer to give her another ride home. She wouldn't leave now, or ever. She refused to go anywhere with him.

"Miss Millerson. How nice to find you alone. I hoped we might enjoy lunch together." He approached her desk where he opened the cloth bag in his hand.

"I've already eaten, Mr. Kent."

"Please, call me Eldon." He retrieved a sandwich from his bag. "We can still enjoy the peace and quiet. Just the two of us."

Karen stood. "No. Really. I should go outside and supervise recess." She headed for the aisle, eager to leave Mr. Kent behind.

He reached out and grabbed her wrist. "I think you belong here, with me." Steel edged his voice and his eyes went cold.

She drew in a deep breath and held it. She was trapped in her own classroom. "Mr. Kent, please let go."

He released his hold on her arm but stayed in the aisle.

Desks blocked her escape.

"Why do you pursue me?"

"Because you're beautiful." The low tone of his voice assumed an intimacy that made her skin crawl. "And heaven knows Silver Grove has a pathetic shortage of beautiful women." He produced the box of candy from the day before. "I always get the best. That's how I know you belong with me."

The door slammed.

Karen's gaze darted in that direction. If only a disturbance large enough to pull her away from Eldon Kent would arrive.

"Miss Millerson, Joe and Marty are fightin' again." Tim Hixson stood in the center aisle, his hair tousled from running. In his hand he held a baseball and glove.

"Excuse me." She hiked up her skirt and hurdled over the seat of the front-row desk.

Following Tim outside, Karen scanned the children at play. Everything looked fine until Tim led her around the back of the school. Two boys rolled in the grass. Onlookers ringed the wrestling match.

"What is the meaning of this?" Karen yelled with as much authority as she could muster.

The boys ignored her.

She bent over and grasped thirteen-year-old Marty's upper arms. "Quit right now." She hauled him away from his fourteen-year-old brother Joe. No easy task for a five-foot-three teacher. Marty's weight and height combined with thrashing feet and swinging fists almost toppled her.

"Quit," Karen reached between the pair. "Joe, you go stand by the wall." She hauled Marty to his feet and guided him closer to his brother. "Tell me what happened."

Both boys talked at once and pointed at each other.

"Stop. Start over. One at a time. Joe, you go first."

"Hey, that's not fair. He started it."

Karen glared at Marty. "Joe, continue."

"We were playin' baseball with Tim. Marty overran a base, and I struck him out, but he wouldn't get off the base. He started wrestlin' me 'cause I told him to get out of the game."

"Marty, why didn't you listen?"

"'Cause I ain't out. Everyone knows to run past first base."

How she detested the word "ain't." Someday, it would cease to take up space in Marty's vocabulary. She settled her hands on her hips. "Here's what we'll do. Hand over the ball, glove, and bat. You need to find another way to occupy yourselves at both recesses tomorrow."

"But, Miss Millerson."

Karen shook her head. "When you prove to me you can play together without a fight, I will allow you to play baseball again." She picked the bat off the ground and claimed the glove and ball from Tim. "Ten more minutes until recess is over. Go find something else to do." She turned away from the boys' dejected faces and marched inside.

An empty room awaited her. She stood still and enjoyed the silence. Mr. Kent must have grown tired of waiting on her and decided to eat his lunch elsewhere. Maybe this would be the last she saw of him. Her stomach quivered. He didn't seem to be the type to give up so easily. This last thought coupled with the growing heat of the day made the walls close in on her. She picked up the bell. Conducting classes in the shade of the wide outdoors was a good idea.

"MAMA IS GOING to remake my blue winter dress from last year." Tillie announced from her side of a thriving tomato vine. Visions of the pretty dress took shape in her imagination. "She's borrowing a pattern from Sally Hixson." She placed a ripe tomato in the bushel basket at her feet. "It'll have the latest style. Straight skirt, pleats over the shoulders, buttons down the front. I can't wait." Tillie picked another tomato and put it in the basket with the others.

"Will she have it finished by Saturday?" Logan asked from the other side of the vine. He reached to place huge, juicy-looking tomato in the basket.

"No. It won't be a summer dress."

"Andrew will miss out seeing you in it, then." Logan's brows rose, giving him a scheming look.

"Not if he keeps courting me." Tillie returned his smirk. "I already have a dress to wear on Saturday. It's two years old, but Mama alters it for me each spring."

"I'm sure you'll look wonderful no matter what you are wearing." The vine empty of ripe produce, Logan moved the half-full basket to another vine, this one closer to the fence.

"Thanks." Tillie's cheeks flushed. She darted a smile to her big brother. She loved times like this when she had Logan all to herself. During these times with him, she almost forgot her pain. His attention restored to Tillie a tolerable level of comfort. She sought out opportunities to spend time with him. Always, they ended too soon.

"You and Mama should have a nice supply of tomatoes to can tomorrow," Logan said while he worked. "What does Mama plan to do with them?"

"Make stewed tomatoes. She brought the jars up from the cellar this morning." Tillie dropped two more tomatoes into the basket.

"I noticed." Logan said the words to Tillie, but his attention rested somewhere over her left shoulder. He rose to his feet, his focus still in the distance. Grasping the fence, he sucked in a long, slow breath.

Tillie swiveled. What had captured Logan's interest so completely? Expecting to see the cows in places they didn't belong, a visiting neighbor, or according to Logan's face, the blooming of a rare and delicate flower, Tillie glanced over her left shoulder. Nothing more than Miss Karen Millerson walking the lane. The teacher arrived home again after a day of school wasn't worth bringing their project to a halt.

Logan waved and called out. "Hey, Karen."

She returned the wave, adjusted her course, and came in their direction.

Logan leaned over the fence. "How was your day?"

The fair skin around Karen's eyes creased.

"You look troubled," Logan said. "Didn't the pump work?"

"The pump is fine."

"Did the windows stay up?"

"Two of them needed propped up on books, but yes, we got along fine with the windows."

"Did someone get hurt?"

Karen shook her head while biting her lip.

"What is it?"

"Eldon Kent. He came to the school again today."

During the exchange, Tillie studied Karen. She wore a ruffled blouse with lace at the collar and on the cuffs. Satin ribbon formed an angular design on her dark skirt. A cummerbund embellished her trim waist. Although designed as a simple outfit appropriate for the school room, it still spoke of fine style, the style that girls who could afford new clothing wore.

Tillie hung her head. To think a made-over dress excited her. Held up next to Karen's clothing, Tillie's few dresses belonged in Mama's rag box. Nothing in her wardrobe possessed the taste of this newcomer to their household. The pitiful work dress she wore now didn't even know the meaning of the word "style." At least it was mostly hidden behind her apron. Continuing with her work, Tillie fought the shame that tried to cloak her.

"He wanted to eat lunch with me." Karen's voice wavered.

Logan sucked in another breath, quick and impatient.

"I'm concerned he wants to court me." Karen's distressed gaze fixed on Logan's face.

Logan nodded. His clear blue eyes dimmed. "It worries me too."

Tillie stood. She tapped Logan's shoulder. "The basket is full. Could you please carry it to the house?"

"I'll get to it later." He held his hand in the air as though to push her away. His eyes still on Karen, he asked, "What do you think we should do?"

The question wasn't meant for Tillie, but she knew her answer. Get rid of Karen, make her go away. She interrupted their work and stole Logan's attention. Scowling, Tillie crossed her arms.

"I don't know." Karen's voice rose. "On Monday he came at the end of the day. Today he came at noon. I never know when he'll come. When he does, each day is different, catching me off guard."

"Do you want him to court you?"

"No." Karen spoke the word forcefully, determined. "But he doesn't seem to get the message."

"All right, then. Plan on me picking you up at school every day."

"Every day?"

"Yes."

"But you shouldn't have to leave your work."

"I want to. This plan may not prevent Eldon from coming to school, but it'll send the message that he's not welcome."

Karen bit her lip for a moment as though thinking over the prospect. She must have approved because relief relaxed her features. "Thank you. I appreciate your thoughtfulness. Truly."

Tillie turned away. The whole exchange made her nauseous. When Logan persuaded her and Mama to board the teacher, he'd said they'd hardly notice another person in the house at all. But he'd been wrong. Logan noticed her. And now, so did Tillie.

Logan exited the garden without another look at Tillie. The full basket of ripe produce forgotten, he strolled at Karen's side, talking with her in low tones.

Tillie turned to the tomato patch. She'd been the one at Logan's side when she entered the garden an hour ago. Now she worked alone. Mama needed one more bushel in order to begin tomorrow's work, so Tillie knelt down to reach for a bright red tomato hanging from the flourishing green vine. This job would take forever with no one to help her, and a heavy heart slowing her movements.

CHAPTER TEN

"*T*eacher, what's your favorite subject in school?"

Karen swallowed a bite of the roast beef sandwich Mrs. De Witt packed for her earlier that morning. Her mouth empty, she answered Lacy Jones's question. "Let's see." She studied the cottonwood branches above. "I believe I enjoy reading most of all."

"Oh, Cal hates to read." Lacy screwed up her face. "No way would he give up fishing or field work for a book." She took a bite of the half-eaten apple turnover in her hand.

Chuckles arose from Alice Hinkley and Sarah Hixson, the other girls who shared the quilt spread on the grass.

"Then he hasn't read poetry or history or adventure." Karen's animated voice produced awe on Lacy's face.

"My favorite is poetry," Alice Hinkley said.

"Yes, I can believe it is." Karen smiled at the fifth-grade girl who, in spite of her young age, already possessed an appreciation for lyrical passages. With her mother acting as her piano teacher, Alice's gifts were channeled in the direction of music.

"Do you like poetry, Miss Millerson?" Alice reached in her lunch pail and pulled out a thick sandwich.

"Yes. In fact, I plan to read a sample of Tennyson to you after recess."

Alice's eyes lit up.

Karen raised her gaze to the white plumes of cloud that billowed overhead, blocking the sun. Today's heat grew more oppressive with each hour that passed. Only when a slight breeze stirred did she enjoy a reprieve.

So far this week, the students had conducted themselves well in her outdoor classroom. Karen planned to hold classes outside again. If work got done in a timely manner, she might even dismiss early so the children could contend with the heat seated by a shaded stream or on a front porch instead of in a stuffy classroom.

Karen scanned the yard. The boys had finished their lunches and were engaged in a horseshoe toss, the compromise that resulted from the disagreement in the baseball game. If the boys could handle themselves during this recess, she might let them have their gear back.

Sarah stood. "Come on, let's play." She helped each girl stand. The three of them took off in the direction of the swing.

A sigh escaped Karen's lips. She much preferred eating her lunch with grade school girls than with Eldon Kent. He'd stayed away today. She stood and brushed crumbs from her dark skirt. Oh, the day was warm. Karen fanned her face and righted her petticoat. Perspiration dampened her neck and legs. How wonderful it would be if a refreshing breeze would blow in and cool her down. But nothing about this day produced anything cool. The ground radiated heat. The pump handle seared her hands. Even the water she drew from the pump tasted like it came from a stove top.

The children labored in their play. They, too, felt the heat. The time had come to cut recess short and gather everyone in the shade. She scurried inside for her poetry book. The place the book usually occupied on the corner of her desk was vacant. Karen examined each book shelf and opened her desk drawers. No book.

Her gaze caught the corner of a red cover with gold letters on the spine under the globe. She raced to the corner. Wednesday afternoon's use of the globe had required a stack of books, including the one on poetry, in order to prop the globe up high enough for the boys in the back to see. She grasped the book and laid it on the corner of her desk in plain view.

A glance at the clock indicated that too much time had passed during her search. Recess ran late. Karen rushed outdoors to call the students.

Her steps faltered after one glance at the horizon. The innocent white clouds from only moments ago had turned dark. Their black bottoms hovered low to the ground. Panic threaded through her chest. She must get her students sheltered, but she didn't know where. The school building had no basement. Two outhouses and a building that doubled as a small barn and coal storage were the only other shelters on the property. None of them were capable of standing through a storm. The main level of the school building itself was her best choice. She gulped at the reality of weathering a storm on the ground level.

The breeze stilled. The afternoon turned as dark as evening dusk. More than a simple rainstorm was headed their way.

"Children!" Her call died. The heavy air sucked up her voice. She tried again. "Children, come inside!" Her effort to arrest their attention failed.

The younger students continued to romp around the yard, oblivious in their play. Older students faced west and watched the sky. Wisps of gray swirled beneath the dark clouds.

"Teacher, look." Kelvin Kent turned while pointing west.

Karen waved a frantic hand toward the school. Her movements stiffened like she was in slow motion.

Kelvin backed away from the spot near the road where he stood with a cluster of cousins. They followed his lead.

The eerie sky boiled overhead. Images of that mangy bull from her first night in town flashed through her mind. She'd been able to run away from it. Why couldn't she run now? One glance at the scared faces coming her way answered the question. The safety of all these children depended on her. The weight of responsibility combined with the fear threatening to freeze her joints made the job of taking even one step nearly impossible.

At least she could still talk. As the children filed through the door she held open for them, Karen pointed to the front of the room. "Get down on your knees under my desk. No distractions. Go now."

The students filed through the door and down the aisle in quick succession. Marty Kent brought up the rear of the line without the other two buddies in his gang.

"Where are Tim and Joe?" Karen demanded.

Marty shrugged. "Last I saw 'em they were out behind the shed."

They were probably devising some new plan for mischief when they should be paying attention. Typical behavior.

Karen called to the oldest girl in the school, Tom Hinkley's fourteen-year-old daughter. "Faye, please help the students kneel down. I must go outside to find Tim and Joe."

"I will, Teacher." Faye's reply carried through the eerie stillness.

Karen plodded out the door. Chills ran down her back. The children. She must help the children. She forced her legs to a jog.

Her back went rigid and all her muscles tensed, bringing her to a stop. A smoky, finger-like cloud descended and began to raise dust on the horizon. Screams ripped from her lungs.

LOGAN FINISHED his noon meal and rushed to the oat field. One more examination of the plump, bearded heads assured him the oat crop was ripe and perfect for cutting. Satisfaction flowed deep and brought a smile. A bountiful harvest meant large profit. And profit meant freedom. If he took the entire income to the bank, he'd find release from his obligation to Eldon. A savory thought. The future looked bright for the De Witt family.

A song rose from his heart and hummed on his lips as he sauntered into the barnyard. The tune faded when he noticed the sunlight. It looked strange, like the golden rays were forced through a black filter. He'd been so engrossed in his plans he failed to notice the darkness gathering above. Heavy clouds swirled low to the western horizon. Logan ran to the chicken coop where he chased the hens and rooster to shelter. He rushed on to the horse barn and, after moving fence posts and buckets inside, secured the doors. Before sprinting to the house, he shuttered the windows on the dairy barn and latched the door.

The sky continued to darken. A light wind drew his attention to the windmill. It turned when the breeze blew, but stopped and remained still for several moments. Another light wind blew, but this time the windmill turned in the opposite direction. Then it stilled. The confused windmill spun the pattern three more times before the wind quit and the air settled heavy around him. No birds chirped. No cows lowed. No leaves rustled. The hairs on Logan's arms stood on end.

He leaped onto the porch and threw open the door.

"Mama, I want you and Tillie to get underground. Now."

The women turned and stared at him like he was a crazy man.

"Go to the cellar. We're in for some violent weather." He assisted Mama in untying her apron and pulled the heavy boiling water bath brimming with full jars of tomatoes off the stove.

Tillie dropped the knife she'd used to slice the tomatoes and rushed for the back porch.

Logan guided Mama in the same direction. Then he lifted the square in the floor exposing a ladder.

Tillie went down first. Her head disappeared from sight as Mama stepped onto the first rung.

Logan rummaged around in a cupboard for matches and candles. "Here, take these." He handed them down to Tillie.

"Aren't you coming?" The alarm in Tillie's voice matched the sense of danger in his heart.

"No. I'm headed to the school. Karen may not know what to do in a storm."

"But—"

"Please watch over Mama for me."

Mama's voice carried up the ladder. "Bring Karen and the children to the farm, dear."

"I'll try. But don't wait for us. Both of you stay in the cellar until I come home. Understand?" He hung around long enough to see Mama and Tillie nod. "Good." He replaced the cellar lid and bolted from the house.

Daylight disappeared.

Logan's chest heaved. He ran on. Karen needed him.

Gray clouds swirled together and twisted along the ground. It cut a path straight for the school.

A scream tore the air. He'd heard it for the first time the night Vern's cows stood on the road.

Karen.

Logan careened into the school yard.

Her hands shot to her mouth as she stood near two boys wrestling beside the shed.

He yelled her name.

She turned.

A gust of wind jolted him and blew dirt in his eyes. He leaped into a run once more.

"Take Joe to the school." Karen yelled above the noise of the wind. "I'll bring Tim."

"Where are the others?" Logan stared at her, willing her to assure him everyone was accounted for.

"Inside." She nudged Joe in his direction. "Hurry!"

Karen's command of the situation warmed him. This city girl possessed a level head.

A gust of wind howled around them. Logan's heart skipped a

HOPE FOR TOMORROW

few beats. "Come on. None of you should still be out here. Let's go!" He took off on a run dragging Joe by the wrist.

Karen and Tim kept pace with him.

The screeching wind resisted every movement up the steps. Finally reaching the top one, Logan pulled the door open far enough for Tim, then Joe, followed by Karen to squeeze through. The door slammed shut. He pulled on it again, but the wind sealed it tight.

"Logan!" Karen's muffled voice from inside the school screamed his name.

Dirt scoured the side of his face. He must get inside or prepare to fly.

He yanked on the door with all his might. It inched open allowing just enough space for him to slip through.

A loud crack split the air. A large limb of the cottonwood tree crashed through the roof above the last row of desks.

Screams lifted from the children.

"The twister is here." Karen's lower lip trembled.

"Get down by your desk." He tugged on her hand, but Karen remained still as though nailed to the floor.

"I can't."

"You must." If Karen didn't move, her brief time in Silver Grove would come to an end. The wind would decide where she landed next, not Tom Hinkley.

The pitch of the wind changed. It shrieked and wailed like it was alive and in pain.

He was out of time. If a sloped pasture was the sort of obstacle he faced, he'd lift Karen in his arms again and carry her to where she belonged. But a fallen tree branch and rows of desks separated him from Karen's safety.

A roar with all the force and shrill of a steam engine surrounded the school. Logan wrapped his arm around Karen's waist, pressed her close to his chest, and scrambled under leaves towards the opposite end of the room. "Hang onto me, Karen. Whatever happens, make sure and hang on to me."

Karen's arms locked around his neck.

Logan fought his way against the gusts now tearing through the hole in the roof. He arrived with the teacher in the cluster of students as a deafening crash filled the air. "The roof! It's caving! Get down."

KAREN RELEASED her hold on Logan and knelt with her face pressed against the wooden boards. Wind whipped from all directions. Hard little balls pelted her back. Rain drenched her blouse.

She clutched her hands over her head as the glass cracked and shattered. Trembles overwhelmed her insides until she couldn't stop shaking. This storm would never end. Karen bit her lip to stop the moans rising in her throat.

Logan's strong arm circled her waist, drawing her close to his side. She burrowed deeper into his embrace. The steady beat of his heart helped her relax. If she focused on that safe, predictable rhythm so close to her ear, the fury of the storm couldn't reach her.

They crouched on the floor for what felt like hours. Karen's knees cramped. Still the wind blew. Older sisters spoke in low tones to soothe younger siblings. Finally, the pounding ceased. The winds subsided until only the sound of falling rain remained.

Logan patted her shoulder. "We can get up now."

Karen shifted her weight so that she could push to a standing position, but a section of the roof slanted over her head. She crouched down. "Is anyone hurt?"

The Hinkley girls hunched in one corner with Sarah and Becky Hixson. Five-year-old Ben crowded in at Sarah's side with her arm around him. The six Sanders children occupied the other half of the floor along with their four Kent cousins. Cal Jones hunched near little sister Lacy. Wade Patterson knelt between his two younger siblings. All of them were present and safe. But the younger ones whimpered while the grade school boys stared wide-eyed.

Logan pressed against the shingles brushing his head.

"Let me help." Cal Jones stood along with Wade Patterson. The two boys assisted Logan in moving the fallen roof. It clamored against the stove, freeing Karen and her students to move about. She helped children stand to their feet, gave hugs, and offered comfort.

One of her arms around Mary Ellen and the other around Lizzie, Karen looked out over her destroyed classroom. The windows were all broken. Shattered glass lay in the grass. Curtains hung in shreds at the empty windows where the wind teased them. The walls slanted in on the room under the weight of the large branch and collapsed roof. Melting hail stones, sticks, and soggy papers covered the desks. Shingles were everywhere.

A sob caught in her throat.

"We need to move everyone into the yard before the walls fall in," Logan said. "Follow me to a window."

Logan crawled through first. He stood on the grass and helped Lizzie then Mary Ellen out of the building. Karen received assistance next.

The smaller students followed with help from the older ones. Eighth grade boys Wade and Cal came last. A creak and a loud groan of wet wood echoed across the lawn. Everyone turned in time to see the school walls waver then fall in a heap. The stove pipe protruded through the rubble and wet papers flapped in the resulting gust.

Karen clutched her throat.

Logan scanned the entire group. "Please stay here. I'll go to the farm for the wagon so that we can take everyone home."

Before he could take even one step, a stream of wagons rolled down the road and turned into the school yard. Fathers jumped out and hurried to the children.

"Thank God you're all safe." Vern parted with his usual reserve and released a praise that multiplied tears in Karen's eyes.

Tom went down on one knee and opened his arms wide to welcome all three of his daughters in a tight embrace.

Clyde ruffled his sons' hair and reached to hug his daughters.

Leo Sanders, Evan Kent, and Roy Jones followed behind the other men seeking out their offspring.

"Daddy!" Lacy squealed and hurdled into her father's arms.

The men compared stories of damage at their farms as they gathered their children together.

After everyone returned to the road, Logan guided Karen through the sodden yard. "Come on. Let's go home. I want to check on Mama and Tillie."

CHAPTER ELEVEN

*L*ogan abandoned the slow pace he'd set to accommodate Karen on the walk to the farm and bounded over the steps. "Mama! Tillie!" he called as he sailed through the kitchen of the unharmed house.

Mama's head appeared after he lifted the cellar door. "We're fine, dear. How about Karen and the children?"

"The school is demolished, but everyone is safe." Logan kept firm hold of Mama's hand to steady her as she stepped off the ladder. "The children are on their way home with their fathers. You should see the school, though. Or what's left of it." He sucked in a deep breath.

Once Tillie emerged, Mama led them to the kitchen. "Let's have some coffee and finish off the apple pie." Mama set cups on the table and tied her apron around her waist. "Did anyone report damage?"

"Yeah. The twister hit the school but missed Clyde's farm. He only has fallen trees and broken windows. It blew the roof off one of Vern's barns, uprooted some trees north of his house, and destroyed one of Evan Kent's cornfields. The worst damage was done on the Hinkley farm where Tom lost his corn crib."

"I'm glad no houses were lost and no one was injured." Mama dished pie onto plates and passed them out.

"Tom will need to cancel classes for a few days until the school can get rebuilt. He called a meeting for tomorrow night to make plans." Logan dried his hands and joined the women at the table.

When the coffee time finished, Logan succumbed to his impatience and went outside to get a look at his own farm. Oak leaves plastered the north side of the house and barns. The windmill, so confused earlier in the day, now lay on its side, a stretch of fence smashed into the mud under its weight.

A few shingles from the house lay strewn across the garden and orchard, but nothing more serious greeted him. A couple of days of repair and the farm would be back to normal.

Even the corn had fared well. Less hail had fallen on Logan's fields than on the school, so beyond a few shredded leaves, the corn survived.

He moved on to the hayfield and was relieved to see it was fine. However, when he checked on the oats, they were flat on the ground. All the ripe and promising heads of grain were pummeled into the mud.

Wrapping his arms around his torso to halt the cramps shrinking his stomach, Logan dared to survey the damage. Nothing could be salvaged. Not even for bedding. He swallowed hard.

Without those oats, he had no way to pay the bank. His crop, his plans, his family's financial security were all ruined. The storm had taken the very resource he needed most and left him stripped and destitute. He trudged to the dairy barn under his own storm cloud. Mama and Tillie would lose their home for sure. In the barn, Logan slapped the high-hipped rump of a Holstein. The cow turned large brown eyes on him and mooed softly as though to assure him nothing was amiss. He wanted a bit of her calm. She complacently wagged her tail, unaware the world had changed. Unless he figured out a way to hang on at the bank, nothing would be the same again. Not for him or for Mama and Tillie or even for the cows. Without those oats, the only other source of income he had was the sale of the dairy herd.

Logan lowered himself onto the milking stool. He had no other option but to sell out before the inevitable bankruptcy overtook him. But these were Dad's cows. They belonged here. The family needed them, depended on them, just like the cows needed and depended on Dad and now Logan to care for them. He couldn't sell the herd. There must be another way. This evening's milking wouldn't be one of the last.

THROUGH THE EVENING meal of Mama's delicious roast beef, Logan choked his food down well enough to avoid any one asking questions about his lagging appetite. Karen and Mama kept up a pleasant conversation, but Logan couldn't force himself to enter in. He just wanted to be alone. Skipping dessert, Logan headed for his room where he could take the time to pray. Seated at his desk, he opened his Bible and read from the Psalms. *They are like trees planted by streams of water which yield their fruits in its season and their leaves do not wither. In all they do, they prosper.*

He closed his eyes. Nothing he'd done so far prospered. Maybe he needed to return to his old job.

A knock on the door interrupted his thoughts.

"Come in."

Mama entered and sat on his bed. "What kind of damage did you find?"

Logan blinked in surprise. "How did you know about the damage?"

A smile pulled at one corner of Mama's mouth. "Logan, dear, you forget how much you resemble your father. I could always tell when something bothered him. You're no different."

He scanned the room for an escape from the terrible duty of delivering bad news to his mother.

Mama waited with her gaze fixed on him. He wasn't going anywhere.

"The oats are ruined."

Mama blinked. "Those were intended as payment against the debt."

"Yes."

"What will you do now?"

Logan shrugged. "Try to find a way to hang on, but if I don't I'm forced to sell out."

"The situation is that bad?"

"I'm afraid so."

"Oh, I didn't know."

His throat ached. "I'm thinking I should return to preaching, but I'd have to move back to Oswell City to do it. You and Tillie would have to come along."

"Move so far away?" Mama said the words like they were a diagnosis of some rare and fatal disease.

"Yeah, but all your friends are here and now Andrew wants to court Tillie. Plus, we're boarding the teacher." A sharp pain pierced his gut. Leave Karen behind? Up until now, he'd ignored his own feelings on the subject.

"How much time do you have to decide?" Mama leaned forward. Her hands clutched the quilt so tight her knuckles turned white.

Boy, he hated to ask her to move. But he had to provide for her. What other choice did he have?

"A couple of weeks. I'll see Eldon at the end of the month after I collect Karen's room and board." Logan fiddled with the ribbon marker of his Bible. He could guess how well Eldon would take the news of a damaged crop.

"Will you still let Andrew call on Tillie?"

"Yeah. It's the only thing that's made her happy. Don't want to take that away from her now."

Mama stood and pulled a hankie from her apron pocket. "I trust you to do what's best, dear."

Her simple admission humbled him. Did he know best? What he wanted for them and what actually ended up happening might turn out to be two different things. "Thanks, Mama."

She slipped out the door.

After a long moment of contemplation, Logan turned back to Psalm 1 with renewed interest. He needed to figure out prosperity's secret.

KAREN SCANNED the sanctuary from the De Witt pew. Other families claimed their usual pews proving that week night meetings followed the same tradition as Sunday morning. Down front, Tom Hinkley visited with Clyde and Roy, the other two members of the school board. The meeting would start soon.

The promise of a return to normal brought Karen peace. The memory of her students outside at recess under that dark sky haunted her. Any one of them could have been harmed in the storm. Relief and thankfulness still flowed out of her heart. She didn't know what she would have done if Logan hadn't come. Those wrestling boys in the back yard would've met with a tragic end, right along with herself. If Logan hadn't moved her to safety, the roof would've smashed her.

She ventured a glimpse of his face. Maybe he wasn't as brash in his choice of occupation as she first thought. A man who operated machinery with names like stacker, thresher, or shredder might have some space in his heart to consider the well-being of others after all. Since he held an off-farm job at one time in that town he visited last weekend, Logan might possess more caution than the average farmer.

Karen tilted her head to the side. He was beginning to mean more to her than the handsome young man who offered her a place to stay. His concern for her went beyond the surface kindness he showed as the recipient of her room and board payments. He'd risked danger to come to the school.

And then the wind shut him out. No amount of pushing on the door made any difference. She hadn't been strong enough to help him. It wouldn't bother her so much if she didn't care.

But she did. And now she sat here in church by his side.

At the last minute, Sandy chose to stay home. Karen fought her desire for Sandy's presence in the De Witt pew. If Logan's mother were here, they'd look less like a couple. Dressed in his dark suit, shaved, and with his waves of hair slicked back, Logan fulfilled the part of a suitor. Her thoughts really shouldn't race down that trail, but she couldn't stop them. He'd searched her out with that sensitive gaze of his when she came down for supper. To top it off, he acted the gentleman through the meal and the ride to church.

Perhaps he shouldn't have come to the school to help her. If he'd stayed away, her heart wouldn't have this excuse to misbehave like one of the mischievous boys in her classroom.

Karen turned her attention to the front of the church when the school board chairman stepped forward.

Tom cleared his throat. "Good evening. Glad to see ya here tonight. Thanks for comin' out. I see we have Miss Millerson with us. Thanks for bringin' her, Logan."

People turned and smiled at her.

"Roy and Clyde figured repairs to the school will take about a week. We need to give the place a chance to dry out before we replace the shingles, repair the roof, and order in new glass." Tom stopped to make eye contact with the school board.

"Dependin' how long the railroad takes to get the glass and shingles here, we'll start school up again in a week," Clyde said.

"Maybe if we save the window repair until last, we can stick to that plan. The kids can still have class without any glass in the windows," Tom said.

"For as hot as it's been, they might prefer windows with no

glass now that the storm passed through and cooled the air down." Roy chuckled.

Murmurs of agreement rippled across the room.

Tom held up his hands. "Men, what do you say? Can I plan on your help in the mornings tomorrow and next week? Workin' half-days gives us time to tend to our own storm damage."

Fathers nodded their consent. So did Logan.

Karen peered at him. He didn't have any children to benefit from a repaired school. "Why do you want to help?" The words slipped out before she could stop them.

The shadow she'd detected on the afternoon of his surprise return dimmed his eyes again. "I may not be a married man with children, but I still enjoy an excuse to leave the farm now and then."

His unspoken wishes lingered in her mind, bringing an ache to her throat.

Tom's voice cut into her thoughts. "All right. Let's meet at the school after chores tomorrow morning. Bring your tools and any children who want to help." Tom turned to Clyde. "Can we use your wagon?"

Clyde nodded.

"Good." Tom turned back to the gathering. "I'll put a notice at the hardware store sometime the end of next week to announce the start of school."

Clyde stood. "Sally and Lucy put together a coffee time. You're welcome downstairs for cookies following the meeting."

Tom held his hands up again. "Meeting adjourned."

Karen stood and inched toward the center aisle behind Logan.

"Mr. Hinkley, if there's anything you'd like for me to help with, I'm willing," Karen said as he passed by.

"That's mighty nice, Miss Millerson."

Pete joined them.

Tom scratched his head. "Maybe at some point you'll want to

check your books and see how wet they got in the rain. They might need time to dry out."

"Yes. Good idea. As soon as the site is clear enough for me to work there, I'll come."

He shook her hand. "If you'll excuse me, Lucy is waitin' for me downstairs."

"Certainly." Karen stepped out of the way.

"I hope none of your books are damaged, Karen." Logan put his hands in his pockets.

"I'm sure they are, but I'll check into it as soon as I can and replace them if necessary."

Logan glanced at Pete. "You might have some books she could borrow. Maybe you'd like to show Karen your collection sometime."

Pete waved his hand like no one cared. "Oh, I think she'd be much more impressed with yours." He turned to Karen. "You might have to wait a few days for Logan's books to get here, but I'm sure he has a much better library than I do."

"You have a library?" She hadn't planned to sound so incredulous, but farm boys hated to read. Karen couldn't imagine why this one would possess an entire library. "Where is it? Do you store books in the barn?"

Pete chuckled and jabbed a thumb in Logan's direction. "Who, Reverend De Witt here? Nah. The barn's too small for his supply of reading material."

"Come on, Pete." Red stained Logan's face.

Karen's gaze darted between the two men. "Reverend. What are you talking about?"

Pete lost his smile. "Didn't he tell you?"

"Tell me what?" Karen's pulse throbbed in her ears.

Pete turned to his friend with mock tsk-tsk noises. "Logan, you've been keeping this young lady in the dark."

Logan shrugged. "It never came up."

"She needs to know." Pete rocked back on his heels and

crossed his arms, his enjoyment of his buddy's discomfort evident on his face. "Where do you store your books, Pastor Logan?"

He tugged at his collar. "Currently, they're all housed in my study at the Oswell City church."

This new information circuited all the way through Karen's brain, surged in her veins, and set her heart on a race. Logan De Witt was a preacher. Memories of the past days spent with the De Witt family assaulted her. Logan's offer to pray for her on the eve of the first day of school. His consistent show of kindness and compassion. And of course, his voice. It could belong to no one else but a preacher.

Karen covered her mouth before she spewed harsh words due to the years of fear and pain harbored in her heart. Logan De Witt, the farming preacher, was the most dangerous man she'd ever met. The inroads he'd already made into her heart promised to inflict more misery than any threshing accident or an untimely death or her father's terrible decisions.

But she still could find safety from all these things in her teaching career. She must focus on it and forget all about Logan and his daredevil persona. In need of privacy to sort it all out, she clutched her skirts and fled the church.

CHAPTER TWELVE

"*Y*ou never told her?" Pete gawked at him like he would a dim-witted child.

"Didn't have a chance. We've had other, more critical matters to deal with." Like Eldon Kent and violent storms. Warning Karen of his vocation was the least of his worries. Besides, he enjoyed the friendship that had grown between them. She saw him as he was, struggling and grieving just like anyone else.

"She didn't take it so well." Pete's voice softened. Gone was his previous swagger.

"Now you know why I fail whenever you try to set me up." He held Pete's gaze.

"You won't stay single forever." Pete stepped closer and squeezed his shoulder. "Don't let her get away."

Logan frowned.

A tiny smile lifted a corner of Pete's mouth. "The girl is eating her heart out over you."

Sometimes Pete didn't know what he was talking about. At least he saved those moments of insanity for discourses he held out of the pulpit. Too bad Logan had been his choice for this one.

Logan shuffled away from Pete and down the aisle. He'd better seek out Karen. He may not have much experience with women, but he knew enough to believe that any time a young lady high-tailed it out of church, it was because he'd said something offensive.

He stumbled upon her seated in the swing on Pete's back porch. A rather intimate setting for after dark, and not one he would have chosen. But, Karen's restored state of mind held utmost priority. He sucked it up and eased in next to her. "What did I say?"

She traced a fold in her blue skirt. The same skirt she'd worn for her introduction to Vern's bull. Mama had worked wonders on it. All traces of mud were gone. "I didn't know you were a preacher."

"I'm sorry. I didn't think the little detail all that important."

Karen turned to him. "Why are you farming, Logan?"

"Mama and Tillie were left alone on the farm with no one to take care of them after Dad's death. So, I asked for some time off and came home."

"You were the pastor of a church when your father died?"

"Yes. In fact, that's where I went on my recent trip." He could supply Karen with much more information about his time in Oswell City, but she needed his assistance right now. He'd keep his disappointments to himself.

"Do you intend to return to preaching someday?" She asked the question as though fearful of his answer.

Now that Pete had so blatantly exposed him, honesty was his only choice. "I want to, but I'm testing it out. If a replacement is found, I'll stay on the farm. If not, then I'll return. I'm waiting on God's direction right now."

Karen's eyes widened. She turned back to her crease-folding.

Late season crickets chirped in the grasses of the cemetery, filling the silence that deepened between them.

"So, you left a job you love to take care of your mother and sister." Karen's voice held no accusation, only the tone of a woman trying to solve a mystery.

"Yeah, I guess so."

The moon slipped out from behind a cloud and cast a soft glow on Karen's features.

"Sounds like something you would do."

Her mouth tilted only inches away from his own. With her face tipped back, her lips made an easy target for a kiss.

Kissing. Now where did that idea come from? He hadn't thought about kissing in years. Not since the days of Pete's sorry match-making. He exhaled until the last ounce of air left his lungs. The moonlit night was getting to him. Rubbing his hands together, Logan cleared his throat. "Does it matter to you if I farm or not?"

"Oh, yes." The words sounded like they escaped before she had time to censor them. "I mean, I think everyone should do what God asks them to do. He's asked me to teach. If He wants you on the farm, then that's where you belong."

"Wise words, Karen." He shifted in his seat. "Tell me what you think I should do."

"Oh, I wouldn't know. Only you can hear God's call on your life."

"Tell me what you'd want it to be, then."

She bit her lip and took her time providing him with an answer. "You should do what makes you happy." She glanced up at him again.

Oh, those lips. Closer than the last time, he was sure. How easy to cup her chin and close the distance between them. She still might choose to leave. He held a piece of news that possessed the power to shatter any hopes he'd had the nerve to dream up.

He inhaled. "Karen, I have something to tell you."

"What is it?"

"Clyde stopped me after the meeting. He said Tom involved him and Roy in the search for a teacher to replace you but didn't find one. Neither did they find another position for you. With school already started, all the positions are filled."

Karen's focus left his face and shifted to the sky where tiny points of light twinkled through the darkness. A small breeze caught a tendril of hair and teased her cheek with it.

Logan should've been the one with the good sense to brush her cheek, not the wind. He sucked in a deep breath and shifted in his seat again. He needed to get out of here.

He pushed off the swing and stood up. "Tom wanted me to let you know that the school board won't hold you here. If you don't want to spend a whole year teaching country school, then you're free to leave."

"But Silver Grove won't have a teacher."

"I know, but they want to be fair." Tom's grace held a high cost for Logan. If Karen left and deprived him of the extra income, he'd have to sell the farm for sure.

KAREN HEARD the sincerity in his voice, and she cherished it. He'd always acted kind toward her, but this announcement proved to her that Logan was capable of acting in the interest of the good of others instead of being driven by his own. But that's how Father had acted all the while involved in a cover-up. Would Logan behave differently? His friend had just revealed him as a preacher, a profession Logan avoided telling her about. Maybe he didn't want her to know because, like Father, he had areas of his life he wished to keep concealed.

In spite of all that, she needed to pursue her career. Silver Grove was now her only option. Before tonight, Karen would have jumped at the release his offer promised her. Now she wasn't so sure.

She met Logan's gaze. He waited for an answer.

"I'll stay."

"I thought you made it clear to Tom that you refused to teach anywhere but a high school."

"I did, but I've changed my mind."

He studied her as though her new attitude was due to a mysterious injury. "You're sure about this."

"Yes." The faces of the Hinkley sisters, five-year-old Ben Hixson, and even the incorrigible Emmett filled her mind. "Trust me, Logan. I have good reasons. I'm learning to love the students here and want to see Silver Grove's school stay in session."

"You're a high school teacher and yet you want to teach country school." Leaning against the porch pillar, Logan crossed his arms over his chest.

Karen might as well be ten years old. "I have nowhere else to go."

If she was a specimen under a microscope, then Logan would have already learned all he could ever know for as close as he scrutinized her. She refused to say any more.

After a long time, he backed away from the pillar and inhaled. "Well, I sure could use the money. We have the room, so if you want to stay in Silver Grove, Miss Millerson, then my home is yours." With a little flourish of his hand, he motioned in the air before him as though rolling out a grand and royal carpet.

A floaty little feeling fluttered in her stomach. What if those gracious words belonged to an upright, truthful preacher? There were some in the world. Just because her father messed up didn't mean all preachers acted that way. Now that she'd chosen to stay in Logan's home, she'd have lots of time to study him.

LOGAN SAT AT HIS DESK, the farm account books spread open before him. If concentration could squeeze answers out of a sheet of paper, he'd have finished this job much sooner. He erased a number, filled the space with a different figure, and studied. The sum still fell short of what the bank demanded. Another dollar amount may work as a possibility. He erased and scratched. Still no improvement.

He dropped the pencil and massaged his temples. Regardless what he tried, the numbers sent him the same message. He needed more money. He knew what the shortage meant, a trip to the bank first thing Monday morning. Trying to forget what he read on the page, he squeezed his eyes shut. This couldn't be how God intended for his stay on the farm to come to a close.

There must be another way, but Logan had reached a dead end.

"Logan, dear." Mama's voice rang in the stair well.

He pushed away from his desk and poked his head into the hall.

"Pete's here. He brought the mail and has a letter for you."

Logan motioned for his friend to climb the stairs. Maybe Pete would have a genius idea to solve his problems. "Have a seat," he said, pointing to his chair at the desk. Logan settled on the bed.

Pete handed over an envelope postmarked Oswell City. Tingles erupted over Logan's shoulders and down his back. In one swift second, he ripped the envelope, unfolded the letter, and began to read.

Dear Pastor Logan,

We've found a young man willing to fill in as your substitute. Perhaps you remember Dan Kramer. His wife is Clara Zahn, daughter of the family who owns the café here in town. They're waiting to go to the mission field so Dan was quite happy to have this opportunity to minister. They can stay in town until March but are willing to accommodate your schedule.

Let's keep in touch.

Sincerely,

Paul

Logan stared at the words on the paper until they blurred. Dizziness assaulted his head while his heart shrank. Boy, would he miss Oswell City. The letter was so final. So much for holding out for the day when he'd need to return as soon as possible. Leaving the financial stresses and ruined crops behind lined up with his plan much better than replacing him did.

"What's it say?"

Logan blinked. He'd forgotten all about Pete seated across from him. He handed Pete the note so he could read for himself.

Pete glanced up. "Sounds like you're staying."

"Sure does." Logan took the letter and folded it up. "At least the church will be taken care of. I was concerned about them getting left without a pastor." That prayer may have an answer, but the answer created more problems. Without the faint promise of his preaching job waiting for his return, Logan had nothing to fill his need to provide for Mama and Tillie, or to guarantee his removal from the farm.

Logan settled into his seat at the desk after Pete left. He must make the best of things now. The sale of the farm loomed as his only option. But then what would they do? He'd have to find a job in town. Mama and Tillie would still end up moving out of their home. Pain pricked his heart. His departure from the farm had forced Dad to borrow money in the first place, so the responsibility to make things right with the bank belonged to him.

Through the rest of the day while he repaired the windmill and repositioned it once again to catch the breeze, Logan prayed for God to give him peace about the decision to sell.

None came. Through the milking, supper, and the quiet hours of the night, his unease persisted. Early Sunday morning, he got up, knelt down at the side of his bed, and prayed some more. As he spent time in the barn for the morning milking, Logan continued his silent petitions for God's direction, provision, and peace.

"You look like you didn't sleep so well last night, dear," Mama said when he entered the kitchen for breakfast. "Something wrong?"

Everything was wrong. He dropped into his chair at the table and sipped coffee. "You and I need to talk. I'm going to the bank tomorrow to visit with Eldon about a sale."

Mama moaned. "I hoped you'd changed your mind."

"Wish I could, but I don't have a choice."

"What about Karen?"

"I don't know. Guess we'll work it out as we go." The vague answer held promise of a happy ending, but his gut told him otherwise. Only days ago, she'd made the decision to stay in Silver Grove and teach at their tiny school. He'd rather do anything but wreck her plans. If he had to stay, he wanted her here too. The truth made his heart pound. Karen had begun to rival Pete for the title of "best friend." A farm sale would break up more than their livelihood. It would also interfere with a vital source of encouragement. He polished off a pancake, gulped his coffee, and headed to his room to dress for church.

Mama and Karen stood in the kitchen when he entered. Karen wore her exquisite Sunday dress again, complete with hat, gloves, and curls. What a sight to behold. He may not have many more chances to enjoy the pleasure. He wanted to memorize everything about her, but his pulse took off on a run.

"You look beautiful, Karen." Wow. Not one stutter. He grinned.

Her cheeks tinted pink and a shy smile claimed her lips. "Thanks, Logan."

He turned to Mama. "You look nice, too, Mama."

"Thank you, dear." She blushed a little.

When was the last time anyone had complemented Mama on her looks? Probably not since Dad died. Logan made a mental note to do it more often.

All the way to church, pink and lace brushed his pant leg, his waist, and his sleeve. But really, it wasn't so bad. He could get used to this. Too bad the inevitable farm sale would prevent it.

CHAPTER THIRTEEN

"*H*ey, Logan. Come to my study. I need to ask you something." Pete strode over to where he stood after the morning service making plans with Tom, Clyde, and Vern for rebuilding the school.

"What's on your mind?"

Not until they'd reached Pete's study behind closed doors did he answer. "You remember that church out in the country east of Bridgewater Springs?"

"Yeah. Meadow Creek Chapel. What about it?"

"Did you see the paper?"

"No. I haven't been to town yet this week to pick up our copy."

Pete laid the latest copy of the *Bridgewater Times* on his desk. The front page story sported the title, *Chapel Destroyed in Thursday's Tornado.*

Logan's jaw went slack. His gaze returned to Pete's face.

"They contacted me asking to use our church until theirs is rebuilt. I offered it for Sunday afternoons, and they agreed. The five-mile drive should work out as long as the weather holds. Along with a place to meet, they also need a preacher. Meadow Creek has been without for the summer and the rebuilding will delay the search. I've got plenty to do preparing for my own congregation, so I wondered if you wanted the job."

"Me?"

"You'd receive a weekly salary and could start next Sunday. What do you say?" Pete leaned against the wall. He crossed one of his ankles over the other and awaited an answer.

More money. Made from preaching, of all things. God was big. And good. Very, very good. He grinned. "It's a deal. Tell them I'll do it."

Pete smiled. "Wonderful. I'll drive over myself to deliver the news." He tossed the newspaper on a shelf and turned back to Logan. "There's one thing you should know."

"What's that?"

"You'll need to provide the music."

"Isn't Lucy Hinkley available?"

"No. She'll continue to play for our morning services."

"Oh." Maybe this arrangement wasn't as good as he thought.

"But I know of someone else who might work out better." Pete stroked his mustache and humor glimmered in his eyes.

"Who?"

"Ask Karen." Sneaky Pete turned matchmaker again.

"Now, wait a minute." Logan held his hand up as though to stop an advancing foe.

Pete chuckled. "I'm not trying to set you up."

Logan raised his eyebrow.

Pete shook his head. "Seriously. Have you heard her sing?"

"Uh, well no."

"Go to school on a Wednesday morning sometime. I drove past last week around nine o'clock. She had the windows open so her voice drifted out to the road. She must have been teaching music to her class. Anyway, can I just tell you the girl is talented?"

Talented, beautiful, and caring. A woman he'd thought about kissing. Boy, she was wearing him down. He cleared his throat. If Pete knew where his mind had been, he'd never hear the end of it.

MICHELLE DE BRUIN

All he wanted to do was follow God's leading. Logan was still single because God wanted it that way.

A knock came at the door.

"Come in," Pete called.

The door opened, and Karen entered. Her gaze rested on Logan. "Your mother is ready to go home. She sent me to ask how much longer you need for your meeting."

"Tell her I'll be right there." So much for avoiding temptations. She'd found him.

Karen smiled first at him and then at Pete.

After she left, Pete clicked his tongue. "She's gorgeous."

"I've heard you say that before."

"I'll say it again. Don't let her get away."

Logan scowled. "I thought you said you weren't matchmaking."

A smile tugged at one corner of Pete's mouth. "I won't have to this time."

"May I remind you that she is my boarder? Even if I did care for her in the way you hope, I couldn't do anything about it." The speech was meant to ward Pete off of any more attempts to throw him and Karen together, but it left a sad little ache in a forgotten corner of his heart.

"God has a way of working things out."

All God had worked out so far included a clear message that Logan should focus on him instead of on courtship. If Logan hoped to attain any degree of success, then obedience must extend beyond his effort at honorable living arrangements. "Maybe that's true for others, but it doesn't seem to be the case for me."

Pete shoved off the wall. "Ask her to help you on Sundays. See what she says."

Logan shook his head. He'd already taken far too many risks in the past.

SEATED at the table in the farmhouse dining room, Karen cut her roast beef into small pieces.

"You and Andrew have a good time Friday night?" Logan asked his sister.

"Yes." Her face colored. "He wants to come again next Friday."

"What did you tell him?"

"I said yes. Is that all right with you?"

Logan winked. "He's your beau, Tillie."

"I know, but do you like him?"

"I do. I think he's a fine young man."

"Then I like him, too."

Logan buttered a slice of bread. "I had a talk with Pete after church this morning."

"Why did it take so long?" Sandy asked.

"He offered me a job."

Sandy's eyes widened. "He and Anna are leaving?"

"No. Nothing like that. He showed me an article in the newspaper. Thursday's storm leveled the chapel in Meadow Creek."

"That's terrible," Karen said.

"Yes. They need a place to meet while the chapel is rebuilt. Since they also need a preacher, Pete suggested that I take the job." Logan spooned corn onto his china plate.

"Are you going to do it?" Sandy asked, pouring water from the cut glass pitcher.

"I am. Starting next Sunday afternoon." Logan forked his third helping of meat onto his plate.

"Does this change your mind about that trip to the bank tomorrow?"

"Sure does." He helped himself to his second heaping mound of potatoes.

"Will you have enough time through harvest to prepare sermons?" Sandy asked, her voice skeptical.

"I'll make time." He reached for the gravy boat. "The letter

Pete delivered yesterday held the news that Oswell City found someone to replace me. I'm staying here with you." A river of gravy ran down one side of the potatoes and smothered the meat. "Nothing will change except my need to spend time in study and prayer."

"You do that anyway, dear." A self-satisfied smile spread across Sandy's face. She looked the happiest Karen had ever seen her.

"I'm not sure how well this income will make up for the loss of the oat crop, but coupled with the milk sales and Karen's room and board, it's the best option I have."

"It sounds like a good one to me."

The room grew hot and stuffy. In the days following the storm, life might stay the same for the De Witt family, but for her, everything had changed. She taught country school, not high school. Her residence was a small room in an old-fashioned farmhouse, not a comfortable house on a city street. And now Logan announced that he was staying in Silver Grove, on the farm, and in her life. The last time she'd shared a home with a preacher, her whole family suffered scandal complete with their names in the paper and a near brush with prison for her father. Karen prayed those days were behind her forever.

After the meal ended and Karen assisted the other women with dish washing, she settled in the parlor to enjoy one of the Jane Austin books in her collection. She'd read *Emma* dozens of times before, but she never got tired of the genteel world portrayed in the story. Spending a Sunday afternoon with the characters she found in the pages helped Karen feel a little less homesick.

Two chapters later, Logan arrived in the parlor. He claimed the rocking chair and opened his Bible. With his head bent over the book, he read with his full focus on the pages.

Thoughts of the destroyed chapel returned. Logan might be a preacher and she might regret the time she'd have to spend with him to accomplish the ideas taking shape in her mind, but those poor people needed assistance. She cleared her throat to get his attention.

Logan glanced up.

"I want to help."

His brow furrowed. "Help with what?"

"The services for those people who lost their church building to the storm."

Logan sucked in a breath while his gaze left her face.

"What's wrong?"

He turned to her again, his brow still furrowed. "I can't ask that of you."

"You aren't the one asking, I am."

"Then the answer is no." He shook his head.

"Why? Surely they need a Sunday school teacher or at least someone to greet them at the door." *Emma* slid off her lap and thumped on the floor.

Logan flipped a few pages in the Bible. Either he was stalling for time or searching for a verse to give as an answer. "I must stay focused on the work the Lord has given me to do. He wants me to serve Him unattached." He rubbed the back of his neck and glanced at her. "I mean, I wish you could . . . but . . ."

Perspiration glistened above his twisted brow. The poor man must suffer from some sort of ailment. Her question required only for him to assign her a task. Surely that wasn't such a difficult job to make him break out in a sweat.

He bent down to retrieve her abandoned book and gave it to her. After wiping his forehead with a white handkerchief, he returned his attention to the Bible in his lap.

Their conversation had clearly come to a close. Karen found the page where she'd stopped reading. She resumed the story in the place where Emma's sister and her family visit for Christmas. Karen's thoughts turned to her own sister Julia, her little nephew Ben, and Julia's lawyer husband Arthur. The birth of their baby lay less than two months into the future. Karen doubted she'd get to see them at Christmas. Heaviness weighted her chest. Those people in Meadow Creek probably felt the same way about their church. Like her, they'd been severed from something very important to them. She had to try again. Closing her book, she leaned toward Logan. "There must be something I can do."

Logan swallowed. Once. Twice. "Pete had mentioned that I'd have no one to lead the singing."

"I love to sing."

Logan's attention never left the Scriptures as he fiddled with his tie until it loosened away from his collar.

Karen left her place on the love seat and knelt beside the rocking chair to gain his attention once more. "What were you planning to do without anyone to help with the singing?"

He shrugged. "I'd do it, I guess."

"Is that what happens in Oswell City?"

"No. We have a pipe organ. Apparently, the Meadow Creek congregation doesn't have anyone who plays." He flipped a page and kept reading.

"Do you enjoy singing?"

His eyes moved from side to side following a line of print on the page, never once looking in her direction. "No. I'm perfectly content to let the organist take care of all the music."

Karen stood. "May I please come? Maybe you can put me on trial for a month or so. After that, we'll reevaluate if we feel this isn't working out."

Logan tugged at his tie again, loosening it even further. Unbuttoning his top button, he blew out a puff of air that scattered the blond strands fanned at his hairline. With slow movements, he closed the Bible and raised his head until meeting her gaze. "All right. Sounds fair. Four Sundays. You don't need to do any more." He offered a faint smile, more perspiration glistening on his forehead.

CHAPTER FOURTEEN

*T*illie stared at Mama while choking on a sip of milk. "What did you say?"

Mama set her coffee cup down on the table. "I said that Karen and I talked and it's been decided that she is going to assist with the meal preparation and laundry so that you and I can work on canning the tomatoes."

"With all the time off while the school is getting rebuilt, I'll be available to help you in the kitchen and to learn from you." Karen's eyes took on a shine.

"Can't you cook?" Tillie asked.

"No. I never learned, but I've always wanted to know how."

"You're the same age as me and can't cook?" She sniffed and tossed her napkin on the table. "Some girls our age are already keeping their own houses." She peered at Karen. "How come no one showed you?"

"Uncle Henry and Aunt Fran hired a cook and a full time kitchen staff. They prepare the meals and see to all the kitchen tasks." Karen took a breath. "And, well, we're not the same age. I'm older than you."

"That's even worse. A woman older than me who can't cook."

Tillie reached for a biscuit and lavished butter on it as though the creamy topping could somehow cover this terrible disgrace.

"Don't be too hard on her, Tillie. Karen spent all her spare time studying to become a teacher." Logan's voice melted her irritation a slight degree.

Tillie took a bite of her biscuit, but she stared at Karen with the desire to prove just how ignorant this so-called teacher really was.

"Well then, it's time someone taught you." Mama piled her silverware onto her plate and pushed away from the table. "Tillie, if you could please fetch one of your aprons and give it to Karen, we'll wash up these dishes and get to work."

Tillie shoved away from the table and returned with a red gingham apron. She slipped it around Karen's waist and tied the strings in the back while holding her tongue against the gross injustice. Why did she have to be the one to train a spoiled rich girl how to cook? Mama sure knew how to make her life miserable. With an exaggerated tug, Tillie tightened the loops in the apron strings cinching Karen's middle.

Karen sucked in a breath. Towel in hand, Tillie strutted to Mama's side, ready to dry the dishes.

Logan carried his empty coffee cup to the sink where it sank into the suds.

"Thank you, dear." Mama tilted her head to receive a light kiss on the cheek.

"Have fun, ladies." He grinned and disappeared onto the back porch.

"Tillie, please go outside and butcher a chicken. I'd like to teach Karen how to fry it."

She gritted her teeth against more complaints and left the house.

THE DOOR SLAMMED, and Sandy turned to Karen. "You'll get used

to Tillie. So, you said at breakfast that you're older than her."
Sandy's tone of voice held a bit of a question, inviting Karen to
supply her with more information.

"Yes. I'm twenty-five."

Sandy swung around to gape at her. "Oh, Karen. I'm so sorry."

"Why?" Surely Sandy didn't feel the need to lament Karen's
old age.

Sandy shook her head. "When my husband and I agreed to
board the teacher, we assumed, based on the age of past teachers,
that you were fresh out of high school."

"Your husband?"

"John. He's gone now."

Karen nodded. The information lined up with the facts Logan
had shared with her in the swing Friday night.

"How did you become the teacher in Silver Grove?"

"I came to Iowa planning to teach at the new high school in
Bridgewater Springs. When I arrived in Silver Grove, Tom
Hinkley informed me of a change of plans."

"You must have been disappointed."

"I was. But I want the opportunity to teach, so I'm happy to
stay here." Karen lifted the lid on the speckled pot. Steam and heat
rolled over her face. "I didn't have a chance to tell you when
Logan introduced us." She shared a smile with Sandy as memories
of her muddy skirt and bandaged ankle returned.

"So, tell me about yourself. I understand you are from Chicago." Sandy moved to the cupboard with a stack of clean dishes.

"Right. My own father died four years ago. He'd worked as a
salesman before his death." Karen shuddered. She wanted to forget
everything from his earlier years as a preacher. But Sandy didn't
need to know all that. Her own son was a preacher. Some things
were better left in the past. "My sister got married shortly after his
death, but Mother and I moved in with her brother and his wife.
They paid for my teacher training at Illinois State Normal Univer-
sity. This qualified me to teach in a high school."

"You left home and ended up here with us."

"Correct."

Sandy brushed a strand of hair out of her eyes. "You and Logan have something in common. He wasn't planning on an extended stay on the farm either. But I'm happy you're here. We'll try our best to help you feel at home."

"You've already done a wonderful job."

Tillie returned with the chicken as Sandy finished the dishes. She went to the pantry and returned carrying a jar of dark red fruit. "Let's also make cherry pie for dessert."

Karen's mouth watered. "I love cherry pie."

"So does Logan. It's his favorite." Tillie's eyes squinted. "You'll probably mess it up since you've never made it before."

"You're right. I've never done this before." Karen glanced around the kitchen at the stove where a fire blazed, the chicken in the sink, and the fruit in the jar that somehow had to get onto a plate in the form of a pie. Maybe she couldn't cook this meal, even with all of Sandy's careful instructions.

Karen squared her shoulders, Sandy's words still on her mind. *"You and Logan have something in common. He wasn't planning on an extended stay on the farm either."* Unexpected circumstances had interrupted her well-intentioned plans too. This first meal she'd ever cooked on her own could act as her way of letting him know she cared. He wasn't alone in his attempts to find the good in the difficulties he now shouldered. He had her support as well as her appreciation for the sacrifices he'd made.

Karen smoothed her borrowed apron. "I can do this."

Tillie peered at her. "We'll see."

Sandy slid the cookbook closer to Karen. "Here's the recipe."

Karen scanned the words, their meanings taking longer to sink in than a phrase of Shakespeare.

Tillie smirked. "She'll never make cherry pie like I can. The way Logan likes it."

Karen fought the wish to compete with Tillie's lofty boast.

She'd make pie to Logan's tastes in spite of anything Tillie might say. Her heart would dictate the quality of her work, not Tillie.

"Karen will do just fine. She needs your encouragement, Tillie, not your criticism. Why don't you get busy filling more jars?" Sandy set a crock of lard and a canister of flour on the table.

Sandy checked the recipe one more time. "You're all set. Tillie and I are nearby if you have any questions."

She'd figure this out on her own. She'd made her way through all of her teacher's training with honors using that attitude. She could find success again.

From what she read, the lard came first. Karen went in search of a butter knife. It worked well to get the lard out of the crock, but instead of going into the measuring cup where it belonged, the lard plopped on the floor along with the clattering knife.

Tillie turned around. "You're making a mess!" She rushed to her knees and scraped up the splat of lard. She threw it in the slop bucket and pushed Karen out of the way. "Let me do it."

"No, Tillie. Karen needs the practice. Fixing the meal is her job. Your job is to get another batch of jars ready for the canner." Sandy frowned at her and ladled tomato slices into a jar.

"But she drops everything." Tillie crossed her arms.

"She'll get better."

"I don't want to eat a thing she cooks if it all has to go on the floor first." Tillie muttered to herself on her return trip to the stove.

Her mother gave her a stern look. "That's enough."

Karen loosened another slab of lard from the side of the crock. This time, it landed in the measuring cup.

For the next hour, she worked on the pie. By the time she layered everything in the pan, the crust felt thick in places but dry and crumbly in others. She put it in the oven anyway. It would bake and taste just wonderful, she was sure of it.

Following Sandy's example, Karen peeled and sliced the potatoes and prepared the chicken.

"Tillie and I need to go out to the garden for more tomatoes."

Sandy set up the ironing board. "Karen, would you want to start ironing?"

"Sure."

"Begin with Tillie's dresses and Logan's white shirt." Sandy heated an iron on the stove's surface. After a few moments she flicked water on the iron. It sizzled. "That should work." She motioned to Tillie to follow her outside.

The kitchen to herself, Karen scooted the ironing board closer to the stove. Now she wouldn't need to move even one step between the oven and the iron while she worked. She smiled. Tillie and her mother would be quite impressed with all the work she would accomplish.

She took the iron by the wooden handle, reached for the first dress, and laid it out on the ironing board. The pressed floral cotton on one of Tillie's work dresses brought another smile. With slow, deliberate glides of the iron over the material, she worked to make the flounce and sleeves just right. When the dress met her approval, she hung it on a hanger.

Karen heated the iron again and reached for Logan's shirt. The mud stains glared up at her as an unwelcome reminder that she had done the permanent damage. Successive washings and exposure to bright sunshine had done nothing to fade the splotches. Karen passed the iron over them. If only the simple movement erased the stain. She arranged the shirt so that one sleeve lay flat and pressed it with the iron.

A smoky odor stung her nose. She jerked the iron away from the shirt sleeve. Maybe the iron overheated on the stove and scorched the fabric. But the shirt was fine.

Maybe the chicken needed flipped. She scanned the stove. The chicken sizzled deliciously in the pan. She moved it to the counter anyway. Smoke spewed around the exposed burner. More wisps of smoke surrounded the oven door. The pie! She couldn't let it burn. Tillie would gloat. More than that, all of Karen's efforts to cook Logan and his family a satisfying meal would fail. She yanked the door open and stared into the haze. What should she do, reach blindly into the stove and pull the pie out, or wait for the smoke to clear? A flame, fanned to life from the sudden rush of air into the oven, licked the nearest object, and scorched to a crispy brown all her dreams of domestic competence.

CHAPTER FIFTEEN

he repairs to the farm completed, Logan returned his tools and bin of nails to the barn and headed for the house to prepare for a quick trip to town. He entered the back porch and claimed the usual upturned bucket as a seat to remove his boots. Voices from the kitchen reached his ears and slowed his movements.

"Ruined! How could you?" Tillie's voice rose beyond the point of exasperation.

"Make another one." Mama's words rang with fatigue.

Muffled sobs followed. Karen's?

What was going on in there? The women were busy with another ordinary day of garden work and kitchen tasks, but the bits of conversation told him a war had been fought and all three of them had come out the losers.

Logan rushed into the kitchen.

The scene brought on a laugh and a groan at the same time.

His white dress shirt hung from Karen's grasp, the cuff of one sleeve missing and the remaining edges of fabric charred. His stomach lurched. He needed that shirt Sunday. It was the only one he'd brought with him from Oswell City. What should he wear now, a faded shirt he wore around the farm? Most of them had tattered sleeves or patches on the front. He couldn't show up looking like a scarecrow.

"Look at what she's done to your shirt. Just look!" Tillie whipped the poor garment away from Karen and shoved it into his face. She pointed to the crispy edges, evidence of a recent and blazing flame.

"I'm so sorry, Logan." Karen choked the words out with great effort.

Mama handed her a handkerchief, and she used it to wipe her eyes.

His heart thumped. Hang the shirt and the irate sister. He wanted to gather Karen into his arms and whisper soothing words into her ear like he'd done during the storm. Words that said he cared more about her than any old piece of clothing. He'd figure out a way to replace the shirt. But how to repair Karen's sense of confidence? Another matter entirely.

He cleared his throat. "You could use a break. Karen, let's take a trip over to the school and check on your library. Then we'll stop at the post office. Why don't you come along, Tillie?"

She crossed her arms, wadding the precious garment in the process, and gave a haughty shake of her head.

He bit back a groan. "I only need to mail a letter so the trip will be a quick one. Please come."

Tillie glared at him.

"I'll drop you off at the mercantile before I go to the post office." Boy, he hated bribery, but no other method worked on Tillie when she'd made up her mind to defy.

She relaxed, and her glare melted away, but the lift of her chin remained. A look passed between Karen and Tillie, one that hinted at rivalry.

Goosebumps broke out on the back of his neck. Far more than his dress shirt hung in the balance here. He yearned to decipher the invisible contest charging the air.

A glance at Mama provided him with no further clues. She busied herself opening the oven door. "I'll take care of the pie. It looks fine."

"Of course it does." Tillie put her hands on her hips. "She got all excited about a little filling that dripped onto the bottom of the oven. Happens all the time. Not worth causing a disaster."

Mama straightened and looked at Tillie. "Why don't you go upstairs and get ready for the trip to town?"

Logan's fist tightened. He'd forgotten how much a kid sister tried the nerves. "Be ready in ten minutes." He sprinted up the stairs for the letter he'd penned earlier in the day requesting a shipment of books from Oswell City and slipped out of the house to hitch up the horse.

WHEN HE RETURNED HOME, the table was set with plates, silverware and glasses.

Mama held a hot pad out to Karen. "The only thing left to do is make the gravy. I've been keeping the chicken warm, and I must say it looks very tasty."

The aromas hanging in the air certainly lived up to Mama's description. Logan's stomach grumbled as he dried his hands and took a seat.

Tillie leaned over and stage whispered. "She cooked the whole meal." The expression on her face betrayed her doubts on the edible quality of the food Mama and Karen placed on the table.

"Let's pray." Logan reached for Tillie's hand on his right and Karen's hand on his left. His mouth invited God's blessing while his mind asked for some added grace should Tillie's doubts get proven true.

But the unspoken prayer wasn't needed. A few bites into his fried chicken and mashed potatoes proved Karen's abilities. "This food is really good."

Karen's face turned a deep pink. "The potatoes are a little lumpy."

"And the chicken is dry." Tillie puckered while Mama frowned at her.

"Didn't affect the taste any. You should cook for us more often." He helped himself to a second piece of chicken.

"Wait until you sample her cherry pie." Tillie's voice held the tone of a condemning judge, but Logan's mouth watered. Fried chicken and fresh cherry pie. Life didn't get any better.

"Any damage to your books?" Mama asked.

"Yes, unfortunately. The reading primers had begun to mildew. Those books were on the shelf closest to the windows. Mr. Hinkley said he'd request a new supply from the superintendent."

"Will they arrive in time for school Monday?"

"Not sure. I may need to improvise in the meantime." Karen wiped her mouth.

"The children may need a few days to adjust to the school routine, anyway," Mama said.

Karen leaned back in her chair. "So will the teacher."

Silence settled while Logan polished off his meal.

Mama smiled and stood. "Let's cut in to that pie, girls."

"Bet it didn't turn out." Tillie jutted her chin.

Karen straightened and glared with the most condescending school-teacher expression Logan had ever seen. She reached for her fork. "It might be the best you ever tasted."

Mama set a golden crusted pie before him. "Help yourself to the first slice, dear." She handed him the spatula.

His gaze flicked from one face to the next. Mama always served the dessert. Why did she want him to do it this time?

Three women, two with anticipation and one with distrust present in their eyes waited on him. He'd better not waste time asking questions.

"Well, all right." He sank the spatula into the crust and cut a wedge. Dark red filling dripped from the side as he lifted it from the pan. "My favorite."

"Karen made it." Pleasure eased the tired lines in Mama's face. Tillie snorted.

He settled the slice on his plate and pushed the pie pan over to Tillie. "Go ahead and take some."

"I'll wait." She shook her head and she whispered. "Take a bite."

Karen's face blanched white as her gaze stuck on the pie slice.

Had something gone wrong during the baking? Did they want him to sample it to declare it safe before anyone else risked eating a portion? He lifted his fork and cut a bite. Well, if the women wanted to poison him, at least they'd chosen a tasty way to deliver the venom. A man could eat cherry pie for a long time before regret caught up with him.

Logan chewed the bite in his mouth, a doughy patch sticking to his teeth. But the warm filling delighted his taste buds. The gravy may contain a few lumps, and Tillie may have known what she was talking about in saying the chicken tasted dry. But he couldn't disappoint the need for approval hanging on Karen's features. "Excellent," he said, cutting off a second bite of pie. "You did a wonderful job." A smile at Karen made her face flush again.

"Hard to believe." Tillie pushed the pie pan away as though it really did contain something poisonous.

He sank his fork into his dessert and scarfed down the entire slice in five bites.

AFTER DARK, Mama and Tillie lit a lamp and retreated to the sewing machine while Karen occupied the love seat in the parlor reading a book. Left alone at the kitchen table, Logan opened the Bible and made notes on the Scripture he planned to preach from Sunday. Two years ago, he'd used the same passage to write a sermon for his Oswell City congregation. The points he'd made returning to his memory, he wrote them down and added a few new thoughts.

Engrossed in the Psalms, he sat with his head bent over his notes when Karen's voice startled him.

"Thanks for taking me to the school today."

He glanced up.

She retrieved a glass from the cupboard, pumped water into it, and took a drink.

"You're welcome. Glad Tom can replace the damaged readers." Her presence in the kitchen jogged his memory. He marked the verse where he'd gotten interrupted and closed the Bible. "I discovered a package in the mail when I stopped at the post office. It's on the table." He jerked his head in the direction of the dining room.

Her brow furrowed, Karen left the room and soon returned with the package. She turned it over and pressed it with her fingers. "It's for you." She held it out to him.

"It has a Chicago return address."

"Yes. Mother sent it."

He took the package and studied it. Why would her mother send him anything? She didn't even know him except for whatever Karen may write in her letters.

"Open it."

Of course. A man could expect nothing less from a young woman full of surprises. This package probably contained another one. He turned it over and ripped off one side.

Folds of tissue paper spilled out. He sorted through them until uncovering the parcel. "Wow. A new shirt!" He stared at Karen.

Karen sat down. "After I stained your last one, I wrote to Mother and asked her to replace it."

"How did you know my size?" His chest tingled.

"I peeked at the collar that night while it hung over the stove to dry."

Leaning back in his chair, he laid the new garment over his notes on the table. He unfolded it and smoothed the faint wrinkles from the bright white fabric.

"Little did I know I'd go on to completely ruin your shirt today."

He grinned while taking in every last detail of the gift. An embroidered monogram, *LDW,* embellished the crisp white pocket.

"I'm so glad it came this week. I'd begun to wonder if Mother forgot."

Boy, he'd look sharp with this new shirt under his black suit. "This shirt is nicer than the one you replaced."

Karen fingered a cuff. "I let Mother decide what to send."

"Tell your mother she has great taste." He recalled a fleeting memory of Dad pecking Mama's cheek with a kiss after she'd given him a gift he treasured. Karen deserved the same. He yearned to act on the gratitude swelling in his heart.

He couldn't. His life headed in the wrong direction for that sort of thing. Bachelorhood still called, and for good reasons. Even though Teacher Karen may have taught him a little more about women, he must remember their living arrangements. Tom might have made a concession allowing him to escort her places like a family member would, but nowhere did the agreement permit kisses. Even chaste and thankful ones.

He'd have to settle for words only.

CHAPTER SIXTEEN

On Monday, Logan scooted up to the hot food set on the table for the noon meal.

"You should help Karen learn how to make an angel food cake when she comes home from school. We need it for dessert after supper tonight." Mama slid a recipe card across the dinner table in Tillie's direction.

Angel food. Yes, a fitting dessert for Karen to bake.

Tillie scanned the card. "Karen can't do any of these things!" Her raised voice penetrated Logan's thoughts.

"That's why you need to help her." Mama never missed a beat spooning green beans onto her plate.

"You saw her wreck Logan's shirt."

"But the pie turned out fine. So did the fried chicken. Plus, Logan has a new shirt now."

"He does?" Tillie turned incredulous eyes on him.

"Yeah. Karen asked her mother to send me a new one from Chicago." He fought the grin covering his face as well as the pride swelling his chest.

"Come on, Tillie. Teaching Karen how to make angel food

cake should be easy for you." Mama's voice held a note of pleading.

"That cake uses a whole dozen eggs. I don't want her to waste food."

"She won't with your expert guidance."

"Angel food is my specialty."

"Right along with your success at baking pie."

Mama deserved his support. Logan chimed in. "Look at how Karen's cherry pie turned out. I'd be happy to sample more."

Tillie glared at him. "She'll never cook as good as me."

"Maybe not. You have more practice, but at least Karen will gain some useful skills while living with us should she ever have her own kitchen someday." Mama reached out and squeezed Tillie's hand.

Tillie snorted. "A spoiled, pampered girl like her? She'll never lower herself to mundane kitchen tasks. All she'll do is return to her rich family, whoever they are, and get someone else to do it."

"Don't underestimate your influence, Tillie."

Now Logan understood why Mama was so determined to get Tillie to coach Karen. She saw Tillie's tutelage of Karen as a way to restore Tillie's faith in herself and her world. Maybe the effort would get her to go to church again. He silently cheered Mama on.

"After learning from a good teacher like you, Karen might find that she likes to cook."

Tillie shrugged off Mama's words. "A teacher needing someone to teach her. I never saw the like. She's smart in all the wrong things. Fancy clothes and teacher training haven't gotten her anywhere."

Words of disagreement pressed his tongue, but Logan managed to hold them back. Tillie could learn a thing or two from Karen, but now wasn't the time to strike up a debate. How he'd love to see the day when Tillie would come to appreciate Karen for more than just a rival to outdo. "Come to town with me."

The suggestion drew Mama's attention. "I didn't know you need to make a trip today."

"Karen gave me our first month's payment for room and board, so I want to stop at the bank. I also want to check at the post office and see if my books have come yet." He glanced at Tillie. "You'll get half an hour at the mercantile."

She blushed. "Well, I guess I could ride along." She turned to Mama. "Do you mind if I leave you to do the sewing alone?"

"Not at all. A change of scenery and some of Andrew's company will be good for you."

An hour later, Tillie at the mercantile with Mama's list, Logan stepped into Eldon's office armed with Karen's payment. He slapped the bills onto the desk. "I'd like to apply this to my account, please."

Eldon reached for the money and fanned the bills out like a hand of cards. He scowled. "Hardly worth your trip to town."

"Every little bit helps."

Eldon peered at him. "You think you'll pay that interest down by bringing petty little piles of money like this in here?" He wadded up the cash and threw it in a drawer.

Heat simmered in Logan's gut. Did Karen's hard-earned salary mean so little to him that he'd scorn this small profit from the effort she made to teach and discipline his passel of wily nephews? And after he'd worked so hard to get her attention. If he could just give Eldon a piece of his mind, he had a speech ready to spew.

Eldon folded his hands on the desk and gawked at him with patronizing victory.

The heat on Logan's insides went from a simmer to a boil. Nothing about Eldon had changed from school days. He'd actually grown worse. Refusing to let Eldon score, Logan reached for his black account book, one of many on the stack. He opened it and slid the book across the desk. "Record it. I'd sure hate for your numbers to come up shorter than mine."

A glare was the only response he received. Logan handed him

the pen. Eldon grasped it and waved it in a show of malice. "I'll write it down this once, but don't waste my time with measly sums of money. Bring me enough to prove you want to get rid of that debt."

Logan clenched his fist, struggling with the desire to pound it into Eldon. Of course he wanted to get out of debt. The faster he did, the quicker he could rid himself of Eldon. He gritted his teeth. "You'll get your money. I'll come back after harvest." He turned and stomped out of the building and down the street, shoved open the post office door, and approached the counter.

"Good afternoon. What can I help ya with?" The postmaster greeted him.

Logan sucked in a deep breath. This trip to the post office was already helping him forget about Eldon. "I'd like to check on a shipment coming to me from Oswell City. Has anything arrived yet?"

"Let me take a look." He left the counter for a back room and appeared again carrying a box. "This box is heavy. What'd those people ship you? Bricks?"

Logan grinned. "Books."

The postmaster heaved the burden over the counter. "Glad you're the one who has to haul them things home instead of me." He reached for an envelope that had slipped from the top of the box. "Don't forget this. A letter came for ya."

Logan scanned the return address. It revealed Dan as the sender. He slipped the envelope into his bibs pocket and picked up the box of books. "Thanks."

The postman waved on his way to help another customer.

At the wagon, Logan pushed the box of books under the seat and leaned against the side. He tore the envelope, unfolded the enclosed paper, and read.

Hi, Logan:

Hope you received your books. I sent them the same day I mailed this letter, so if you haven't seen them yet, let me know.

I write because a couple has made a request for a December 21 wedding. I'd love to perform the ceremony, but I'm leaving town to spend a couple of days with family to celebrate the Christmas holiday. I wondered if there was any way you could get to Oswell City to do the wedding.

Logan paused. Of course he'd return. He continued reading.

The couple getting married would know you much better than they know me. When I told them I'd write you and ask, they were in favor of the change. The groom is Brandt Koelman, one of the lawyers in town. The bride is Lorraine Ellenbroek, the mayor's daughter.

Logan read the last sentence aloud, his stomach twisting every which way. So Lorraine was getting married after all. What a fool he'd been. Lorraine never cared for him. He slapped the letter against his thigh.

Maybe he should tell Dan "no." He shook his head. As Logan's last-minute replacement, Dan deserved to spend his holiday with family. The unwelcome task fell to Logan.

He sighed. This letter came as yet another sign that bachelorhood was still the best plan for him. Lorraine refused him because he might move away from her hometown. Before Lorraine were the girls that Pete thought perfect for him. First had been Cecile, the sister of a buddy from his seminary class. She'd been a talented vocalist. Before her was Florence, a good friend of Anna Betten. She'd been the daughter of a wealthy family. Logan could never provide Florence with the material wealth she was accustomed to, and she knew it. Their courtship lasted a total of two months, long enough for Florence to discover his mind couldn't be changed to pursue business like her father.

Now Karen had come into his life. Beautiful, talented, and wealthy, she possessed the same traits as each young woman from his past. His shoulders slumped. If history was any indicator of future success, then he'd never know the pleasure of a deeper relationship with a woman like Karen.

He wadded up the letter and pitched it in the wagon. It bounced off the box of books, a crinkled, ruined mess. Just like his attempts at courtship. His whole frame stiffened. He'd steer clear of young women in the future. Courtship and the inevitable marriage had no place in his life. It may have taken him a while to catch on, but he'd learned his lesson now, and learned it well.

"MIND IF I JOIN YOU?" Karen entered the kitchen that evening, a stack of books and papers tucked in her grasp.

Logan glanced from the Bible to her face. "No. Not at all."

She claimed the chair across from him. "I have test papers to grade. Your mother and Tillie are still hanging the upstairs drapes so the kitchen is actually a quieter place to read than my room tonight."

He laughed softly. "I had the same problem. Give them a few days and the fall cleaning should be complete."

Fall cleaning. Now she knew what to call the flurry of dusting, furniture rearranging, and rug beating she'd witnessed the past week.

Karen arranged her stack of papers according to grade level and began checking answers. Sensing Logan's gaze on her, she tried to ignore him. Her cheeks began to heat. Could he see straight through her to the feelings for him crowding her heart? Surely not. Logan was so perceptive, though. One look like he gave her now might be all he needed to detect the truth. She shifted in her seat and tried to concentrate, but her mind remained fixed on the man across the table from her and not on Tim Hixson's math test.

Her attention crept to his face. Logan's gaze held all the fondness of an admirer. Did feelings for her take up space in his heart? Her breath caught at the possibility. She should focus on Tim's test before she blurted the question.

Logan cleared his throat. "How's Tim's math?"

"Average." She paused in marking checks through the numbers. "Tim could be a good student, but he tends to get nervous and then he stutters."

"I can relate," Logan said with a flat voice.

"Those Kent boys think it's a big joke to pull Tim into their stunts because he acts guilty even when he isn't. They cut up and pull pranks and then blame Tim. Well, I'm catching on. Those boys won't get by with their shenanigans any longer."

She heaved a deep breath and took a paper off the next pile.

"Lacy Jones." Logan read the name upside down from across the table.

"She needs to be given a chance, but writing and comprehension are so difficult for her." Karen laid her pen down and glanced at Logan. "Know what I'd like to do?"

He shook his head.

"I want to take her to the city. Buy her a pretty dress and let her attend one of Mother's parties. Instead, Lacy has to live a life filled with hard work, faded patched dresses, and limited opportunities."

"Like Tillie." Logan's voice turned quiet and thoughtful. "I wish to do the same things for Tillie sometimes. Take her to Oswell City with me. Give her a taste of town living." He waved his pencil in an act of dismissal. "But she wouldn't go."

"Why not?" Who in their right mind would turn down the chance to experience living in town?

"Andrew Carter." Logan grinned and wiggled his eyebrows.

"I see." She shared his smile.

He bent over the Bible and resumed his study.

Karen attempted to do the same as she returned to Lacy's math test.

The kitchen reposed in a comfortable silence. The kerosene lamp burned at one corner of the table and cast a soft glow over the stove and the polished wood of the chairs. Sweet whiffs of apple pie still hung in the air. An occasional thump or scrape from the work going on above added to the homey feel.

She stole a glimpse of Logan as he studied. His comment about the reason for his trip to town that afternoon still lingered in her mind. He'd said he took her payment to the bank and deposited it. Handing some of her salary over to a preacher at the end of the past month had wreaked havoc on her conscience. What he might do with her money she could only imagine, and none of the ideas coming to mind were good.

Lamplight glistened on a blond wave of hair that flopped over Logan's forehead. In one hand, he held his pencil ready to jot down a thought. His other hand propped against his chin. Lines of concentration creased his brow and happiness glowed in his eyes. He looked innocent enough. Maybe he had nothing to hide. He seemed honest on the outside. How wonderful if that honesty penetrated his insides too.

The thought pricked her. It shouldn't matter, but her heart wasn't listening. Those feelings for him were growing stronger, unconcerned about his choice of vocation. Both the preaching and the farming. If he really was everything he appeared to be, then life with a man like him would satisfy her every wish. She might even be able to overlook the fact that he wasn't a professor or some other esteemed person worthy of her family's respect.

Karen returned to her work. It was no use. He'd never change. Neither would she. If only her life thus far hadn't implanted in her terror of the very things Logan represented, like accidents, untimely deaths, and scandal. Then she'd be free to follow her heart's leading. But her overgrown fears hid from view the path to the security she'd searched for so long. She may never discover it.

He laid his pencil down and turned a page. "I think you can find a way." His gaze met hers.

"A way for what?" Her heart thumped. Had he been reading her mind instead of the Bible?

"To take Lacy to a party."

"Oh." She exhaled. "In the city?"

"No. Right here in Silver Grove."

Light dawned. "We should host a party at the school."

Logan smiled. "A fall party. You'll want to wait until harvest is nearing the end so that all the parents can come."

"We could play games."

"I'll help you find supplies for them."

"We can also provide the food."

"The desserts. Have Tillie help you make the pies. Give her a sense of purpose."

"We'll help Lacy."

"We'll help Tillie." Logan's smile grew when he spoke at the same time she did.

Karen face heated.

LOGAN'S INSIDES glowed when Karen blushed. Five minutes ago, he'd had no one but the apostle Paul on his mind. Now that Karen shared the table with him, the letters to Timothy had somehow lost their appeal. He may have resolved to avoid eligible young women, but that decision sure didn't seem to have any affect where Karen was concerned.

She delighted him, unsettled him, and fascinated him by turn. How in the world was a man to concentrate on sermon writing with such a captivating young woman seated across from him? He wanted to jump out of his seat, manufacture another crisis, and hold her again. The day of the storm stayed with him and kept fresh the feel of Karen in his arms. She seemed to have taken the whole incident in stride whereas he'd been left with a memory impossible to erase.

He forced his attention back to the Scriptures. Experience taught him that dreaming proved to be a fast road to disappointment. He'd better not indulge in that silliness again.

Footsteps stomped down the stairs to the kitchen. Tillie trudged across the room to the ice box. She tugged the door open and grabbed a chunk of ice. "This bee sting on my head is acting up again. I shouldn't have listened to you and agreed to a trip to town." She held the ice to her head and scowled at Karen. "What are you doing in here?"

"My room is too noisy to concentrate and get my work done since you and your mother are still hanging the drapes."

"Don't you know we have to get the cleaning done?" Tillie's voice sounded like it wanted to shout.

Karen stiffened. Her mouth opened and then closed again. She assumed the look of the condescending school teacher. Her voice held enough ice to retire the chunk in Tillie's hand. "Your brother and I are working on plans for a fall party at the school."

Tillie huffed. "Go outside and leave Logan alone. At least Mama and I don't hover around the table wasting his time when he needs to study."

Tillie had gone too far. He didn't want Karen to leave the kitchen, and she hadn't wasted his time. He stood. "Tillie, you need to apologize or leave the room."

She threw a glare at him. "You always take her side. No fair."

Logan returned her glare. "Apologize or leave."

Her eyes rolled to her lids, and her head bobbed from side to side. Impatience edged her voice. "Sorry."

When had Tillie grown so childish? He'd agreed to board the teacher based on the idea that Tillie would want her for a friend. What had gone wrong?

CHAPTER SEVENTEEN

*L*ogan stood at the basin washing his hands while he listened to Karen recount the events of her day to Mama.

"Those boys never let up." Karen darted her hands into the air. Her skirt swirled around her ankles as she moved about the kitchen.

"What happened?"

"Marty and Emmett devised the wonderful idea to build a fort with some branches and dirt clods. Of course they pulled Tim in on their plan."

Logan reclined in his chair and reached for a slice of cinnamon bread. He took a bite, thankful the chewing would prevent his mouth from smiling. Karen's story humored him, but the hint of sarcasm in her voice entertained him more. He didn't dare laugh in the face of Karen's agitation. Two more big bites kept his mouth occupied.

"The fort had actually been good for the boys. I've lost Cal and Wade to the harvesting work on their father's farms. That seemed to make a difference. These older boys have helped create games at recess for the younger ones to play. Since they aren't at school right now, the only other activities the boys want to join in with are whatever Marty and Emmett are doing in their fort." Karen brought two filled coffee mugs to the table.

"It sounds like they adjusted well to Cal and Wade being gone." Mama reached for a mug.

"Yes, they did. I would've been content to allow them to play in their fort the entire autumn, but I learned today that Jake Fuller received a shipment of sling shots at the hardware store. Most of the boys have one, brought it with them to school, and shared with whoever didn't have a sling shot." Karen trembled as she reached for a slice of bread, broke off a piece, and put it in her mouth.

"How many boys are playing recess games at the fort?" Mama motioned to Tillie, inviting her to take her seat at the table when she emerged from the room that contained the sewing machine.

"Ten. The girls have enjoyed a little peace and quiet in their games on the school's front yard since the fort is in the back."

"That's quite a few. I can see why the girls are feeling more relaxed." Mama poured more coffee into her cup.

"Until recess this afternoon." Karen shook her head and her eyes slid closed like she tried to block an exasperating memory from her mind. "I heard screaming coming from the direction of the fort so went to check. Lacy Jones sat on the ground covering her face. She'd been hit in the eye with a rock from Emmett's sling shot."

"The poor girl," Mama said.

"Yes. I sent Carrie Kent home to ask her father to fetch the doctor. Since the Kents live the closest to town, I hoped this would save time. Lacy was in pain."

"Eye injuries can be serious."

"I haven't heard the doctor's diagnosis on Lacy since he drove her home as soon as he arrived at school." Karen sipped her coffee. "After that happened, the story came out. The entire brigade of fort occupants has been shooting at the girls for the past two days whenever the girls venture into the yard behind the school."

"Do the girls need to go in that area of the school yard? If the fort has been a good way for the boys to spend their recess, then why can't they continue their play separate from the girls?" Mama reached for a slice of bread.

"It's not that easy. You see, the fort is along the path the girls must take to their outhouse. They can't avoid it." Karen's cheeks stained pink. From her frustration or a bit of embarrassment, Logan couldn't tell.

Memories of his own country school days came rushing back. He'd been guilty of a few pranks against the girls. The laughter he'd done so well repressing began to gush forth. He quickly reached for another slice of bread and took a huge bite to hide it.

"What did you do?" Mama asked.

"I confiscated their sling shots. That put an end to the fun right away. I suppose I'll have to assign cleaning duty again, but that's becoming a problem. Marty and Emmett get in trouble so often that I'm running out of jobs for them. Ours will be the cleanest school in the entire county. But nothing else works. They hate cleaning so that is the best punishment I can come up with."

Karen fell silent while she finished her bread. "I'd like to visit Lacy this evening. I'm concerned for her. Of course something like this would happen to her. She already has so many struggles. An accident will set her back." Karen's voice trembled.

He didn't feel like laughing anymore. "I can take you. Right after I finish the milking and we eat supper, I could drive you over to the Jones' place."

Tillie turned to him with a frown. "But you said you would bring those trunks down from the attic for me that Mama wanted cleaned out."

"I did, but now Karen has an emergency."

Tillie shot out of her chair and marched to the sink.

"Those trunks aren't urgent. I'll get them from the attic tomorrow."

Tillie sloshed water around with more vehemence that one small cup required. "You always listen to Karen instead of me."

Her words pierced him. "That's not true."

"Yes it is." Tillie turned from the sink and pointed in Karen's direction, soap suds dripping from her hand. "Just last night, you forced me to apologize to her when she'd been just as rude."

The color faded from Karen's face.

"You know, if Dad was still here, he'd drop everything to help me." Tillie's eyes turned watery.

"You don't understand, Tillie." Logan tried to keep the edge of irritation out of his voice but it sneaked in anyway.

"I do understand." Tillie moved to where he sat and looked down at him, her eyes full of sorrow. "When you said you were staying home with us, you told Mama that we could keep our home and that nothing would change."

"I did."

"But you were wrong. Everything has changed. Why did you lie to us?" The tears coursed down Tillie's cheeks as she spun away from him and fled the house. The slam of the back porch door put a definite exclamation mark at the end of her heated question.

Mama darted out of her chair and opened the door. "Tillie, Come back!" she called.

"I'll go find her." Logan scooted away from the table.

Karen muttered in a low voice. "I hate the way she treats you."

It didn't feel so good to him, either. But Logan wasn't Tillie's biggest problem. Bitterness was. A general dislike of Karen provided the root. Now it spread to more areas of her life. If something didn't happen to reverse its course, Tillie would completely succumb to the poison eating away at her soul.

Mama returned, rubbing her forehead. "Tillie has changed since your father died. Some days I hardly know how to handle her. Karen, I'm so sorry that Tillie gives you such a hard time."

Karen nodded, a look of sympathy mixed with the frustration already present on her face.

"Where are those trunks, Mama?" Logan stood.

She led the way upstairs and pointed at the ceiling. "Under the south window."

Logan pulled down the ladder and climbed. In the attic, he crawled around until locating the trunks. He worked at getting both of the awkward and heavy items into hallway.

"Thank you, dear. I'll have Tillie go through them tonight while you and Karen are at the Jones'." Mama's words assured him of her approval. He hadn't gone looking for it, but her quiet acknowledgement of Karen's need to visit a student let him know where Mama stood in relation to Tillie.

He nodded. "I'm going to start the milking now."

Mama knelt down to open one of the trunks.

When he returned to the kitchen, Logan leaned against the wall and watched Karen as she washed the dishes. She handled Tillie's outbursts as well as anyone could expect, but if her patience, like his, was starting to wane, then she'd need a little support. He'd give it. They'd share Tillie's wrath. He walked up behind her and placed his hands on her shoulders.

Karen stiffened but turned around. Her gaze met his.

He said nothing. No words could explain away Tillie's actions. All he could do was assure Karen that he, like Tillie, recognized what grew between them. Karen mattered to him. In his eyes, she wasn't the stranger needing a place to stay. She'd become his friend, a dear friend. She could count on him.

She must have gotten the message because she reached up and covered one of his hands with her own.

Logan gave her a wink before he turned away. He'd rather stay in the kitchen with Karen, but Tillie roamed about somewhere. She needed some of his assurance too.

LOGAN DISCOVERED Tillie in the apple orchard perched on an over-turned bushel basket in the grass. Other baskets were stacked beside the trunks of the trees in preparation of the swiftly approaching day when Mama and Tillie would begin picking the apples.

"I'm not Dad." Logan spoke in a quiet voice. "When he was alive, I looked up to him and wanted to be like him, but I'll never be Dad."

"You took his place." Tillie sniffed. "Life should return to normal now."

Logan lifted a basket off the stack and used it for a seat. "Think about it, Tillie. Is that at all realistic? No one can make that happen. Even if Dad was still alive, your life would keep changing."

Tillie stared at the grass beneath her feet.

Logan dared to keep talking in the silence. "Sudden losses like the one you've experienced are never easy, but you have to accept it and find the strength to move on."

A breath shuddered through Tillie's frame as a clue that she listened even though she may not agree.

He stood up, drawing Tillie with him. "I helped you by getting those trunks down from the attic before I came outside."

"You did?" She ventured a glance at him.

Logan nodded. "Now I'd like for you to help me." He led her away from the orchard.

"Where are we going?"

"Do you remember your jobs at milking time? I'd like to have your company in the barn." Logan was jerked to a halt in the middle of the lane.

Tillie dug her heels into the dirt, pulling her away from him. "No way. I can't go in that barn. Not ever again." Tears fogged her voice and collected in her eyes.

Logan kept firm hold on her hand. "It's time. You need to face your loss, Tillie."

"No!" She writhed in an effort to free herself from his grasp.

"Do you think it's been any easier for Mama?"

This got her attention. She paused.

"Or for me?" He swallowed. "We're hurting too. But do you see us taking it out on others?"

"You just want me to help you so I'll be nice to Karen." Tillie's eyes narrowed.

"This has nothing to do with Karen. I want what's best for you."

"And you think that dragging me back to the place where Dad died is good for me?" Tillie's lower lip trembled.

"I'm not trying to drag you anywhere. I want you to be free again." Tears threatened to fog his voice too. "Where's the Tillie I've always known? I've lost her."

Her cold expression faltered, and tears began to stream down her face. Logan drew her into an embrace, holding her for a long while as she cried.

Tillie drew in a shaky breath. "I wish I could help you, Logan. You know I've always enjoyed milking time."

Yes, he knew. She'd been toting pails for Dad ever since she started to walk. He stroked her back, but she pulled away.

"I'm going inside."

After she disappeared into the house, he entered the barn, praying for the day when he had his kid sister back.

THAT EVENING AT SUPPER, Logan went through the motions of eating, but his thoughts were on Mama. Weariness carved deep lines in her face. This fatigue resulted from more than a full day of kitchen work. Weeks of enduring conflict and dealing with her grief probably provided the reasons instead. Tillie's absence from the supper table didn't help. After Tillie resisted his persuasion to come to the barn, she'd disappeared. No one had seen her since. She should've come to supper. Mama didn't need the extra strain of worrying about Tillie.

He went to his room for the letter with the news of Lorraine's wedding. Returning to the kitchen, he claimed his seat once more. "Mama, I have an invitation for you." He slid the sheet of paper across the table in her direction.

She picked up the letter and read it. "You have friends in Oswell City getting married. What does this have to do with me?"

"I want you to come along. The wedding is in December. I'll be gone four days. You'll get a much deserved break if you go with me."

"What makes you think I need a break?"

"You'll have extra work during harvest. You're already tired now. This trip to Oswell City will give you a chance to rest." Logan took the letter when she returned it to him and folded it up.

"Oswell City is so far away. I don't know that I want to travel such a long way from home." Mama lifted her glass for a drink.

"You'll be with me. We'll stay at the parsonage."

Mama glanced over at Karen. "What about the girls? I'm not sure it's a good idea to leave Tillie for so long."

Logan rubbed his forehead. Mama made a good point. He'd failed to consider how the absence of both him and Mama would affect Karen. She'd get left behind with no allies. "We'll need to explain our trip to Tillie and set some rules."

"Maybe Pete and Anna would be willing to check in on us or have us over for evening meals." Karen smiled at Mama. "I think you should go. Logan is right. You deserve a chance to rest."

"But right before Christmas." Mama shook her head. "Who will do all of the baking and decorating?"

"Tillie and I will do it. The preparations for Christmas will get Tillie's mind on something that might cheer her up." Karen's straight forward assessment of the situation eased the lines around Mama's eyes and mouth.

"Well, I guess if it will help Tillie." Mama's voice trailed off while she considered the idea.

Logan leaned forward. "I'll get Vern to do the milking. Maybe he can check in on Karen and Tillie, too, and make sure they don't run into trouble."

Mama's gaze traveled between Logan and Karen. "How can I argue with that? Both of you already have my trip all worked out. Sounds like I'm on my way."

"You won't be sorry. Tillie and I will take care of everything."

CHAPTER EIGHTEEN

*L*ogan listened as Karen sang the last phrase of the hymn at Sunday's afternoon service. Now came the preaching. Four weeks as Meadow Creek's pastor should've been plenty of time to train his tongue to quit stuttering, but it had only grown worse.

His self-appointed song leader bestowed a glittering smile on him as she passed by to take her seat. It was a smile that seemed to ask if he was having as much fun as she was. Sure. Loads of fun. Logan nodded back with raised brows. All she had to do was sing a line of music with everyone else joining in. But he must get his words out with clarity while the room full of people sat in silence. No small task for a preacher trying to avoid the source of his jitters in the first place, who happened to be the gorgeous blonde sitting in the front pew.

This afternoon's service marked the last one of Karen's requested trial run. Logan stood and released the breath he'd been holding. He could do this. If he kept his attention on the Bible lying open on the pulpit, he'd make it through with flying colors.

Logan took his place behind the pulpit. "The Lord of the Word from M . . . Matthew seven twenty-four verses. I mean the Word of the Lord from Matthew seven, verse twenty-four through twenty-nine." Logan's face heated. He was losing ground. Fast. Worse than the poor man in today's passage who built his house on the sand. He cleared his throat, catching a glimpse of Karen in the meantime.

She still smiled.

Boy, the sanctuary felt hot. He'd sure love to remove his suit coat right now. He sucked in a deep breath. "Therefore, whosoever hears these sayings of mine, and does them, will be like a wise man which built his house upon a rock. The rain descended, and the floods came, and the winds blew, and beat upon that house." Whew. Prayers answered. Did Karen still smile at him? He shouldn't glance that way. It might ruin his record. He took another breath and read to the end of the chapter.

He exhaled and scanned every other pew in the room except Karen's. In the row halfway to the back on the left where a mother and her three children usually sat, he noticed that only two of the children were in church today. The little girl was missing. As he began the sermon, Logan made a mental note to check up on them before they headed home.

When he ended the prayer after the sermon, Karen came to stand next to him so that she could sing the last hymn. She leaned close and whispered in his ear. "Did you notice the Harper family?"

"Yes." He whispered back. "The daughter was absent. I'll try to talk to them before they leave."

As Karen sang the last notes, he stretched out his arms, bumping Karen's shoulder. His tongue went stiff. "The L . . . Lord bless y . . . you and keep you." He swallowed. Two more phrases. He could do it. "The Lord fake his mace to shine upon you." A groan worked its way up his throat. He swallowed. Groaning was even more irreverent than all his stumbling. He kept going. "The Lord lift his countenance upon you and give you peace." He lowered his arms, careful to avoid Karen on the way down. He'd left out some words, but the omission meant he could flee the pulpit faster.

Which he did.

The only problem was that Karen left with him, strolling at his side the entire length of the aisle. If they hadn't resembled Pete and Anna on past Sundays, they did now.

Logan indulged in that groan as he stationed himself, with Karen at his side, to greet people on their way out.

The Harper family filed past him in line. "Nice to see you today, Mrs. Harper. I noticed your daughter is absent."

The woman nodded. "Agnes. She's down with pneumonia. Has been since Tuesday."

Logan's heart clenched. What a difficulty for a mother to bear. "Well, Mrs. Harper—"

"We will certainly pray for you," Karen said. "I'm sorry to hear that Agnes is sick."

Logan's jaw went slack. That's what he was going to say. She stole his line and spoke it with more feeling than he ever could.

He forced a smile and shook the hand of an older man who followed Mrs. Harper.

"You do a marvelous job singing, Mrs. De Witt." The old man reached to shake Karen's hand.

Logan's stomach lurched. "Mrs. De Witt?"

Karen's glittering smile appeared again. She laughed.

This afternoon was going from bad to worse. "She's our local school teacher, not my—"

"Oh, so your wife teaches too?" The old man raised his eyes to the sky as though praising the Lord for his wonderful provisions. "My, what a talented young lady you are," he said to Karen. Then he patted Logan's shoulder. "She's a keeper, Reverend De Witt. Yes, a keeper if you ask me." He moved on down the steps.

"No. Wait. You don't understand. She's—" Logan called after him, but a vice clenched his middle so tight Logan thought he might suffocate. He turned to Karen with his mouth hanging open.

She, too, patted his shoulder. He caught her understanding in the simple gesture, but it failed to calm him. "Let it go, Logan. He's already gone. He'll probably forget anyway. What's it hurt?"

Well, if she must know, the old man's assumptions were far from the truth for one thing. Logan's gaze returned to the man's retreating back. Maybe Logan should call out to him once more and make him see things as they are. But even then, one fact would only lead to another. After all, he couldn't possibly explain away Karen's weekly appearance at his side or the way she smiled at him just now, or the way his heart felt squeezed even tighter than his lungs.

Logan shook his head to clear it. More people awaited his greeting. Karen capably did the job of shaking hands and expressing pleasure in seeing them today. She was a natural. This was yet another fact for which he'd have trouble giving a proper explanation. Reaching for the hand of another parishioner, Logan tried to push his discomfort away, but it kept creeping back in. Thank goodness this was Karen's last Sunday. He'd never welcomed the ending of anything else this much in his entire life.

THAT EVENING while Logan was in the barn doing the milking, a horse and rider raced into the farmyard. Karen hastened to open the door.

The rider stood on the porch. He was a large man with the smell of alcohol hanging heavy around him. "I'm lookin' for the preacher. He's gotta come quick. My little girl is awful sick."

"Your little girl?"

"Yeah. We're from Meadow Creek. My wife's been bringin' the young 'uns over here for church on Sunday."

"Oh, you're Agnes's father."

The man nodded emphatically.

"Well, please come in." Karen moved to the side so that the

147

man had room to pass through. "Reverend De Witt is in the barn. Let me get my coat, and I'll take you to him."

She discovered Logan in the fourth stall on the left, the tune of *Amazing Grace*, one of the hymns she'd sung that morning, humming from his lips. "Logan. Mr. Harper is here to see you."

Logan straightened his tall frame from the milking stool and reached to shake the man's hand. "Good evening, sir."

"You Reverend De Witt?"

"I am."

"You gotta come quick. Agnes is worse."

"Have you called the doctor?" Logan's warm voice had the same soothing effect on the anxious father that it had on Karen's own emotions whenever she was scared about something.

"Yeah. He's at our house now. We're afraid she's not gonna make it."

If ever Karen was in need of Logan's comforting voice, it was now. "What? That darling little girl is on the verge of—" Karen couldn't bring herself to say the word.

"Give me directions to your place. I have three more cows to milk, and then I'll come," Logan said.

The man nodded. He proceeded to give Logan directions, and then he raced out of the barn.

He turned to Karen. "You should come with me."

"I'd love to. You know I would. But you could travel much faster alone."

"The doctor is there, so I can afford to take the time I'd need to bring you along." Logan grinned at her and then reclaimed the milking stool, his hands working in a steady rhythm beneath the cow.

Karen's heart stirred. How did one young man store up so much joy and compassion to give away to everyone he met? And here he sat, humming again as though his supply still overflowed. Maybe it did. A sudden desire to know Logan better overwhelmed her heart. She wanted a share in what seemed for him so natural and so easy.

But where should she start? One simple action came to mind and blurted from her mouth. "May I pray for you?"

His motions stilled. He glanced at her. "What did you say?"

Karen blushed. "I asked if I could pray for you. You'll need God to sustain you."

A wide smile stretched Logan's mouth when he rose from the stool. "That's exactly what I need, Karen. I'd be honored to have you pray for me."

She ventured to clasp his hands. Karen's heart skipped a few beats, and her voice wavered as she asked God to give Logan strength and an extra measure of love for this family as he ministered through what may become a very long night.

HALF AN HOUR LATER, Karen climbed in the buggy with Logan and traveled the five miles to Meadow Creek. They passed a large, stone building situated along a stream. Through the trees was another building with a water wheel. The quaint, serene scene in the peach glow of the evening sunshine led Karen to wonder if she'd ever return to the city. A little more each day, her heart was at home in this out-of-the-way place she'd dreaded so much in the beginning. The word "beautiful" whispered across her lips, both as an indicator of the view before her and of the sense of belonging within.

Logan pointed. "That's the grain mill. Local farmers bring their corn and wheat there to grind it into flour and livestock feed. The Carters sell some of the flour in our Silver Grove store. On the return trip, the delivery wagon stops at our farm, among others, to pick up cans of milk to take to the creamery in Bridgewater Springs."

Karen nodded at Logan's explanation. They drove through a

village, smaller even than Silver Grove. Karen tried to guess the size of this school. It couldn't be more than a dozen children.

On the edge of the small village was a square of bare earth surrounded by uneven stacks of lumber and shattered windows.

Logan pointed again. "That's where the church stood. It was the only building in town leveled. Others lost roofs or siding, but that damage has been repaired."

Karen surveyed the twisted tree trunks and branches with wilted leaves piled off to the side, her heart swelling. She turned to Logan. "It makes the work we've done together on Sundays all that more important, doesn't it?"

He nodded. "Yeah. I've been happy to be their pastor. It's helped me too." His cheeks flamed into a bright red. Not even the sun exposure he received in the summer hayfield could turn them such a ruby color. "Thanks for leading the singing these past weeks. You did much better than I would have."

Memories of that afternoon's service returned. "I'm sorry I didn't take the misunderstanding more seriously."

"You didn't need to." He turned to her. "You're right. It doesn't matter. He probably wouldn't have listened anyway." His mouth stretched into a crooked, ornery-looking grin. "Let's hope the rest of the congregation doesn't get the wrong idea."

"It won't matter after today, since I may not be going with you anymore." The four weeks were up. Her trial run was over, and Logan had said nothing about wanting her assistance to continue.

A quarter of a mile from town, they pulled into the yard of a rundown shack. A limp curtain hung at one window. Bottles littered the ground around the front step. Mr. Harper sat there with a half empty bottle in his hand.

"Hey, Rev." He held his hand out to shake Logan's. The rest of the word "reverend" and Logan's last name never came out of his mouth. Perhaps all those syllables required too much work for a man as inebriated as Mr. Harper.

Logan took the man's hand and shook it with the same kindness he'd shown in all of his actions toward Karen on her first night in town.

She smiled to herself as she followed Logan and the other man into the dimly lit house. Agnes's younger brothers sat on two of the chairs at the table. Karen should've brought some of her picture books along. She couldn't guess at how a mother would entertain little ones in such stark surroundings.

Karen followed Logan and Mr. Harper into a bedroom lit by a flickering lamp in the corner near the bed where Agnes lay. She covered her mouth. "Oh, Agnes!"

Logan's arm circled her waist.

She wanted to stay in his embrace, but her concern for Agnes propelled her forward. Karen touched the girl's forehead. It burned.

"She has a serious case. I've seen worse, but her fever is high." The young, dark-haired doctor rolled his sleeves down. He reached to shake Logan's hand. "Make sure to bathe her face and neck as often as you can." He turned to address Mrs. Harper. "Try giving her some of this." He handed a small vial to her. "I'll stop in first thing in the morning."

CHAPTER NINETEEN

*A*s the doctor left, Karen went out to the kitchen with Logan while the parents stayed with Agnes. Logan settled into an empty chair at the table and gave his attention to the lad in the nearest chair. "And how old might you be, young man?"

The little boy held up three pudgy fingers.

"He's just the baby but I'm six." The other dark-haired boy at the table sat up straight and jabbed his thumb at his chest.

"Oh, I see. I bet you love stories."

"Sure do." Big Brother was determined to carry on a grown-up conversation, man to man.

"Maybe you'd like to hear this one." Logan's tone carried a hint of mystery.

"Whatcha got?" Big Brother scrambled off his chair and around the table to Logan.

He opened the Bible he brought with him. "A story about a little man like you who climbed a really big tree so he could see an important person who came to town. Would you like to hear it?"

"Yeah!" Big brother made a fearless climb onto Logan's knee.

"Me too. Me too." Not wanting to get left out, Little Brother reached for Logan.

Logan settled him on the other knee and started reading, the intonation of his voice captivating his young audience.

Tears blurred Karen's eyes. She'd not witnessed Logan's interaction with small children before. He possessed all the traits of an excellent teacher. But even more than all that, Logan De Witt had the word "father" written all over him. Karen turned away. She must get busy with something before she threw all her caution to the wind and forgot why she'd stayed in Silver Grove.

She searched the kitchen to determine how recently anyone had eaten. From the evidence she found in a cold pot and a few dirty dishes, hours had passed since the last meal.

Karen set to work, the clinks of pans forming a background harmony to Logan's story. She could get used to this. Family gathered at the table while she fixed a meal. Even in a dingy little cabin. It worked because Logan was there.

She paused, suddenly in need of fresh air. "I'm going outside."

Outdoors, she stood under the one large tree in the yard and gazed to the sky. The need for material comforts and modern conveniences no longer pulled on her heart. Something within her had changed. She gulped in the clear autumn air, trying to make sense of her thoughts.

The door pounded shut behind her. After a moment, a warm hand settled on her shoulder. Logan had found her.

"What were you doing in there?" Logan's voice murmured near her ear.

"Cooking. Thanks to your mother, I know enough so that I might provide this family with their supper."

"I'm proud of you."

The words startled her. After her attempts at cooking food for him had turned out dry chicken, lumpy gravy, and chewy pie crust, he could still say that. "Thank you."

Logan glanced at the shack. "I'm concerned about Mr. Harper. I'd like to see him come to Christ."

Her heart thumped. "I didn't know he was so, well, such a

153

drunk." She struggled to put a refined spin on the crude reality. "I'd like to see him come to Christ too."

"Would you pray about that?"

The sense of sharing in something serious and important with Logan brought weightlessness to her chest. "I will."

"Good." He grinned at her and spoke barely above a whisper. "I couldn't leave him in better hands." Logan's grin disappeared into a sober expression. His brows formed a straight line above his eyes while his gaze traveled to her mouth and got stuck there.

A breeze blew in and tousled Logan's hair. He blinked and smiled as though enjoying a private joke. "We should go inside. I promised Agnes's brothers another story. Goliath this time." His smile grew as he turned toward the house.

Karen followed. Too bad time refused to stand still. If it did, this evening she shared with Logan would be a perfect time to stop the clock.

Two faint chimes rang out from another room in the house, interrupting her quiet conversation with Mrs. Harper.

"Karen, could you please take over now? I'd like to talk with the Harpers." Logan approached her with the water basin in his hand. His shirt sleeves were rolled up, and the wave of hair on his forehead frizzed as much as it did after an entire day spent working in the field.

"Is something wrong?" Karen's heart rate sped up.

"No. I want to take a little time to share the gospel with them." He set the basin on the table and wrung out the cloth.

"Her fever still hasn't broken then." Karen murmured the words that they'd been working against all night.

Logan shook his head. He stepped nearer and whispered for Karen's ears only. "She's in delirium. The past hour I've spent in there bathing her face hasn't made any difference in her thrashing."

Karen closed her eyes against the truth. She sent up another prayer for this family. The squeak of the pump reached her ears. Still praying, Karen went to the sink where Logan filled the basin with fresh water. She stuck her hand in. The Harpers possessed a deep well. The water chilled her fingers.

"I'll carry this to the bedroom for you." Logan picked up the brimming full basin and led the way.

Down on her knees, Karen labored over the little girl clawing the quilts and heaving in breaths. Agnes had to recover. She just had to. This innocent child shouldn't die of a fever in a rundown, overcrowded shack to be forgotten by the world before she had the chance to grow up and live her life.

At three o'clock, Logan came to the bedroom. "I'm going to hitch up so we can go home. The cows need milked at five and school starts for you at eight-thirty."

She stood, her knees sore. "Oh, Agnes," she whispered. "I hate to leave you. Please get better. You have to recover. Please recover."

The little girl continued to roll around and breathe heavily.

When Logan came to the house for her, he shook hands once more with Mr. Harper. His wife was too distraught to join them so Mr. Harper stood alone in the kitchen, bottle in hand and words slurred. "Thanks, Rev. Glad ya came. We needed ya."

"My pleasure." Logan graced the man with one of his radiant smiles. "I'll ride over sometime in the afternoon and check on you."

The man nodded and waved his bottle in the air as his good-bye salute.

Logan helped Karen into the waiting buggy. He jumped in and guided the horse down the dark road. Crickets whirred in the ditches. The scent of fresh cut hay hung in the air. Staying awake was so much work with eyes as heavy as hers. She dozed twice, her head bouncing until it snapped upright, bringing her awake again. If she only had somewhere to rest it, she might snooze for a little while so she could stay alert during the remainder of the ride home. A perfect resting place near her side attracted her. She allowed her head to fall until it landed on Logan's firm, muscular shoulder.

"Wake up, Karen. We're home." Logan's voice registered in her mind.

Karen straightened and looked around through drowsy eyes. The buggy sat in the De Witt lane. Surely she hadn't slept through the entire ride to the farm.

Logan left his seat and tied the reins to the fence post. He came around to Karen's side. "Would you like for me to carry you inside?"

His question brought her fully awake. She had no sprained ankle, only a bad case of grogginess which she could shake off easy enough. "Thank you, no." She slid to the wheel where he waited.

She took his hand and allowed him to assist her to the ground.

"It's four o'clock in the morning. Why don't you go upstairs and catch a couple hours of sleep before you need to go to school?" Logan searched her face.

"That sounds wonderful, but what are you going to do?" Karen shouldn't fall asleep again if Logan could not.

"I'll put the buggy away and then get an early start on the milking. After breakfast I'll have some time to catch a nap." He moved to the post and untied the reins.

Karen nodded and entered the house. She crept up the stairs, careful not to wake Sandy or Tillie. Her own bed looked marvelous. She couldn't wait to lie down in it. Karen removed her coat, then her dress, and took advantage of some rest, her thoughts fixed on the little girl struggling with fever.

TWO DAYS LATER, Logan stepped out of the hardware store with the can of grease, rubber belts, and the variety of tools he'd purchased to prepare for harvest.

"Hey, Reverend De Witt!" The call from the direction of the train station caught his attention.

Logan snapped his head up.

Mr. Harper lumbered toward him, waving his hand in the air. "Got a minute?"

"I do." Logan set his load down on the walk. "What's on your mind today, Mr. Harper?"

Catching his breath, Mr. Harper leaned against the brick building. "Agnes is feelin' better. Her fever broke yesterday afternoon."

"That's wonderful news. I'll let Miss Millerson know. She'll be happy to hear."

The man sobered. "I've been thinkin' about what woulda happened to her if she didn't make it." He twisted his mustache for a moment. "I mean, my wife brings the kids to your Sunday services. Is that enough? If Agnes woulda died, would she of gone to Heaven?"

Their prayers were getting answered. He cleared his throat and matched Mr. Harper's seriousness. "Attending church on Sunday isn't enough. A person goes to Heaven because they believe in Jesus Christ and the salvation He offers. Does Agnes believe in Jesus?"

Mr. Harper scratched his head. "Well now, I ain't so sure." He studied Logan through glassy eyes. "Would you ask her sometime? I'd love to know if my little girl is fit for Heaven."

"I'll do that." Logan shook his hand. "Maybe you'd like to be there when I ask her."

"Oh, church goin' ain't for me." Mr. Harper shook his head. "My wife, she took the kids to Sunday School. After she got to know some folks, she decided to keep bringin' 'em over here to

Silver Grove." Mr. Harper tugged on his suspenders. "But, me, I don't need no Sunday School. That sorta thing is for the kids."

"The gift of salvation extends to you, too, Mr. Harper, whether you hear it in Sunday School, sitting in a pew, or right here on the street. All you need to do is tell God you believe in Jesus' death on the cross and then invite him into your heart." The man's eyes cleared a bit. "Are you ready to do that today?"

"Nah. Nothin's gonna happen to me. I don't get sick like my young 'uns do. I don't expect to need to think about Heaven for myself for a good long time." He straightened away from the wall.

"You don't need to wait for your body to get sick. Our spirits are already sick before Jesus saves us."

Mr. Harper shuffled his feet. "Yeah, well. I don't know. Maybe I'll uh, I'll think about it some." He slapped Logan's back. "Nice runnin' into ya, Rev." He moved on down the street.

Logan watched him go, a sense of gratitude stirring his heart. His decision to stay in Silver Grove might have been the right one after all. God was certainly at work in this man's heart, and he'd chosen Logan as the instrument through which to proclaim the truth.

Picking up his parcels, Logan strode to his wagon. If he hadn't chosen to stay on the farm, he wouldn't be here to accept this preaching job at the time when Meadow Creek's church blew down. And if Logan wasn't here to preach the gospel, men like Mr. Harper may not have anywhere to turn. When they ran into a crisis, like Agnes's pneumonia, no one would be available to walk with the family through their difficulties.

A spring entered Logan's step. God still called out to him with kingdom work to do. The only thing that had changed for Logan was his location. Preaching, praying, and counseling were still very much in demand, and God needed Logan to keep doing it.

Logan drew in a deep breath and smiled to the sky. *Thank you, Lord, for making Your way clear to me. I'm happy to stay in Silver Grove unless or until You tell me to go.*

CHAPTER TWENTY

*A*fter a day of testing her students in history, Karen walked the road to the farm. The chug of a steam engine carried through the air. A familiar fear quickened her heart as she hurried down the lane. Moving parts, flapping belts, and the sounds of crushing and grinding gears flooded her ears as she took in the activity going on in the corn field. This couldn't happen again. Not to Logan. She took off running across the shorn field in a frantic search for him.

"Logan! Where are you?" Her gaze roamed over the plodding horses and the startled men. "Logan! I can't see you!" She ran to the opposite side of the dusty monstrosity chewing grain.

Two hands gripped her upper arms from behind.

She screamed once more before turning around.

Logan stood near, still holding her arms. "Settle down, Karen. You'll spook the horses."

She shook her head and opened her mouth to try to speak.

"What's the matter?" Logan frowned. "Did something happen at school?"

She gave another shake of her head.

Logan lowered his voice. "Eldon didn't come to school again, did he?"

"No." She choked it out.

"Then what is it?" A bit of a smile pulled at Logan's mouth.

Neighbor men closed in from every side, all of them watching her.

She drew in a deep breath. She must look so silly bolting across the field and screaming out Logan's name. Taking a step back far enough to remove her from Logan's grasp, she gathered her wits. "Nothing. Really. I'm sorry. I just got scared is all." She gestured to the machine. "I feared you might be hurt."

Logan waved the men back to their jobs. He moved a distance with her away from the work site until the sounds of the machine faded behind them. "I'm fine, as you can see." He motioned to his overall-covered form. "Go on in the house and get calmed down. I'll be in for supper."

Karen nodded. Logan's unruffled manner restored her own peace of mind. She attempted a little smile, which Logan returned. He retraced his steps to the work site. Following his advice was a good idea. But first, she must let him know that she didn't want him to suffer any injuries.

Three large steps and she caught up to him. He turned around with a question in his eyes when she grasped his hand.

"Don't let anything happen to you." Her voice wavered. The plea asked so much more than for safety in the field. It requested that he somehow assure her nothing would steal him away.

"THE MEN WILL BE WORKING until after dark, so we must eat without Logan and keep his food warm for when he comes in later." Sandy set the table while she talked. "Karen, would you please clean up the kitchen so that I can do the milking? Tillie will help him scoop the ears into the crib when the wagon returns to the yard. We'll need to follow this schedule until the work is done since Logan must help on the harvest crew at the other farms."

Sandy's words informed her that her worries had only begun. Only a small amount of food reached Karen's stomach during the meal. Logan's life would be in danger for many days to come.

The harvest crew worked at the De Witt farm for two more days. Each evening, Karen breathed a sigh of relief when Logan finally came in the house, well and whole although quite dusty and tired, and took his seat at the table.

Her focus returned to her classroom when the harvest work moved on to the Patterson farm. But her peace was short-lived. Saturday afternoon, a horse and rider raced up the lane. Karen recognized the rider as Vern Patterson's oldest son, Wade. She opened the door to him as her stomach plummeted. Wade wouldn't leave his father's farm before the work was done unless he had a good reason. Karen didn't want to learn what that reason might be.

Sandy and Tillie left their laundry tasks and joined her.

"I've brought a message. Mr. De Witt's been injured. Dad went to town for the doctor. We wanted you to know. We'll be bringin' Mr. De Witt home as soon as we can." He turned around, got on his horse, and galloped down the lane.

Sandy sank into a chair and silently wiped her eyes. Tillie paced. "I can't believe this. First we lose Dad, and now we might lose Logan too."

"Don't say such things, dear." Sandy motioned for her to sit down. "We shouldn't expect the worst. Logan might be just fine." Her voice turned quiet, ominous. "But farm accidents are usually serious." She wiped her eyes again.

Tears flowed from Karen's eyes too. She sat in Logan's chair at the table. The location comforted her and also provided her with the perfect view of the road. Soon he'd be home. That meant he was still alive, but it also might mean that he could still lose his life.

Karen heeded Sandy's words to Tillie and pushed those kinds of thoughts from her mind.

A wagon rolled down the lane. Karen joined the other women as they watched out the window. Tom Hinkley climbed down off the seat. He went around to the back and helped someone sit up. It was Logan.

Karen examined his appearance. No bandages on his head. No blood. He walked around the wagon, shook hands with Tom Hinkley, and made his way to the house. He looked perfectly fine.

"Thank God." Sandy's words echoed Karen's thoughts. She ran to the open door as Logan entered and held up his left hand.

"It's nothing more than a finger injury. I'll be fine."

"Will you lose it?" Sandy inspected the bandaged hand.

"No. The doctor stitched it up."

Tillie threw herself into his embrace. "I was so worried."

"I knew you would be, so I insisted they bring me home sooner than the doctor wanted." Logan moved to the wash basin and sank his right hand into the water he poured from the pitcher. "Give it a few days, and I'll be back to normal."

"What happened, dear?" Sandy came to the wash stand to assist him in cleaning his bandaged hand.

"Got it caught between the cogs on one of the wheels in the husker-shredder when tightening a belt. I'm glad Vern saw it happen and could help me get my hand out. If he hadn't been there, I could've damaged my entire hand." Logan accepted the towel his mother handed to him. "I'm beat. Getting stitched up is more tiring than a whole week of harvest. Could you please get some bath water ready for me? I want to clean up and go to bed."

"I'll do it." Karen forced the words from her mouth. She went to the porch for the large metal tub and returned to the kitchen. Like on the day of that storm, all of her movements were in slow motion.

Karen stood at the stove dipping water from the copper boiler into the tub as Sandy and Tillie left the kitchen with baskets of damp clothes to hang on the line. The whole situation crushed her. Shaking began in her legs and extended up to her hands until she dropped the dipper on the stove with a clang. Tears streamed from her eyes, making her vision blur. She leaned against the sink to stop herself from collapsing on the floor.

Logan turned to her. "Karen?"

She wiped her eyes, but her legs would not stop shaking.

He rushed over to her and took her in his arms.

Leaning against him, Karen gained the strength to talk. "I was so scared."

He smoothed her hair with his uninjured hand. "Shh. It's all right. I'm here now."

"That terrible day just kept worrying me all week. The worst happened. It could've happened to you." Karen began to weep.

"What terrible day?"

"Ella's brother. He was in an accident too."

"Tell me about it."

Karen sniffled. "Ella was a good friend from college. She'd invited me to visit her during our summer vacation. While I was there, her brother. He . . ." The image of the injured man and the tortured cries of Ella and her sisters flooded Karen's memory as if it was happening all over again.

Logan held her much the same as he did on the day of the storm. Steady. Close.

"They were threshing. He got his leg caught. Mangled to the knee."

"I'm sorry." Logan's voice reached her ears, low and soothing.

"The doctor came but couldn't save him. He was young. Like you. He left behind a wife and three small children." She buried her face in his dusty shirt. "Oh, Logan. It was so terrible."

"It still bothers you."

"Yes. I still see Ella's sister-in-law, working over him alongside the doctor. Crumpling in pain when he died." A sob caught in her throat. "It reminds me so much of Mother when she lost Father."

"I'm sorry." Logan continued to hold her and let her cry. The moisture from her tears mixed with the dust of his shirtfront. Still he didn't let her go.

Karen leaned on him until the tears were exhausted. Her soul a bit more settled, she breathed in slowly, enjoying the quiet.

The back door thumped closed. The footsteps of Sandy and Tillie pounded on the floor of the back porch. Karen pulled away from him as they entered the room. "I'll be fine. Your bath water is ready, so I'll carry it up for you." She'd be able to follow through if her legs didn't start shaking again. Logan may survive this accident, but if he kept farming, he'd for sure suffer another and then another. If she allowed her feelings for him to continue on at the same rate they'd enjoyed this far, eventually what happened to Ella's sister would happen to her. Then Karen would be in the same predicament as Mother with no support and dependent on others to take care of her.

Karen's back straightened as she climbed the stairs. Those things would never happen to her. She had her teaching career, after all. Karen couldn't decide which was worse. Caring for a man who operated dangerous machinery with the power to kill him. Or a man who possessed the sort of power to injure, cut off family members from one another, and kill the trust of an entire community. Her wish to know Logan, the preaching farmer with an insatiable craving for hazardous endeavors, must cease. A teaching career promised her much more stability.

CHAPTER TWENTY-ONE

"*B*ut Logan, it's Sunday afternoon."

Logan made the last twist in the blue striped tie at his neck while he looked into the small mirror on the parlor wall.

Karen sat on the love seat. The mirror reflected her face over his right shoulder. Her eyes held a pleading look.

His tie in place, he turned around. "I realize that, but I think it's unnecessary for you to come along anymore." Unnecessary was an understatement. Use of the word "unwise" or even "dangerous" fit much better. The last thing he needed while attempting to preach stutter-free was Karen's alluring presence in church.

"How will I find out more news about Agnes? I've been dying to know how that little girl is doing." Karen stood and looked him in the eye.

"I'll tell you when I come home."

Karen frowned.

He should make it up to her somehow. "Tell you what. The weather is still fine today. When I come home, I'll take you on a nice, long walk along the creek and supply you with every last detail."

The expression on Karen's face told him the plan was less than fair.

"See you at four." Leaving the parlor, he picked up his Bible and his sheet of notes on the way out the door.

After the service, Logan stood at the church door, shaking hands like he did every week, but the more people he talked to, the more he believed he'd made a terrible mistake by leaving Karen at home.

She waited for him in the porch swing when he came to the house after bedding down the horse. He rubbed his forehead. His face must look like he'd spent hours in the sun.

"Did you find out about Agnes?" Karen leaned forward.

"I did." Mrs. Harper had been quite generous in providing him with updates.

She searched his face. "What's wrong?"

Logan ran a hand through his hair. Boy, he didn't want to talk about this.

Karen stood. Her brow furrowed. "Something happened. What is it?"

He sucked in as big of a breath as both lungs could hold. "Uh, well, everyone noticed you were gone today."

A large smile spread across her face. She nodded as though prompting him to continue.

"When I greeted people after the service they kept asking me why, uh . . . why Mrs. De Witt hadn't come today." His cheeks burned.

Karen's eyes widened. Then she sputtered with a laugh refusing to stay held in.

"We need to straighten this out, Karen. I shouldn't have let it go as long as I did."

She turned serious. "Apparently that older gentleman sang my praises to more people than just you."

He gulped. "Apparently." Logan led her down the steps to begin the promised walk through the pasture. "I suppose you should come along next week to help me explain the truth." A grin claimed his lips. "You'll have two jobs."

Karen rewarded him with a beautiful smile. "I'd be honored, Reverend De Witt."

KAREN DESCENDED the stairs to the kitchen at one-thirty the following Sunday afternoon. She still wore her Sunday dress. The weather had cooled enough for her rose-colored summer dress and hat to stay in the closet. Today, she wore a burgundy dress with long sleeves. Ivory lace trimmed her neckline and embellished her hat.

Logan glanced up from the notes he organized. Pure enjoyment swept over his face. "I believe I like this dress just as well as your summer one."

His compliment made glad little tingles break out on her arms. "Thank you."

He picked up his notes and Bible from the table. Then he moved to the door. He held it open with a grin on his face. "After you, Mrs. De Witt," he whispered when she passed in front of him.

The teasing reminded her of her reason for going along with him today. "What do you plan to say?" she asked when he got in the buggy.

"I don't know. I've never been in this kind of situation before." The flaming of his cheeks told her that he'd rather not say anything but instead forget the whole thing.

"We must tell the truth," Karen said in an attempt to console him. "The Harpers know I'm not your wife. Maybe they've had a chance to correct some of their neighbors."

"Possibly, but the congregation still needs to hear it from us." Logan tapped the horse with the reins.

At the church, Logan helped her to the ground. She walked with him inside and down the center aisle. Taking her usual seat in the front pew, Karen smiled up at Logan, but he refused to look at her.

Karen's chin dropped to her chest, and her cheeks burned. If she hadn't insisted on helping him, none of this would've happened. Logan wouldn't be in the middle of a serious misunderstanding requiring an awkward and painful explanation.

And yet, if Karen hadn't asked to help, she wouldn't have met Agnes. Neither would Logan have asked her to pray for him or for Mr. Harper. Karen lifted her head. Good had come of her wishes even if they made things more difficult for Logan.

He cleared his throat. "Good afternoon. I would like to open worship with the verses of Psalm eight." Logan picked up his Bible and read in his warm voice.

Karen closed her eyes. She could like him. Very easily. She already did. Too much.

"Let's pray." Logan led the congregation in prayer.

This was her cue. Karen left her seat and joined him at the pulpit.

"Mr. Harper is here," Logan whispered after the amen. "Halfway back on the right side."

Karen scanned the area Logan indicated. There he was, all dressed up, seated next to his wife and with no bottle in his hand. Agnes sat next to him. The little girl looked wonderful.

The service proceeded in the same way as all of the ones past except for how it ended.

When Karen finished singing the last hymn, Logan kept her at his side.

He cleared his throat. "Um, I have a quick announcement to make. I'm sorry to detain you for these additional minutes, but I feel it's important to tell you the truth." He had the attention of every last person in the room, including Karen's. Logan shot a nervous glance her direction and continued. "I learned last week that during this past month we've been together, the conclusion has been drawn that I'm married. That isn't true. I want to tell you because my assistant deserves to be known to you for who she really is." Logan stopped to rub his forehead. Perspiration glistened on his skin. This speech was costing him. "I should have made a proper introduction on the first day, but I failed to do so." He took a step back and gestured to Karen. "This beautiful and talented young woman who has been leading our singing each week is the teacher for Silver Grove's School, Miss Karen Millerson. She isn't my wife. Rather, she's boarding with my family for the school year and wanted to help minister to you on Sundays."

A few claps rippled through the sanctuary.

Logan inhaled and raised his arms. "And now, the Lord bless you and keep you. The Lord make his face to shine upon you and be gracious to you. The Lord lift his countenance upon you and give you peace." He left the pulpit.

Karen followed.

At the back of the church, they stood outside in the breeze and sunshine to await parishioners. Logan turned to her with a wide grin on his face. "Did you hear that?"

"Your explanation? I thought you did a marvelous job."

"Thanks. I meant the service. The Scripture reading, sermon, and benediction."

"Yes, I heard them. You were wonderful, as usual." Why would Logan feel the need to draw attention to his preaching? He never did that.

"Karen, I didn't stutter. I made it all the way through an entire service and that uncomfortable explanation about us and didn't stutter." His grin grew. "This is the first time ever."

His meaning registered in her mind. "I didn't realize you struggled so much."

He gave a nod, a serious expression replaced his grin. "Every week for the last three years until today. And I think I have you to thank for it."

"Me?" Karen rested her hand on the bodice of her dress.

169

"Your prayers mean more than you'll ever know." Logan gazed deeply into her eyes.

People approached, so Logan turned away and began to shake hands.

A group of three older women formed the beginning of the line. One of them patted Logan on the cheek with her white-gloved hand. "Now, Reverend De Witt, you may try to get us to believe you aren't married to this young lady, but you should be."

Logan's eyebrows rose.

"She's good for you. It's obvious to us you belong together." She gave him one more little pat and, amidst the chipper agreement of her friends, moved on.

Logan pulled at his collar. This afternoon should end so that they could go home and stop being the target of other people's opinions.

Near the end of the line, the Harper family appeared. Agnes reached up and gave Karen a tight hug. "I'm all better, Miss Millerson."

"Your news makes me so happy." Karen returned the hug before Agnes pulled away.

"I knew you were a teacher all the time. Mama told me." Agnes looked up at her mother.

Mrs. Harper's cheeks turned pink. "We didn't know our neighbors were thinkin' that way about ya."

"Doesn't matter." Logan waved his hand in the air. "I wanted everyone to hear it from me."

"My husband wants to see you. He's waiting around inside." Mrs. Harper glanced at the doors to the church.

"I'll meet with him as soon as I can." Logan gave her a smile.

"We'll be over by the wagon until you're through." She gathered her children and led them around the corner of the building.

"What do you suppose he wants?" Logan asked when everyone left.

Karen couldn't answer. She only shook her head while she went with Logan inside.

"YOU WIFE SAID you were looking for me." Karen sat down on the front pew as Logan shook Mr. Harper's hand.

"Yeah." Mr. Harper scratched the side of his head. "I keep thinkin' about what you said when we met in town."

Logan settled onto the step to the pulpit, facing them. "How can I help you?"

"I know what you said about me is true. My soul is sick. I've been hopin' that whiskey or my work at the mill or even my kids woulda made me feel better, but they don't. I keep drinkin' and drinkin' hopin' that'll make it all right, but I feel worse." Mr. Harper rubbed his palms on his thighs. "I don't know what to do. I can't keep goin' on like this. Agnes gettin' sick scared me half to death. What if she died from that fever?"

Logan grasped one of the man's wrists. "Salvation is your answer. Like I said on Wednesday, it's a gift. All you need to do is accept."

"Does it stop the pain?"

"What pain?"

"The pain of havin' nothin'. I work and work but it don't add up." He shook his head.

Logan glanced at Karen. He nodded.

She took his silent action as her cue to join in. "Mr. Harper, you're talking about the emptiness we all feel when we don't have Christ in our lives. You've tried to fill it with all the wrong things. If you ask Him to live in your heart, you will be filled, healed, and at peace."

Mr. Harper focused on the floor. Everything she'd said appeared to be finding a landing place on his insides.

"Would you like to try?" she asked.

Mr. Harper gave a shaky nod. "Yeah, Okay. But I don't know what to do. Can ya help me?"

Karen tilted her head in Logan's direction as her cue that he should take over now.

Logan leaned forward. "Just pray what I pray. I'll go first." He closed his eyes.

Karen did too. Not because she needed to say the same things Mr. Harper needed to say, but to ask God to give Logan the right words to use.

"Lord Jesus, I need You. Thank You for dying on the cross for my sins. I ask You right now to come live in my heart. It's empty and it needs Your healing and Your peace." Logan paused to allow Mr. Harper to take his turn. He continued. "Please forgive my sins and prepare a place for me in Heaven someday. Amen."

Mr. Harper repeated after Logan. Both men opened their eyes.

A big smile claimed Mr. Harper's face. "Thanks. I'm feelin' better already." He shook Logan's hand. "But what about Agnes and her brothers? How can I know they have Jesus in their hearts, too?"

"Share with them what you did just now. If they haven't already prayed that prayer, then ask them to do it too."

"Yeah. You're right. I'll do that." He stood. "See ya next week. I can't wait to come back."

"I'll keep praying for you, Mr. Harper."

"So will I." Karen waved to the man on his way out the door.

Logan turned to her. "You make an amazing assistant."

Karen blushed. "I've tried my best." If only those words were as effective in her heart as they were on Sunday afternoons. All her efforts to hold herself at a distance from him were daily becoming unacquainted with success.

CHAPTER TWENTY-TWO

"$\mathcal{T}$he fall party is this Friday night." Karen scanned the schoolroom on Tuesday afternoon to ensure all paid attention. "The notes I sent home to your mothers last week asked them to contribute dishes to our potluck meal."

Heads lifted. Whispers between Becky and Mary Ellen in the second grade row ceased. Karen hid a smile. Talk of food usually worked in securing her students' attention. "I need you to bring replies to school tomorrow so I know how much food we'll have." She reached for a copy of the flier she'd send home with the children and read from it. "The party begins at six o'clock with games. Mr. De Witt will supply those for us. The meal begins at seven with dessert to follow."

They will have desserts if Tillie cooperates. So far, she'd rejected Karen's request for help with the baking. If Logan hadn't suggested Tillie help with the party, Karen would've asked the mothers of her students for baked goods. That course of action would have been much easier.

How she'd love to have Tillie as a friend, but she was getting so weary of the younger girl's resentment. Maybe this party could somehow bring them together.

Karen turned her thoughts back to her classroom. "Please remember to talk to your mothers this evening. Class dismissed."

Amid the racket of nineteen energetic bodies crowding toward the door, one of her least favorite people appeared.

"I heard of your party and want to offer my services." Eldon Kent advanced toward her.

Karen's heart pounded. She took two steps backwards to create more space between them, but he only stood that much closer. He had a genius for appearing when she least wanted him around. She glanced at the clock. Logan would arrive any minute to take her home.

Eldon could help by staying away. The words formed on the tip of her tongue. Swallowing them, she quickly dreamed up something more diplomatic. "Thank you, but I have all the plans made." Her voice shook. He stood too close for her to draw in a decent breath.

"I could provide prizes for the winners of your games."

He saw her as a prize, and he wouldn't win at this game. "We won't be giving out any prizes." She tried to step around him, but he leaned on her desk, blocking the way.

Boots clumped on the floor at the back of the room. Karen glanced over Eldon's shoulder.

Logan.

Her heart leaped and her lungs constricted. She was free.

"Afternoon, Eldon." Logan's words held a frigid tone. Unnatural coming from a man who possessed the warmest voice she'd ever heard. "What do you want here with Miss Millerson?"

Karen cheered Logan's use of her professional title. It was one more way to push Eldon at a distance where he belonged.

"I came to offer my help for her party Friday night." Eldon's words came out as cold as Logan's.

Logan shoved past Eldon and stood protectively at her side. "Got it covered. Thanks all the same."

If Eldon was a gracious man, he would have conceded at this

point, but instead he scowled at Logan and attempted one more ploy. "I had also hoped Karen would allow me to act as her escort Friday evening." His features hardened. "But I know when I've been shown up." Steel entered his gaze and his words as he left. "I'll see you Friday."

"Sorry I'm late." Logan reached into his pocket. "I have something for you. I went to town to check the mail and discovered this." He handed her an envelope.

Karen took it and read the return address. "It's from Mother." She flipped it over, tore it open, and read Mother's script.

"What's it say?"

"My sister Julia had her baby last Saturday. It's a boy. They named him Sam." Karen finished reading and glanced up at Logan. A few tears gathered in the corners of her eyes. "I wish I could meet him. Knowing Julia would have her baby this far into the school year made leaving home even harder." Karen folded up the letter and returned it to the envelope. The good news from home pushed all thoughts of Eldon from her mind.

WEDNESDAY AFTERNOON, Logan strode down the hall to Eldon's office.

Eldon answered his knock. "Good afternoon. Please come in." The cordial words would've been charming spoken by anyone else. Coming from Eldon, they held a note of haughtiness.

Logan took his usual seat and laid the mountain of cash on Eldon's desk.

His eyes gleamed as he snatched at the money. "You listened and brought me a large amount." If Eldon had ever learned to say "thank you," he may have risked it now. Instead, he leaned back in his seat and counted.

Logan waited. He knew how much he'd brought and could have easily told Eldon but refrained. Eldon had to count it all himself before trusting any number, spoken by a dependable customer or otherwise.

Eldon reached for the last bill and took up his pen. "This payment will make a significant reduction in the accrued interest." He wrote a dollar amount in Logan's ledger. Finished writing, he laid the pen down, and scrutinized Logan. "You realize you only have two months to eliminate the interest."

Logan nodded. Hadn't he stayed up half the night prior and agonized over the obvious fact?

"Do you have a plan?" Eldon shoved the book over to Logan.

"The same one I told you about this summer."

Eldon squinted. "Unless you have another corn crop hiding somewhere, you'll have to pay the bank every last cent of your income."

Logan squinted back. Was this Eldon's little payback for Logan's attempt at keeping him away from Karen? Maybe, but Logan didn't have time to speculate about how Eldon did banking. Everything he said was true. Logan had to pay the bank that much to make the end-of-year interest deadline.

He studied the account book. Christmas would be slim at the De Witt home this year. Too slim. He wanted Mama and Tillie to have nice gifts of new clothing or household decorations. Something frivolous. The just-because kind of gifts that spoke of his love for them.

The numbers glaring up at him were too unforgiving for that sort of holiday. His family would be fortunate to eke by with a tree cut from his own pasture the way things were going. Logan pushed the book towards Eldon and stood. "It's the only plan I have. We have to make it work. I'll see you in a month."

Logan strode out of the bank, shaking his head and muttering to himself. Eldon was the most disagreeable, uncooperative person he'd ever met. If any other bank existed in town, Logan would've gladly moved all of his accounts elsewhere.

LOGAN RETURNED to a farmhouse vibrating with noise and action. He entered a kitchen hazed with flour dust and a little smoke from the stove. Karen must be in charge of the baking temperature again. He stood at the wash stand and sloshed water over his hands and arms. He'd sure appreciate it if the project under way involved none of his clothing this time.

Karen beamed at him. "Pie number six coming out of the oven." She opened the oven door, allowing the delicious scent of sweet baked cherries to escape and waft over to him, tempting his appetite.

He dried off and went to her. "Let me have a taste."

She straightened and almost bumped his chest with the hot pie plate. Her cheeks flushed pink, whether from the oven's heat or his nearness, he couldn't say. "Later." She tried to smile, but her mouth dropped open in a small gasp.

An undercurrent passed between them, almost knocking him over with its strength. They weren't speaking about pie at all. He didn't desire a sampling of the dessert. He hungered instead for a taste of life with Karen as more than his boarder, his Sunday assistant, or even as his friend. Living arrangements and his best reasons for choosing the single life suddenly lost their essential flavor.

"Save some for me."

"I plan to." A slight smile stretched across her red lips. Cherry red lips.

Another delicacy he wanted to taste.

Karen's blush deepened like she'd seen his thoughts.

He winked.

"Take that pie to the table and let it cool with the others." Tillie's command dragged him back into reality. She pointed her dough-crusted finger at a line of pies on the end of the table closest to the open window.

Karen slid the cherry pie from the stovetop and hastened across the room. Mama turned from the sink where she washed mixing bowls and slipped another pie into the oven.

The evening milking awaited him, so Logan fled the kitchen. If he planned to escort Karen Friday night, he needed some practice forcing his brain to think of her as Teacher Karen. He'd grown more comfortable with her lately, as long as he remembered to think of her as the professional who instructed children. She was Teacher Karen, someone who had in common with him only the goal of influencing lives and nothing more. She might be everything he wanted in a woman but to him she could be nothing more than Teacher Karen, Boarder Karen, Friend Karen.

Now that her trial period of going along with him on Sunday afternoons was finished, he could stick to his plan of heeding the apostle Paul's words without any speeches given in defense of his single status. It was well to remain unmarried. He could focus even easier on the Lord's affairs and pleasing Him without any distraction.

He must make every effort so that their relationship fell within the proper confines. Rides in his buggy were strictly for the practical purpose of transporting her to and from church and school just like he would any member of his household. That is what Tom Hinkley asked of him on the first day. Meals were shared in this context as were any of their other interactions.

Sharing books in the evenings and on Sundays was coincidence. It happened only because they lived in the same house and not because Logan in any way looked forward to the coziness of sharing the parlor with Karen. Reading was necessary. She did it to prepare lessons. He did it to prepare sermons. Not much space in that scenario for those undercurrents he discovered in the kitchen a few moments ago.

The words of those ladies from Meadow Creek rustled his calm. *"You should be married to this young woman. She's good for you."* Marriage meant family. This was a yearning he didn't dare entertain. The evening spent with Agnes's little brothers awoke a piece of his heart he'd thought had been laid to rest forever.

But he had a family. Mama and Tillie were his family. They needed him in every way. Even if he did have permission to take a wife, the news of it would ask for too much change from them. He shouldn't long for things he could never have.

Eldon needed to remember that lesson too. Karen had been quite clear that Eldon couldn't have her, not her attention or her willingness to attend the party with him.

Why? Was her reluctance because of her dislike of Eldon, or did it have something to do with Logan? Maybe she wanted to make sure Eldon didn't claim her so that she was available for someone else.

Was Logan that someone?

If so, then he'd let her down. He might need to assist with setting up games and moving desks around, but he was still the provider of strength and safety. These were two more practical necessities that slipped neatly into the kind of relationship required between a man and the woman he was offering a place to live. He was still single with no room in his life for romance. Karen was still a teacher paying him for room in his house, not in his heart. One night at a school party wasn't going to change anything.

CHAPTER TWENTY-THREE

"*W*elcome. Thanks for coming." Karen stood at the entrance of the school building, greeting the families of her students. Mothers joined Sandy and Tillie at the food tables, uncovering dishes and organizing a line. Fathers congregated about the room, discussing corn prices and the yield of their crops.

Logan had stayed outside to help the students with a horseshoe toss, bobbing for apples, three-legged races, and croquet. Karen went outside to join the fun as soon as the last family entered.

Tim Hixson, his brother Nick, Kelvin Kent, and his cousin Ned played a game of horseshoes.

"May I play?" Karen asked.

"Sure." Ned handed her a horseshoe explaining the rules.

She waited until Kelvin and Tim had taken their turns, then she threw at the stake in the grass. Out of the corner of her eye, Karen glimpsed Logan as he coached the three Hinkley girls, Evie Patterson, and Lacy Jones on how to hit a croquet ball through a hoop. Lacy giggled when Logan missed on purpose as part of his demonstration.

The boys threw their horseshoes.

"Your turn again, Teacher." Kelvin handed her another horseshoe.

She threw at the rod poking out of the ground a few feet away. Metal clinked as her horseshoe hit the target.

The boys cheered.

"You're great at this game." Tim's thatch of reddish-brown hair bounced around his ears as he thrust his fist in the air and jumped.

"Thank you. This is my first time to play horseshoes."

"You've got the knack."

"Hi, Mr. De Witt." Nick waved at Logan.

Logan ruffled Kelvin's hair. "Who's winning?"

"Miss Millerson," they said in unison.

"Really?" Logan's gaze swung over to her face.

"Beginner's luck." Karen shrugged.

Logan stepped closer and lowered his voice. His gaze trailed off to the left. "Look who's here."

A buggy sporting a single driver pulled into the dusky school yard. Karen recognized it along with the horse. Her stomach dropped. She'd hoped he'd stay home or work late, anything except attend the school party.

Kelvin waved and called out to the driver. "Hi, Uncle Eldon."

Karen whispered to Logan. "Let's go inside."

Logan consulted his watch. "Seven o'clock." He turned to the boys. "Time for supper. Go tell the girls." He offered his arm to Karen and led her to the door.

Once inside, Logan raised his voice. "Miss Millerson has indicated she'd like to start the meal, so let's pray."

The room quieted as people bowed their heads.

Someone's hand grasped her elbow. A scream caught in her throat. She clamped her lips to muffle it.

Logan continued to pray. When he said "amen," Karen opened her eyes.

Eldon stared at her.

"May I escort you through the line?" Eldon almost smiled.

181

Karen resisted the urge to throw a retort out at him. "Uh, no. I—"

"The teacher deserves to go first. Come with me." Eldon tugged on her arm.

For the sake of avoiding a scene, Karen allowed him to pull her along beside him to the front of the room. The success of her party now depended on her toleration of Eldon's company.

LOGAN FROWNED at Eldon's retreating back. He wanted to rush after Karen and pull her to his side where she belonged, but starting a tug-of-war over the teacher was probably a bad idea.

Karen turned around. A pleading look for him to do something haunted her eyes.

He had all kinds of ideas of what to do with the likes of Eldon. But punching a guy out and carrying him back to his buggy dead-man style didn't fit somehow with the rest of the evening's entertainment. Logan sent Karen the most supportive smile he knew how and stayed in his corner of the room, his attention fixed hawk-like on the pair as he waited for Eldon to take a seat. Once he settled, Logan would join them and force Eldon to put up with his company just like Karen was always forced into tolerating Eldon's. Give the guy a taste of his own medicine. That would be a sure way of getting Karen back at Logan's side where she belonged.

Logan leaned against the wall, hands in pockets, and watched as families filed through line behind Miss Millerson and her unwelcome escort. Plates filled, they moved on to seek out places to sit down.

Now was his chance. He eased closer to the food table and stood two people away from reaching for a plate when Pete intercepted his path.

"Looks like Karen has herself a suitor."

All Logan needed now was for his match-maker friend to

come along and magnify his problems. He shifted his weight from one foot to the other. "You should get in line before the food is gone."

"Save a seat for me."

"Isn't Anna here?"

"No. She's not feeling well so stayed home."

Logan placed food on his plate while trying his best to ignore the way Eldon leaned in too close as he kept one hand on her elbow to steer her through the room or how the chairs all around them had already filled.

The role of escort belonged to him. Karen would want it that way. All Logan could do right now was watch from across the room and try to keep his supper down whenever Karen looked his direction with silent torture dimming her eyes.

"You feeling all right tonight?" Pete studied him with a furrowed brow after he sat down.

"Yeah, but I'm not too hungry, I guess." He pushed his food around on his plate and tried to appear interested.

"You seem a little preoccupied."

Had Pete said something? He turned to his friend. "What?" Pete's comment registered in his brain. His cheeks heated. "Oh."

Pete's gaze traveled off Logan's face and around the room as though he searched for clues to Logan's discomfort. "You weren't expecting Eldon to come, were you?"

Logan shrugged. "Oh, I knew he'd come, but I expected to keep her away from him."

"It's rather unusual not to see the two of you together." Pete's quiet voice struck a nerve.

Logan needed fresh air. Eldon had accomplished what Logan thought couldn't be done, whisking Karen away from him. And now he'd pulled it off and left Logan to field Pete's interrogations. The room closed in on him, suffocating him.

Pete went back for seconds. He asked Logan to come along, but the helpings on his plate from the first round still looked too large. Logan shook his head and forced his knotted stomach to accept the food he tried to put in it.

The last bites of Pete's food disappeared as Karen freed herself from Eldon to stand near the food tables.

"Thank you for coming tonight. Your children had a wonderful time helping me plan for this party. I hope you've all experienced it as the occasion of celebration we intended it to be." Karen beckoned to Tillie. "The time has come to serve dessert and I don't want to begin without giving proper credit. All these pies you see here on the table wouldn't have been possible without Tillie's skill at baking and her patience teaching me how to cook. Thanks, Tillie." Karen clapped. Everyone followed her lead. "We have apple, cherry, and peach. So, if my special helper would come up now, we will start serving."

Lacy Jones left her family. She went to Karen, wearing a proud smile and a dress that looked new. The patch covering her eye was the only indicator of the struggles Lacy faced. Logan grinned to himself. It appeared that Karen's dream of taking Lacy to a party in a new dress had come true. She handed Lacy a knife and showed her how to cut the pies into wedges. Tillie scooped them onto plates.

"Want some?" Pete stood and waited for an answer.

"I'll take apple." Since Karen had promised to save some cherry for him, he ventured on to his next favorite.

Soon, Pete returned with slices for both of them. Logan's looked perfect. The top was golden and crusted with cinnamon and sugar. Tender slices of apple spilled out the sides. His mouth watered in spite of the large meal he'd forced down. He forked a bite into his mouth and puckered.

This wasn't apple pie. It tasted too bitter to live up to that description. Logan steeled his nerves and swallowed.

"This stuff's terrible," Pete said under his breath. He laid his fork down before chugging his entire glass of water.

Logan did the same.

Karen arrived. "How did it turn out?" Anticipation of a compliment shone in her eyes.

Logan couldn't give her one. He had to speak the truth, but he didn't know how to do it in a way that wouldn't crush the budding confidence of the tutored cook.

Pete spoke for both of them. "The pie tastes horrible. Too salty."

"What?" Karen snatched up Logan's plate, cut a bite with his fork, and raised it to her mouth.

"Don't!" Tillie lunged and caught the fork mid-air. It fell from Karen's hand and clamored onto the plate. A dive from Logan saved both plate and pie from a tragic end on the hard wood floor.

"It's ruined." Tillie jabbed her finger at Karen. "All because of you." Karen retreated slowly across the room, but Tillie advanced, the tears glistening in her eyes. "You ruined every last one of those pies and then blamed me. Tonight you come in here telling everyone that I made them. I did no such thing! Mama and I are better cooks than that. Now the De Witt women are the laughing-stock of the whole town. See if I ever help you cook again! You are the worst excuse for a teacher I've ever seen. Logan made a huge mistake when he let you stay with us. You've wrecked our family. I want you gone." Tillie ground the last word from clenched teeth and sprinted from the building.

Logan's insides boiled. He had to get himself under control before he hunted Tillie down and said something he'd regret. Tillie had no right to treat Karen in this way.

Pete clutched his shoulder. "You'll get your chance to defend Karen. Let her go this time."

His fists remembered how to relax, and his breathing evened out, but the sight of one lone tear sliding down Karen's cheek pierced his heart, breaking it in a hundred pieces.

Feet thumped and chairs scraped as people milled around. Dishes clinked as the women collected their leftovers. Everyone talked in subdued tones, reminding Logan of the Oswell City sanctuary after a funeral.

Well, something had died here tonight. All his hopes for a relationship between Karen and Tillie, for one. And trust. Tillie didn't trust his judgment. Never had, it sounded. That hurt. How deeply had Tillie hurt Karen? She probably felt as betrayed by his sister as he did.

He felt a tap on his shoulder and looked up. Mama's troubled eyes looked down at him. "I'm going to find Tillie and walk home with her. I've never seen her so upset. Could you please stay and help Karen straighten up?"

Logan nodded. He planned to do that anyway. It was the least he could do for her.

THE SCHOOL CLEARED out one family at a time. The party had drawn to a close anyway with the serving of dessert, now it ended a little more abruptly thanks to Tillie's shocking performance. Logan lit a lantern and went outside to collect the games.

Buggies and wagons left the school yard until silence enveloped him. He loaded his supplies into his wagon until the project was complete. Karen should be ready to go home by now. Most of the desks had been moved back into place by fathers as anxious as Logan to restore the situation. No other work remained.

He darted into the school. The scene that greeted him left him thinking that he should've punched Eldon out when he had the chance.

In the dim glow of the lamp, Eldon leaned over the teacher's desk where Karen sat with one hand propping up her head. His low voice murmured into Karen's ear. His hand rested on her back.

Logan's fist tightened at his side.

"Not tonight, Eldon." Karen shook her head. "I should host another party. You'll have to wait until then."

More murmurs in her ear.

Karen straightened. "I'm not going with you. Logan brought me. I must wait for him."

Logan shuffled his feet to distract Eldon from further pestering Miss Millerson.

Both Eldon and Karen glanced up. Karen's face brightened a fraction, but Eldon scowled.

"Everything all right in here?" Logan allowed his gaze to bore into Eldon. When Eldon didn't move, Logan spoke again. "We need to go home, Karen. Can I help you with anything?" Logan arranged a couple of desks although they were in perfect order already. He didn't care. The activity would send Eldon the message that his fun was over.

Eldon backed away from Karen's desk. "See you soon."

Karen didn't respond.

Logan sensed Eldon's displeasure at his intrusion, but he ignored it. The sooner Eldon left, the quicker Logan could take Karen home.

He moved down the aisle to where Karen sat at her desk.

"Tillie's right. I've made a mess of everything. A party that should have been fun for everyone turned into a disaster, and I'm the one to blame."

He tugged on her arm until she stood and faced him. "You are not to blame."

"I've let the families of my students down." A tear ran down her cheek "And after we planned for so long. The children were so excited."

Logan wiped the tear away.

"I want to make it up to them. I should host another party." Karen sniffed. A breath shuddered through her frame. "But I think I feel worse about Tillie than about the party."

Logan nodded. He hurt too.

"I didn't know she hated me so much."

"It's news to me."

"I've let my students down. I've disappointed their families. Now I find out I'm causing problems for your family. I had no idea." Karen reached for her handkerchief. "Your mother has every right to refuse me any more room and board. She and Tillie may never speak to me again after what happened tonight. I can't blame them. Tillie and I will never be friends now. Maybe you really did make a mistake in boarding me."

The vice got a hold on Logan's heart again. He grasped both of Karen's upper arms. Gazing deeply into her eyes, he used his best persuasive tone of voice. "Boarding you is the best thing that ever happened to us."

More tears flowed over Karen's cheeks, telling him she felt worse, not better like he'd intended. Talking was getting him nowhere. He had to do something more convincing, something that came from him alone so that Karen knew he acted out of his own will without any influence from his family.

Only one course of action came to mind. It was one he'd wanted to take for a long time. Lowering his head, he placed a light kiss on Karen's lips.

Her breath rasped, and her eyes glowed as if she'd found the comfort she sought.

Logan's own breath caught in his throat. The dormant places deep in his heart responded to the touch of Karen's lips. Desire awoke so powerfully he almost couldn't contain it.

Karen's arms circled his neck, sending him a clear message. She wanted more comfort.

Drawing her closer, he lowered his head once more. He took his time exploring her soft lips while savoring their sweetness.

Better than cherry pie. Oh, so much better.

The kiss intensified.

Karen's eager response delighted him. His arms around her and his mouth covering hers answered places in his heart that had waited many silent years for a moment like this one. He didn't want it to end.

But it did. Karen drew back and gazed at him through wide eyes. One last tear remained on her cheek.

A brush of his thumb wiped it away. "Feel better?"

She nodded, jerky at first, like her neck had to remember how to work again.

"Good." He should've found a better word. "Good" might sum up how he felt about Karen's restored state of mind, but it sure fell short of a proper description for the firecrackers going off on his insides.

CHAPTER TWENTY-FOUR

*K*aren rode in the wagon to the farm. Her breathing still hadn't returned to normal. Grateful for the dark of the night, she pressed her lips with the tips of her fingers. Logan had kissed her. Really and truly kissed her. And not on the cheek like he did his mother. This kiss landed square on her mouth and penetrated every last fiber of her being.

In the lane, Logan brought the wagon to a halt. She expected him to follow his usual habit of leaping out to assist her, but he sat still and stared at the reins in his hands. He glanced at her and then returned his focus to the reins. After a silent moment, he crawled from his seat, tied the reins, and came to her side of the wagon. He held his hand out to her like he'd done dozens of times, but this time he didn't let go. Sheltered within the folds of her skirt, his fingers curled around hers during the walk to the house.

Through the journey and arrival at the farm, no words passed between them. But none were needed. The expression in Logan's eyes spoke for him. He had feelings for her. Karen's stomach fluttered. If she didn't already care for him, that kiss would've come as an unwelcome shock. But she'd wanted Logan to kiss her the second time. Nothing else in her entire life brought her such an assurance of security as Logan's kiss.

She shouldn't give her heart to him. Allowing that to happen would strap her to a life of suffering if he died and scandal if he didn't. If only she could somehow return the kiss back to him. Then she'd be free. Oblivious to the knowledge of how well Logan satisfied her hopes. Things such as his call, like hers, to shape and influence lives. And his interests in lofty topics like history and religion. But so much more defined Logan as a man. Like the kindness that marked his every conversation along with the compassion for God's people and the love for God's word that kept him in the pulpit for the Meadow Creek congregation week after week. Karen studied his profile as they crossed the porch. Could such a gentle man really be as dangerous as she first believed?

LOGAN USHERED Karen into a dark kitchen. He wanted to climb the stairs where he might sort through his newly discovered affection for Karen in the quiet of his bedroom. But a lamp glowed in the parlor, reminding him of the conflict requiring his attention. Releasing Karen's hand, he went to the parlor with her. Mama sat on the loveseat talking to Tillie in the low tones of a mother delivering a severe reprimand. Tillie slumped in the rocking chair nearby. The rage appeared to have subsided, and now tears fell like a gentle shower after a thunderstorm.

Tillie lifted her head and glared at Karen.

"We waited for you to come home." Mama's gaze rested on Karen. "Could you please show me where you got your ingredients?"

"Certainly." Karen turned around and led Mama to the kitchen.

Logan took Mama's place on the loveseat. The anger he'd felt at the school heated his insides once more. He glanced at Tillie while trying to keep his voice as soft as possible. "You realize you wrecked Karen's party tonight."

"I didn't mean to." Tillie ventured a glance at him. "I hope you aren't as mad at me as Mama is. She assigned me the job of clearing the cellar of all its cobwebs and spiders before she'll let me spend time with Andrew again."

The anger subsided enough for a grin to tug at his mouth. He couldn't top Mama's methods of discipline. She may have said she didn't know what to do with Tillie, but her handling of this situation proved otherwise. Mama was going to be just fine.

A wail echoed from the pantry.

Logan shifted his attention to the kitchen.

Mama returned to the parlor, a blue striped tin in her hand. "I believe we found the problem."

Tillie frowned. "The sugar tin?"

"Not anymore." Mama took a deep breath. "Since salt went on sale at Carter's store last week, I asked Logan to buy some. The salt tin is too small to hold it all, so I put the extra in this tin. I'm sorry, girls. I didn't even think about them looking the same. I suppose I am to blame. Thanks to me, you dumped heaps of salt into each one of those pies."

Logan could still feel the burn on his tongue. "No wonder they tasted so bad."

"Where's the sugar?" Tillie directed her question at Mama after shooting him a withering look.

"On the top shelf of the pantry. I know to look there but should've told you."

"Yes, you should have, Mama. That wasn't fair." An expression of defeat clouded Tillie's eyes.

Mama set the tin on the table. "I forgot. I'm sorry."

"So am I. It ruined everything." Tillie wiped tears from her face.

Mama straightened. "Let's try to forget the whole thing. You'll make other pies. No one will remember anymore."

"I wish I could believe you." Tears rimmed Tillie's eyes again.

Mama rested her hand on Tillie's arm. "Get a good night's rest, and you'll feel better."

Her words proved false. The next morning, when Logan left his room to do the milking, he discovered Tillie drooped over the kitchen sink and making gut-wrenching noises.

He touched her back. "Tillie?"

"Go away. I'm sick," she choked out.

"You were fine last night. What happened?"

She sagged. "I ate something bad at Karen's party. Whenever I try to help her, something terrible happens to me." She gagged some more. "That girl has wrecked my life. I'm staying as far away from her as I can get."

Another fit of gagging overtook her, so Logan reluctantly backed away, left Tillie alone in her misery, and went to the barn. His plan to board the teacher so that he could provide Tillie with a friend after he left for Oswell City had taken a detour. Logan shook his head. Life looked so different now than it did the day he found out about the teacher coming to stay with them. Karen had actually turned out to be more his friend than Tillie's, if what happened at the school last night qualified as friendship.

KAREN SPENT some time in her room before breakfast. She couldn't bear to think of all the days and hours stretching before her when she must share the table with Logan. The way she kissed him would've left no question in his mind of her feelings. Nothing would be the same now. She couldn't talk to him or even look at him without remembering what she'd done. In need of some time alone, Karen sat at her writing desk.

She pulled out her journal. School kept her so busy that she hadn't used it since the day she left home. In search of a blank page, three little star-shaped petals fell out. They were dry but still held their color. Karen brushed one onto her finger and held it up. The memory of that day came rushing back to her. She'd sat with Julia in the white wicker loveseat on the lawn of Uncle Henry's Michigan Avenue home while guests enjoyed Aunt Fran's garden party. Julia's two-year-old son Ben had picked these flowers just for her. She'd kept them in water while she packed but when they began to wilt, she'd saved these three small petals. They'd traveled with her as a reminder of her search for safety and healing. These were Ben's petals, given to her on her last Sunday in Chicago.

Karen remembered how she felt that day, in need of some security of her own. Her heart pressed her to believe she'd found it with Logan. Sharing his home, his kisses, and even his ministry. She picked up her pen and tried to write, but dizziness assaulted her. Karen was falling with no solid footing to slow her down. She tumbled so far she'd never hit bottom. The kiss at school confirmed the astonishing truth. Somewhere during the course of these Sundays helping Logan and working by his side for the Harpers, she'd managed to fall in love with him.

LOGAN LOWERED his frame onto the milking stool, his thoughts more on last night's surprises than on his work. One swift brush across Karen's mouth for the sake of cheering her up shouldn't snag him like a fish on a hook. But it had. Boy, he'd gone and done it now.

He picked up the stool and the half-full pail. Moving on to the next Holstein, he went to work once more. The whole episode endangered his mission. He must remain unattached in order to better pursue the Lord's work. Karen was quickly becoming as big of a threat to his sense of purpose as Eldon was to her safety. What a mess. If only he'd tried something else to let her know he cared. Then he wouldn't have kissed her. That would've been the smart thing to do. If he hadn't been so impulsive, the desire that surged to life last night wouldn't still be throwing his heart out of rhythm or lingering in his mind, teasing him with the longing to do it again.

The milk pail full, Logan left the stanchion to take it to the house for Mama. With his head bent low as he mulled over his problems, he crashed into an obstacle on the path. He snapped his attention away from the ground.

A petite blonde stared at him.

"Karen!" he yelled, unsure he was quite ready to see her yet today. "What are you doing out here?"

"I was actually on my way to the barn. When I offered to help your mother with breakfast, she asked me to get a pail of milk from you." She pointed to the pail at his side as her voice faded and her cheeks turned pink. "But I can see that you were going to bring it in anyway."

"How about if I give it to you now?" Logan held the pail out in front of him.

Avoiding his gaze, Karen reached for it.

"Something wrong?" When Karen didn't answer, Logan spoke his own thoughts on the previous night's happenings. "I could understand if Tillie's actions at the party still bothered you."

Karen set the pail of milk down and hugged her torso. "The plan to help her turned into a disaster. I want to be a friend to Tillie, but it seems the harder I try, the more I drive her away." Karen rubbed her sleeve. "I don't know. Maybe I should give up."

Logan shook his head. "Tillie needs your friendship whether she knows it or not."

"We're both so different." She let the thought hang.

Logan leaned against the corner of the nearby chicken coop and stuffed his hands in his pockets.

"Tillie could be so much fun. I know we'd have great laughs together over the little things. Julia and I used to do that. We could share stories, our wardrobe, the kitchen, and just spend time together. But I don't know how to get through to her. I saw the anger in her eyes last night. There isn't anything left to do. I've tried to come up with ideas, but as long as Tillie remains sullen and avoids me like she did this morning, nothing will change."

"Give it time. She'll cool off. Andrew is coming over tonight. He always seems to have an uplifting effect on her."

Silence settled as Karen watched the rays of sun break over the stubbled field where golden corn stalks stood such a short time ago. "She's hurting."

"Yes, she is. Her pain has made her bitter. That's probably why she's been so awful to you. I'm sorry."

"It's not your fault."

"In a way it is. I'm the one you pay for room and board. Plus, Tillie is my sister. I feel responsible for how things have turned out."

Karen gave him a smile with a degree of sorrow dimming it. "But there's good in it too. If Tillie comes around, she'll find healing. All of us are waiting to be kind to her and well, to love her, if she'll let us."

Logan smiled. Karen had managed to encourage him yet again. "I've been praying about this for a long time. Will you share it with me?"

"Now?"

"Yeah." He grinned. "And tomorrow and the next day, right up until Tillie decides to change."

Karen drew in a breath.

He held her hands while they took turns petitioning the Lord for Tillie's healing.

When Logan ended the prayer, Karen glanced up at him. "You confuse me."

"Oh, really?"

"You look out for me like a family member. You pick me up every day from school. You partner with me to plan the party, and you ask me to pray with you." Karen looked him in the eye.

He raised a brow, curious where her train of thought might go.

"And yet, you seem well, uncomfortable around me. You

resisted my assistance for the Meadow Creek services until you were forced to take me along to clear up a rumor. Now that it's over, you haven't said one word about wanting my help anymore." Karen took a deep breath. "But last night you kissed me as though I mean as much to you as . . ." She didn't finish.

"Oh, Karen." Logan suddenly felt quite tired. "You mean a great deal to me, more every day it seems. But you see, God has called me to serve Him as a single man."

Karen's mouth hung open. "But I saw you with those Harper children. Don't you ever want to have a family of your own someday?"

He gazed into her eyes. An honest question deserved an honest answer. "I think about it all the time." He filled his lungs with air. "It's the sacrifice I have to make."

"But, Logan." Her hands fluttered in the air as high as her head and settled at her sides again. The gesture made him think of butterflies in the flower garden forced to leave the petals due to an unexpected disturbance. "You don't know what you're missing."

He leaned against the chicken coop again. There stood Karen, inches away from him. She was beautiful, caring, and patient with his sister in a daily hope for friendship. As her response to his kiss confirmed, she was also harboring feelings for him. What man in his right mind would forfeit the chance to pursue her?

Someone like him. As he'd done so many times before, he took full inventory of where his choices had led him, to the places of bachelorhood, devotion, and calling. Joy bubbled within, but Logan couldn't forget the cost. His whole chest ached. "I think I do."

"But surely—" She closed her eyes for a moment. When she opened them, she crossed her arms and held her chin high. "Every person must obey the Lord's leading for that particular life. You know what God asks of you."

He cleared his throat. "Mama probably has breakfast ready by now. Let's get these pails to the house. I'll finish the milking later."

Logan picked up the pail at Karen's feet. His arm nearly circled Karen's waist as he followed the path. He may have allowed it if they weren't walking in full view of the kitchen windows, but he still walked in full view of the Lord. That fact strengthened his resolve to keep his distance.

CHAPTER TWENTY-FIVE

*S*aturday night, Tillie felt well again. How wonderful that she hadn't needed to cancel her plans with Andrew. She scurried around the house ironing her best dress, fussing over her hair, and preparing snacks. Logan and Karen had both been rather quiet at the supper table. A resulting gloom hung about the house. Tillie did everything she could to chase it away as soon as possible. She worked extra hard to make her dress, her hair, and the snacks just right. He'd be so pleased. Last minute, she laid one of Mama's crocheted doilies on the parlor table. The doily was perfect for arranging her snacks in an attractive fashion.

Gravel crunched under buggy wheels in the lane. Tillie hurried to the kitchen and waited for Andrew to enter. Mama cross-stitched by lamplight in the sewing room. Logan and Karen had both retreated to their rooms upstairs, Karen's arms loaded full of books, Logan with his Bible.

Tillie loved having the whole downstairs to herself when Andrew came to call. She must remember to thank Logan and Mama the next time she saw them.

Andrew's footsteps thumped across the porch. His knock came on the door.

Tillie opened the door. "Come in." She pulled him through the dining room and into the parlor. "Have a seat. I have coffee brewed. Let me get you some." She hastened to the kitchen, poured two cups, and returned to the parlor. She handed a cup to Andrew and claimed the space on the love seat next to him.

"How have things been at the store?" She sipped coffee and nibbled from her tray of snacks as she listened.

Andrew recounted tales of deliveries he'd received and the people he'd assisted.

Tillie pointed to his empty cup. "More coffee?"

"No thanks."

"Have a cookie then." She reached for a molasses cookie from the snack tray.

He shook his head and shifted his position. "Tillie, I want to talk something over with you."

Andrew was a solemn young man, but the grave tone of his voice alerted her to trouble. "What is it?"

"Us."

"Us? What about us?"

"We can't continue on like this." Andrew's gaze settled on her face.

"What are you talking about?" His words drove a stake into her heart.

Andrew drew a deep breath. "Part of the reason why I wanted to court you is because you come from a really special family. I've seen the way you've pulled together after your dad died. All of you are so strong in your faith, or at least seem to be." He stopped and drew another deep breath. "Your mother and Logan attend church but you don't. That, well, that concerns me." His earnest, brown eyes searched her face.

Tillie crossed her arms. "God took my dad away from me. He's let me down. I can't keep singing hymns and listening to Reverend Betten when I'm not sure I can believe anymore." Hot tears stung her eyes. The injustice of Dad's death still grated on her soul.

Andrew stood and rubbed the back of his neck. "That's what I'm talking about. I want to marry a woman who will teach our children about faith. That's who I thought you were." He sat down again. "If I'm going to get serious about courting you, then I have to know that you and I share the same wishes for our family someday."

"God means nothing to me." The whispered words sliced her as they slithered up her throat and across her tongue. "He messed up my life, and I don't want anything to do with Him ever again."

Andrew leaned back as though trying to avoid a scorching fire. "I guess I have my answer." He stood. "I'm truly sorry. I'd hoped that . . ." Deep lines etched his face. "I guess I won't call on you anymore. Good-bye, Tillie." The dining room floor boards creaked under his footsteps.

The kitchen door squeaked open and clicked shut.

Buggy wheels crunched the gravel. A horse's whinny faded into the night.

Silence.

He was gone. The only man in her life besides Logan who brought her any happiness at all was gone.

That one last soft place of feeling in her heart turned harder than the rocks that jutted from the barn floor.

Sharper too.

Tillie wanted to throw something or to hit someone. To repay the damage Andrew and Karen and God and the whole world had done to her.

She picked up the glass Andrew left behind on the table and threw it at the ornately papered parlor wall. A satisfying crash announced its shatter in a thousand pieces. The room fell quiet, but Tillie still boiled on the inside. She ran upstairs.

A CRASH FROM THE PARLOR, pounding on the stairs, and the slam of a door startled Logan from his concentration on the book of Acts. It sounded like Tillie's door, but he couldn't imagine why she would be upstairs so early. Surely Andrew hadn't already gone home. He left his lamp-lit desk of notes and Bible and ventured into the hallway.

Karen stood in her doorway, a frown on her otherwise smooth brow. "What's going on?"

Logan shrugged.

Mama appeared on the bottom step. "Andrew left a few minutes ago. I think they had an argument." She craned her neck to look up the stairs at him. "Would you please talk to her, dear?"

He'd signed up for a cozy chat with the apostles this evening, but this sounded more like a lion's den dropped out of Daniel's world. He prayed for God to send an angel or two to come and bail him out or at least to give him the words to say.

Logan inhaled. "I'll try." He cleared his throat and proceeded down the hall. "Tillie?" He spoke in a quiet voice to her closed door.

"Go away. I don't want to talk to anyone." Her voice sounded shredded by heartache.

"Please let me in. I just want to help you."

"No!" An object hit the other side of the door.

Logan looked down the hall, Karen was watching, her eyes dark and her mouth pulled into a straight line.

He turned back to the shut-up room that contained his roaring sister. "All right. I won't make you talk tonight. But tomorrow when Mama, Karen, and I return home from church, you are going to tell me what happened. Understood?" His chest burned. He wanted to barge into Tillie's room and restore her world to the standard of peace he wanted. This was a tall order for a girl who was always finding ways to disrupt it.

A grunt was the only response.

LIGHT STREAMED in Tillie's bedroom window and hurt her eyes when she tried to open them. Swollen and scratchy, they were determined to stay closed. The thump of the kitchen door closing followed by voices in the yard floated to Tillie's ears. She moaned. Sunday morning. Those voices belonged to Mama, Logan, and the teacher. They were probably on their way to church.

Tillie pushed herself to a seated position and squinted at the window. The buggy sat in the lane. Logan stood nearby, wearing his suit. He held Mama steady while she climbed over the wheel. Next he held the teacher's hand while she got in the buggy. Tillie grimaced. She felt sick again. They looked too happy, every one of them. The idea of spending the whole morning at church should bring dread on anyone. If Logan had forced her to go to church, she knew she would have exploded with rage at some point during the useless singing or meaningless sermon. She still wanted to explode.

The horse hooves clomped down the lane. Tillie was home alone. Again. This pattern was beginning to wear her out. Sunday shouldn't come around so often. Sensible people had much better things to do than waste their time sitting around listening to Pastor Betten drone on and on about things that weren't true. Logan really should pursue a different career. He should give up on the preaching and stay on the farm. If he never left again, maybe life would go back to the way things used to be, the way Tillie liked them.

Now that the house was empty, she ventured downstairs and fixed a light breakfast from the leftovers of the food Mama served earlier that morning. Tillie usually cooked the Sunday dinner while Mama was gone to church, but not today. She may not have much say in how things go, but she could at least make this one choice for herself. Her breakfast gone, Tillie went to the parlor for the needlework she liked to stitch in the evenings and took it with her to her room.

As she stitched, memories stole her breath and sharpened the pain already piercing her heart. Everything fell apart on that Sunday morning when she'd left Dad alone in the barn so she could run a pail of milk to the house for Mama. Why couldn't she have seen that Dad wasn't feeling well? She should've noticed the perspiration on his forehead and his slurred speech. This was her last memory of him. By the time she returned to the barn to help him finish the milking, he was sprawled out on the ground with no breath left in him. She should've tried harder, should've taken him with her to the house, anything to keep him from dying and leaving her.

Then Logan came home. Tillie scowled at her door where Logan had stood last night. He should know how much she missed Dad. He should see her constant need for his support and attention. Instead, he lavished both on the teacher.

Tillie produced another scowl, this one directed at the wall that divided her room from Karen's. That girl ruined everything. If she wouldn't have moved in, Tillie might stand a chance at a return to normal. But things had gone beyond the point of what Tillie could tolerate. If there was any way at all to quit sharing her home with the uppity Miss City Girl, Tillie would take it. Maybe Tillie could move out. But that wouldn't work. She had nowhere else to go. If none of the neighbors had room to board the teacher, then they certainly wouldn't have room to spare for her.

Late morning, the same cheery voices disrupted the calm Tillie had almost recovered while she concentrated on the colorful threads she wove into the fabric with her needle. She took a deep breath as footsteps clumped down the hall.

"May I come in?" The closed door muffled Logan's voice.

The word "no" sat on her tongue. She didn't want him here. The way she felt toward him right now, she might do or say something harmful.

She shook off the thought. Logan was too strong and good and kind to suffer a setback from her anger.

"Yes." She spoke the word like a command, but she felt in control of nothing.

The door swished open and clicked closed.

Logan's footsteps thumped in soft rhythm on the floor. She knew they were his, not because she'd heard his voice just now but because they were firm, confident steps. The sound of his footfall brought her comfort even before he sat down next to her. She wanted to lean her head on his shoulder like she'd done with Dad when he was still alive, but the simmer of anger on her insides prevented it.

"Nora told us at church today that Andrew broke up with you."

Tillie figured the truth couldn't stay concealed for long. She laid aside her needlework prepared to endure her brother's wrath.

"She didn't say why. It's your job to tell me what happened."

"Why do you need to know?"

"I don't. You need to let go of it."

Tears burned in Tillie's eyes. She swallowed, opened her mouth in an attempt to talk, and swallowed again. "He's disappointed that I don't go to church."

"Why does this matter to him?"

"He wants a girl who feels the same way he does about God."

"You don't share Andrew's views?"

"No. That's why he left."

"Has turning your back on God made life easier for you?"

Tillie shrugged. "I don't need Him."

Silent minutes stretched between them.

In a low, scratchy voice, Logan spoke. "He loves you, Tillie. Just like Mama and myself and Karen. Come back to Him."

"If He'd give Dad back to me, I might do it."

"That's not how it works."

"Then I guess I don't have a reason to bother with Him." Something Logan had said pricked her memory. "Karen hates me."

"Not true. She wants you for a friend. Told me so yesterday.

That's why she wanted your help making food for the school party. She thought it would be a way to win you over."

Tillie snorted. "I don't need a prissy, spoiled friend like her. I wish she'd just leave me alone."

"I'm worried about you, Tillie. If you keep shutting out the people who care about you, the time will come when you won't remember how to let us back in. Don't let that happen." His voice caught.

She turned to him. Her big, strong, perfect brother had tears in his eyes, for her. Logan felt so strongly about the choices she'd made that he actually broke down. Maybe he cared more than she thought. He'd offered her his compassion. It might be worth gaining more than his exclusive attention.

He rubbed his eyes. "Karen and I are praying for you." Logan stood, squeezed her shoulder, and looked at her with the kindness that made him so special. Then, with a hint of sadness still present in his eyes, he turned and left.

Tillie listened as Logan's footsteps faded away. She wanted to believe him. She wanted to think that Karen really did care about her and that Logan's prayers for her would really change anything. More than that, she wanted God to really be the loving father Logan spoke about. Then she could look to Him for attention and care instead of to all these people in her life who repeatedly let her down. Tillie's heart grew heavy. Believing was just too hard. Logan's words held impossible expectations. She'd never be able to return to God after all that had happened to her. Tillie groaned and lay down. She'd rather struggle to get some sleep than appear downstairs for Sunday dinner. Only when she slept did she find any escape from the pain.

CHAPTER TWENTY-SIX

*L*ogan crawled out from under the wagon. Mud caked his overalls, his hands, even the hair on the back of his head. He wiped his hands on the rain-drenched grass along the path before he dug around in the fence supplies on the wagon bed. Maybe he could find a stretch of wire and a post or two to support the broken front axle.

Of all the times for a break down. The big gala at the hotel started in an hour. Complete with a hired band, full banquet, and silent auction, the evening promised Silver Grove residents a way to raise money for new fire-fighting equipment. Eldon, his father, and his brother Evan planned to give speeches at some point during the evening. Logan intended to enjoy himself in spite of this fact. He'd even gotten his work done on time so he could give the women a much-deserved night out.

Now this. He dragged a fence post and some wire over to the right front wheel. Down on his knees, he worked at tying the post on as a support, but the wagon was too heavy. He needed his jack from the barn. The only choice he had was to leave the broken wagon out here in the field and walk.

Rain continued to fall. Not as a downpour but as a light shower.

Logan hefted himself to his feet and trudged through the growing darkness to the barnyard. He should stop in the house and let Mama and the girls know he'd have to cancel their plans.

They were probably all dressed up and waiting around on him. He winced. Tonight would've been the first time he'd escort Karen somewhere merely for fun, to a place that wasn't routine Sunday morning church or a school function. He doubted he'd get another chance.

A buggy sat in the lane. He'd seen that buggy before, and in places where it didn't belong. He tromped into the house and came face to face with Eldon Kent.

He looked dapper in a dark suit, white shirt, and white bow tie. Not one hair out of place. He was spotless.

Unlike Logan who stood there dripping mud onto Mama's clean kitchen floor. He would have shoved his hands in his pockets, but the movement would only add clumps of mud to the growing puddle on the floor. He chose to glare instead.

"What happened to you?" Mama frowned.

"The axle on the wagon broke. I need to fix it before I start milking." His gaze traveled over Mama and Tillie, both dressed in Sunday best. "I won't be able to take you to town tonight. I'm sorry."

Karen entered from the stairs. She wore a dress of dark red velvet. It set off her fair skin and cherry red lips. His heart lost its rhythm, and his mouth fell open. For a moment, Logan nearly forgot his own last name.

"I'm ready to go." The smile on her face faded. "Oh, my. Are you all right?"

"Yeah, but the wagon is broke down. I won't be able to take you to the hotel."

"Oh." The cheer on her face disappeared.

"Come with me." Eldon approached her." My invitation still stands."

Karen flinched. "I thought I told you 'no' yesterday when you asked."

"He came to the school?" Why hadn't Logan heard about this?

"Yes." Karen gave the answer in a short, impatient syllable.

"You should have sent one of the boys to the farm to get me." Eldon scowled at him.

"I couldn't. They were behind the school playing a game."

Logan heard what Karen didn't say. Eldon had trapped her in the school again.

His jaw clenched. He'd love to push the guy over and smear a little of mud on his dandy outfit.

Eldon's mustache twitched. "I have a place reserved for you at our table. The meal will start soon, and I can't be late."

"I told you, Eldon. I don't want to go with you."

Eldon peered at Logan. "But Logan drives you to church."

"Yes, he does." Karen's voice was strained.

"He also took you to the school party, and he picks you up in the afternoon on week days."

"None of those things have anything to do with you." Karen surveyed Eldon with the look of a teacher searching for a reason to dole out consequences for misbehavior.

Eldon raised a brow. "You'll go places with him, so why won't you go with me?"

Karen's face turned red. She pushed at the air in front of her with her palms flat and spoke in measured tones. "All right. You have a point. If I'm willing to ride with Logan to church and to school, then I should also agree to ride with you to an event your family is hosting." Karen moved to the peg near the door where her long navy coat hung. "I'll get my coat so we can be on our way."

"Let me help you." Eldon rushed to hold her coat.

Karen slipped her arms into the sleeves, buttoned up, and looked at Sandy. "I'm sorry you and Tillie won't be able to go." She turned to Eldon. "Maybe they can come with us."

He shook his head. "Unfortunately, my buggy only has room for two." He opened the door and gestured for Karen to precede him.

Logan exhaled the breath he'd been holding and took the towel Mama handed him. After washing his hands in the basin, he used it to dry off.

Mama sighed. "Well, Tillie. You and I might as well get some supper started."

Tillie reached for an apron. While she tied it on, she said, "I'm glad she's gone. Gives me a chance to breathe once in a while."

When Tillie chose to avoid someone, she followed through. Not one word had she spoken to Karen since last week's school party.

"I'm going back out to fix that wagon and do the milking. I'll be late. Go ahead and start without me."

Mama nodded as she tied an apron over her Sunday dress.

"Sorry about the mess I made." Logan pointed to the puddle around his boots.

Mama waved her hand. "I'll have Tillie get the mop."

Logan trudged out of the house, the mud beginning to dry in a crust on the back of his neck. A warm soak in a bath would feel good right now. He'd be clean and ready to go to a party like Eldon. He'd told the Lord he would give up whatever was required of him in order to stay faithful to his call. This must be how God intended for it to happen. Logan standing by and watching Eldon cart Karen off any old time he felt like showing up and giving her a ride. Maybe God even orchestrated the wagon's break-down so Logan had to stay home without her. Well, he was happy to follow his Lord's leading. God knew that. But Logan never dreamed that the giving up part would feel so miserable.

THE MONTH of November began with Logan's crop safely gathered in the corn crib. The late fall days grew shorter, allowing for the entire household to shift back into their usual roles. Mama and Tillie finished canning the apples and preserving the garden produce. A pumpkin pie, a result of the past week's work, sat on the kitchen counter. Logan couldn't wait to dig in and enjoy a slice. Seated with the women at the dining room table, he was ready to pray and get the meal started so that he could get to the dessert quicker. In the moment when he bowed his head, Logan caught a glimpse of Eldon's buggy through the window. "Oh, no."

"What's wrong?" Mama studied him from the other end of the table.

"Eldon's here." Logan watched Eldon approach the house. "He probably knows we're home."

A knock came on the kitchen door.

Logan exchanged a furtive gaze with Karen. He left his chair and went to the kitchen. "Joining us for Sunday dinner?"

Eldon smoothed his mustache. "No. I came to take Karen to my sister's for our Sunday dinner." He sauntered past Logan and into the dining room.

Logan's blood heated. He was growing tired of Eldon waltzing into his house and stealing Karen away from them like a kidnapper. He moved to the doorway and blocked it.

"I'm not going." Karen's firm answer to Eldon's invite slammed into Logan's ears.

"The children are expecting you." Eldon stated the fact with banker-fashion command.

"I don't care. I'll see them at school tomorrow."

Eldon stiffened. "I want you to spend time with me today."

Karen shook her head.

"Unless there's someone else." While his tone held steel, it whispered of knowledge that perhaps Karen did have other interests.

Her head shaking stopped.

Logan's pulse quickened. He knew Karen's heart. Would she reveal it to Eldon?

Karen's gaze skittered to Logan's face for a moment and then landed on her still-empty plate.

The silence in the room deepened. Even Mama and Tillie stilled their movements. The whole house seemed to hold its breath.

Eldon swung around and analyzed Logan.

He stood still, schooling his features, determined to give nothing away.

Eldon scorned him with the same look he bestowed upon possessors of delinquent accounts. He turned back to Karen.

She crept out of her chair. "Tillie, would you please save a piece of pie for me?"

Tillie turned away.

"Do it please, Tillie." Mama said. She sounded old and tired.

Eldon grasped Karen's elbow. "Let's be on our way, then." He led her from the table, weaseled his way past Logan, and disappeared with Karen out the door.

Logan moved to the window and watched while Eldon helped Karen into his buggy and drove away. Eldon had stolen Karen right out from under his nose. Locked doors worked against thieves, but Logan could think of nothing that might work against unwanted suitors, especially ones as demanding as Eldon.

"Come to the table, dear. The food is getting cold."

Logan heeded Mama's call and sat down. The events of the past three weeks played through his mind while he heaped food on his plate and ate his meal. He'd lain in bed the night of the gala listening for Karen's return and lost sleep for hours afterward trying to forget where she'd been and with whom. Then the next morning at church, all the conversation buzzed around one topic, the teacher. The fact that Karen had attended the gala with Eldon and sat at his side through the banquet created a sensation among the neighbors and townspeople.

The next week it happened again. Saturday night, as Karen read in the parlor, Eldon showed up. And now today, for the third week in a row, Eldon had managed to tear Karen away from them.

They were spending a lot of time together. His stomach hardened, spoiling his appetite for that fine-looking pumpkin pie. Maybe Eldon would wear her down enough that Karen would begin to enjoy his company. She might choose to keep going out with Eldon. Logan didn't want to think about where that left him. All the encouragement, support, and special friendship he enjoyed might get transferred over to Eldon.

He and Karen needed to have a talk, the sooner the better. Logan finished his meal, watching for Karen's return and chiding himself at the same time for expecting her to come home so soon. Still on the lookout, he helped Mama clear the table. No Karen. He studied his sermon notes. No Karen. He replaced his suit coat and tie. No Karen. He left for church and conducted the service in a state of distraction. Maybe he should've continued to take her along. If she went with him, she'd avoid Eldon.

When he arrived home, he found Karen in the parlor with a book. He hastened to her.

"You need to quit going with him." Logan stood before her with his arms crossed over his suit coat.

KAREN PUT her book down and closed her eyes. Logan's command rankled in her spirit. She slowly counted to ten before she said something that hurt him just as much.

Her emotions under control enough to carry on a civil conversation, Karen opened her eyes. "What do you think I've been trying to do? Ever since the day when he stepped foot in my classroom, I've tried to get rid of him."

"You have to tell him." Logan sliced a horizontal line through the air. "Call it off."

If he'd allowed her to attend church with him this afternoon, she might tolerate his preaching at her. "And how am I to accomplish that?" She crossed her arms and her voice rose. "I can't come out and tell him that I . . ." She didn't dare mention to Eldon how she really felt about Logan. Tears formed at the corners of her eyes. Karen blinked. No way did she want Logan to see her crying over this. How silly. She inhaled and leaned forward. "I don't see how you have any right to tell me who I am allowed to court."

"I want what's best for you."

"I find that hard to believe." Karen raised a brow. "If you really wanted what was best, you'd act on your feelings instead of refusing my help on Sundays and standing back, allowing Eldon to step foot in your house week after week. I live here as a member of your household after all. Surely I can expect at least a little intervention from you."

Logan turned away and rubbed the back of his neck.

"When Eldon started showing up at school, I wanted him to stop paying attention to me because I didn't like him. I still don't like him, but you know why I want him to quit pursuing me."

Logan lowered his frame into the rocking chair, his gaze returning to her face. He appeared to read her like he did a passage of Scripture when he studied. Concentration creased his brow. Happiness glowed in his eyes.

"My interests and affection belong to someone else." More of her speech pressed against her throat. She swallowed to keep it in, but the words rushed out anyway. Her voice lowered. "That someone doesn't want me for himself, but he doesn't want Eldon to have me either."

Exhaling a heavy breath, Logan reached for her hand and shifted all of his concentration to caressing her knuckles with his thumb. "Karen, I told you that God hasn't led me to marry. I don't get to serve as a bachelor until I meet the right woman. I must do it because God is the one asking it of me." He paused from talking, but his thumb still moved. "My own wishes must conform to his."

The happiness dimmed, and the shadow of disappointment she'd seen in his eyes in the past returned.

His words poked at her heart. They spoke the truth about her own struggle to conform to God's plans for her. In spite of Eldon's attention to her, so many other events over the past weeks proved to Karen that God was obviously leading her into a deeper relationship with Logan. Eldon's attempts at courtship had worked to deepen her feelings. He'd entered her life and given her a reason to stay in tune with her heart. If Eldon wouldn't work so hard to keep her attention, Karen wouldn't need to constantly ask herself why she didn't want to go with him. But the work was done. Her questions were answered. She wanted Logan.

Giving her heart to him asked of her a huge risk. Logan farmed. It was only a matter of time until a serious accident killed him. He also preached, which meant he might misuse his authority like Father had. Like what happened to Mother, Karen would get dragged into scandal and lose the trust of so many people she counted as friends.

Following God's leading would also jeopardize her teaching career. Karen hadn't been at teacher's college for long before she learned that married women weren't allowed to teach. Saying "yes" to God would mean saying "no" to everything she'd worked for, everything she hoped would bring her security. *"Mr. Harper, you're filling your life with all the wrong things."* Her words to the struggling man slapped her. Trying to fill her life with things that would ease the pain of her father's treatment, she'd done the same as Mr. Harper. Karen had followed her own designs to find healing and peace.

Maybe she could let her pain and her fears go. If she did, God's way might be better. Logan's thumb moved from her knuckles to the back of her hand, his touch soft. *Lord, You can have Your way with me. I give You my whole life. I've held back from You, but not anymore.* He could have her teaching career. Karen winced. She'd also give him those places that were still hurt and searching. The Lord could bring healing and peace in the way he chose.

She might sit here surrendering her life to the Lord, but Logan seemed determined not to cooperate. If Karen's interpretation of God's wishes for her were correct, then they were going completely against what Logan felt God expected of him. Someone must change their mind. Karen had started to change hers. Logan needed to do the same. She turned her hand over and grasped Logan's. "I'm trusting God to meet me in His time and His way. Maybe you should too." She raised her eyes to look at him.

"I'm trying, Karen. If you only knew." His quiet voice was strained.

"Then perhaps we need to pray about us." A smile grew over her face.

But no smile claimed Logan's. He frowned instead and released her hand. "Not sure that would accomplish anything."

Karen gulped and stood up. "Why?"

Logan licked his lips and stood to face her. "Even if God would choose to give us a future together, I'd never be able to provide you with the comfortable lifestyle you are accustomed to."

"Those things don't mean as much to me anymore."

Logan looked at her with a skeptical raise of his brow. "You say that now when you still have everything you brought along from the city and know you'll return there someday. But what would you do if all that was taken away and you had to live on whatever this farm or a job pastoring a small town church provided? You'd see things quite differently."

Karen's stomach tightened. "I'm not sure what I'd do. I've never really thought about it before. The only home I've ever known is Chicago."

Logan nodded. A smile pulled at one corner of his mouth, full of the satisfaction of having proved an important point.

Karen was beginning to get a headache. All their arguing and negotiation counted for less and less as the minutes ticked by. "I don't know what tomorrow holds." Karen approached him and placed her palms on his lapels.

Logan's arms circled her waist just like they did on the night of the school party.

Oh, dear. She belonged here in Logan's embrace with her hand covering his heart. "But I do know how I feel about you. I'm willing to follow the Lord, wherever He might choose to lead." She stretched up on tip-toe and placed a kiss on Logan's cheek.

His jaw trembled. She felt him stiffen and pull away.

Karen stroked his cheek in the place where her kiss landed.

He turned, his lips brushing her forehead. His blue eyes darkened, and his head lowered until his mouth hovered close enough to hers for Karen to feel his breath on her chin.

"No." The word slurred across his lips. "No." Logan uttered it again, a bit stronger this time. "I shouldn't." He shook his head and released his hold on her. He reached for both of her hands and held onto them with the firm grip of a man in need of a solid shelter in a windstorm. Quiet enveloped them as Logan studied her hands. He gazed into her eyes once more. The tempest raged on Logan's insides. Karen saw it in his troubled expression.

Logan dropped his head and let out a deep breath. "The Lord's plans, they are always for the best." He stepped away and left the room.

ANOTHER PAYMENT WAS due at the bank. Eldon already assumed possession of enough of what Logan's household had to offer. He hated the idea of handing over more of his money too. Logan would find the transaction much easier if Eldon would barge into his house and demand it of him in the same way he expected Karen to drop everything and fulfill his every command. That would at least save Logan the misery of yet another meeting.

The teller led Logan down the bank's hall to Eldon's door. "Mr. Kent, a customer is here to see you."

"Send them in." Eldon's muffled response came through the door.

"I brought you my next payment right on time." Logan reached in his coat pocket and slapped the bills onto the surface of Eldon's desk.

Eldon reached for it and counted it. He put the money in a drawer and wrote in Logan's account book. "Next month is your deadline. You need to have all that interest money in here by December 31. With the small amount you brought in today, your next payment will need to be a substantial one." Eldon slammed the book shut. "And don't be late."

Not a chance. Logan would have his money to the bank to clear his name no matter what he must do to make it happen. In spite of his determination, his stomach trembled. One month's payment of Karen's room and board, preaching on Sunday, and milk sales wouldn't meet the total written in Eldon's book. Plus Christmas was coming with its extra grocery supplies and gifts. He still needed more money, and Logan had no idea where to go looking for it.

CHAPTER TWENTY-SEVEN

*K*aren stood before the mirror scrutinizing her reflection. Her burgundy holiday dress draped gracefully over her shoulders and hips. She loved wearing this dress, perhaps because of all the Christmas memories it carried. Last year's dinner parties, banquets, and family gatherings in Chicago saw Karen in this dress. Mother would want to have a new dress made for her if Karen stayed in Chicago this holiday season, but Karen preferred this dress to any other. She remembered Mother, Uncle Henry, and Aunt Fran as she tugged her sleeve and straightened her collar. Her thoughts moved on to her younger sister. Julia and her husband would celebrate this Christmas with a new baby. Karen smiled into the mirror as she imagined how happy Julia must be with her little family. One more pat on a curl of hair. Perfect. She looked her best for a night of festivity.

How she dreaded the thought of spending it with Eldon. Nausea rolled in Karen's stomach. If the Kent family hadn't requested that she sing at the party tonight, Karen would've locked herself in her room or hidden in the barn, anything to avoid another evening in Eldon's company.

Karen frowned into the mirror. Now she must make the best of the situation. In the empty kitchen, Karen slipped into her coat. Eldon's sleigh stopped in the lane as she put on her gloves. He tucked her under a blanket, and then he turned the horses around. The sleigh skimmed along the snow-packed road to town.

"Tonight's event is at the hotel."

Karen nodded. She learned this news on Sunday when his sister-in-law extended the invitation for Karen to be on the program.

"As you know, my father, my brother Evan, and myself own the Silver Grove State Bank."

Yes. Karen knew this fact as well from Evan's children who attended her school.

"Tonight's banquet is the annual Christmas banquet we host as an appreciation for the businessmen of Silver Grove and for their wives. Father, Evan, and I will give a speech after the meal. You will sing two Christmas carols. Then the dance will start."

Dancing. This was the first she'd heard about that portion of the evening. Karen loved to dance, but Eldon didn't fit her ideals of a partner.

"The gala for fundraising employed our local group of instrumentalists, but for this banquet we bring in a string quartet all the way from Des Moines."

Karen heard the message in Eldon's words. This banquet entertained the highest class of folks Silver Grove had to offer. She winced, glad for the darkness to conceal her response. She'd feel at home and enjoy herself at a high-society function if she didn't have to share it with him.

Her thoughts turned to Logan who had shut himself away in his room as soon as darkness fell. To study, he said. Karen almost believed him. She guessed he wanted to avoid Eldon as much as he wanted solitude for his sermon preparation. How much fun tonight would be with Logan as her escort. He'd entertain the entire gathering with stories and laughter. Afterward, they'd share a quiet chat and private jokes in the parlor aglow with lamplight and companionship.

She stole a glimpse of Eldon. His dark suit and hat blended into the black of night around him. His eyes, piercing and cold as the winter air, speared the road before him. No warmth. No humor. And, Karen believed, no heart either.

This was her last time going anywhere with him. Karen turned her gaze away from Eldon's profile and onto the road, content to finish the trip in silence.

At the hotel, Eldon parked the sleigh, blanketed the horse, and offered Karen his arm. She took it, proper and dignified. Karen could be very dignified when her self-worth was on the line. Her regal posture would serve sufficient to pull her through the evening ahead. It had to.

THREE NIGHTS LATER, a knock at the door interrupted Karen's creation of a geography test for use at school the next day. She left the parlor sofa in time to see Logan open the door.

"Hey, Tom." He shook his neighbor's hand. "Good to see you. Please come in."

Mr. Hinkley nodded. He stomped snow from his shoes and let Logan take his coat.

"Good evening, Mr. Hinkley." She shook his hand. "Let me make you some coffee." She took his scarf and handed it to Logan who hung it on a peg with his coat.

"You two the only ones here?" A chair scraped on the floor. Out of the corner of her eye, Karen saw Tom sit at the table.

"No. Mama and Tillie are in the back room at the sewing machine." Logan came over to where she stood. He retrieved cups from a nearby rack. "Something Karen or I can help you with?"

"I have some concerns to talk over with Miss Millerson. Been readin' the paper. Now I reckon the time has come to get a few things out in the open." Mr. Hinkley pulled the newspaper from his vest pocket and slid it across the table.

Both men focused on Karen. Her face heated. "What is it?" She tried hard to sound calm. "Did the honor roll for first quarter finally get published?"

Tom shook his head. "The teacher made the news. Not her students."

Karen hastened to the table, set the steaming coffeepot on a trivet, and grabbed for the paper. Her breath caught. On the front page she found an image that rolled her stomach. Complete with a boldface title and story long enough to cover most of the page, was a photograph of Karen at the Christmas banquet, a plate of food on the table in front of her. That wasn't so bad. The sick feeling came when she saw Eldon seated next to her and how close he leaned toward her. He smiled for the camera like a man intent on courtship.

She choked and shoved the paper at her visitor. "I've seen enough." She dropped into a chair and poured a cup of coffee. At the banquet, she'd tried her best to avoid the camera, but that pesky newspaperman had sneaked a photo just as the meal started. Karen wanted to hunt him down and wring his neck.

Mr. Hinkley reached for the paper and read. "Eldon Kent and his special guest attended the Silver Grove State Bank Christmas Banquet on Saturday night. Miss Millerson has offered her support to Mr. Kent at both of the bank's special events through her attendance at his side." He laid the paper down and looked at her. "Is he courting you?"

"He's trying." The words almost choked her.

A span of silence passed while Mr. Hinkley sipped on his coffee. Half the night seemed to drag by as she waited for Mr. Hinkley to say something.

He finally did after clearing his throat and leaning back in his chair. "Miss Millerson, we have rules here."

"I know."

He peered at her. "When you came, you said you were familiar with the standards for teachers."

"I am."

"Now we don't take too kindly to the teacher of our school steppin' out with a man over and over like this. I could see once in a while to go to church, but doin' it twice and in a big enough way to land your picture in paper could make ya lose your job." Mr. Hinkley met her gaze.

Karen possessed enough propriety to understand how this whole mixed up situation must appear to the school board chairman. People looked up to him. They respected him and trusted his decisions. Allowing the teacher to indulge in unseemly behavior reflected badly on everyone. "I'm sorry, Mr. Hinkley. I hardly know what to say."

Logan must have known, though. He pushed his coffee cup aside and folded his hands on the table. "How well are you acquainted with Eldon Kent?"

"Pretty good. He's my banker." Mr. Hinkley lifted his cup to his mouth.

"He's mine too. I have the privilege of paying Eldon a visit every month to apply money to my account."

"Know the feeling." A wry smile claimed Mr. Hinkley's lips.

"So, how does he act when you go to the bank?"

Mr. Hinkley set his cup on the table and leaned back. "He don't care to ask me much about how things are goin' or about my family or anything like that. He's a likable guy as long as I'm bringin' him money."

"He sounds demanding." Logan reached for the coffee pot and poured more coffee into his cup.

"You got that right." Mr. Hinkley chuckled. "Demanding, impatient, and downright rude sometimes." He shook his head as though recalling an unpleasant memory.

Logan leaned forward. "Tom, please believe me when I tell you that Eldon has been giving Miss Millerson the same treatment."

223

Mr. Hinkley paused. "You don't say."

Logan shook his head once as though the matter contained no negotiation. "I've seen it." He lifted his cup to his mouth and sipped coffee.

Mr. Hinkley turned his attention on Karen. "What sorts of things has Eldon done?"

"He interrupted class one day at the beginning of the year when he came to school with a box of candy and said he wanted to court me."

Mr. Hinkley's mouth slid off to one side of his face.

"After that, he'd show up at school on any day at any time. I never knew when he might appear. Twice, he blocked my exit so I was forced to stay in the building with him."

"How do you explain your choice to go with him to the fundraising gala and the Christmas banquet?" Mr. Hinkley peered at her over the rim of his cup.

Karen shook her head. "It wasn't my choice. Eldon showed up here at the De Witt farm on the night of the gala and would only leave if I went with him. His sister Elsie invited me to sing at the banquet. I didn't feel that I could turn her down since ten of my students are relatives of the Kent family."

"No, ya really can't do that. The Kents and the Sanders are the biggest school supporters. It's only fair you returned the favor." Mr. Hinkley shifted in his chair. "I see your predicament, Miss Millerson. But I'm still the school board chairman, and it's my job to make sure the teacher is behavin' according to the rules." He stood. "One more public outing with Eldon will lead to us askin' for your resignation. Understood?"

Karen nodded. "Yes. I'll stay away from him. You have my word."

A faint smile tugged at Mr. Hinkley's mouth. "Good. You're doin' a good job, and we'd sure hate to lose ya. But rules is rules." He retrieved his coat and scarf from the pegs on the wall. "Good evening, Miss Millerson. Logan." He nodded to each of them and went outside.

Karen twisted her cup around on the table. Mr. Hinkley could've demanded her job from her tonight. He may have accomplished it if not for some expert intervention. She glanced at Logan. "Thanks."

He only winked at her over the brim of his cup.

THE NEXT AFTERNOON, Karen arrived home from school to find Logan pacing the kitchen. He wore his dark suit under a heavy black winter coat. A thick, red scarf hung between the unbuttoned lapels of his coat. The white collar of his shirt made a crisp line at the base of his well-trimmed hairline.

"Ready to go, Mama?" Logan called up the stairs.

"Almost. I need one more dress." Her reply carried to the kitchen.

Logan puffed out his cheeks. He checked his watch and paced again. "We're going to miss the train," he muttered.

Karen removed her coat and hung it on a peg as Tillie entered the room.

"Calm down, Logan. Mama's never traveled as far as Oswell City before." Tillie gave his upper arm a playful punch.

He ignored her and continued to pace.

Sandy descended the stairs with a gray dress slung over one arm. "Help me pack this, would you, dear."

Logan eased the dress out of her grasp and with swift hands, folded it up and laid it on the top of a stack of clothes in the waiting suitcase. He latched it shut and set it on the floor next to two bulging satchels. His arms open, he turned toward Tillie.

She stepped into his embrace. "I'll miss you. Promise you'll come home again."

Logan chuckled. "Of course I'll come home. You and Mama need someone around to tell you what to do."

Tillie punched his arm again, this time with a little more force. "Buy me something."

Affection glowed in his eyes as he smiled down at Tillie. "Christmas is coming."

"I'll remember you said that."

Logan chuckled again and turned toward Karen.

Her chest tightened. How must she say good-bye? Tease him for a gift like Tillie had? Hug him? She cleared her throat when he stepped near. "Did you find my payment?" Asking him about the money she'd left on the table last night before she went to bed might buy her a little time to figure out what to do.

Logan gazed down at her. "I found it. Thanks. I plan to put it in the bank before we catch the train."

Karen twisted her hand in her skirt while her cheeks flamed.

He gathered her in a brief hug. "Good-bye, Karen. I'll miss you."

Tears stung her eyes as her arms circled his waist. "I'll miss you too," she whispered into his coat. The faint scent of his cologne drifted on the woolen fibers. Any other day, the woodsy, spicy fragrance would have promised her the comforts of Sunday buggy rides or sleigh rides to church, meals at the dining room table, and lounging in the parlor with books. Today it taunted her with his long absence.

He backed away and reached for a satchel and the suitcase. "Time to go, Mama. The train won't wait for us."

Sandy carried the other satchel and followed him out the door to the waiting horse and sleigh.

Karen went to the window, pulled back the lace curtain, and watched as the sleigh carried Logan and his mother down the lane. He was gone. Karen brushed at the tears in her eyes before Tillie saw them. The afternoon of their almost-kiss in the parlor came to her memory. He'd found walking away from her nearly impossible, but today he didn't struggle to leave her behind. Maybe he wanted to avoid a show of his feelings for her in front of his family. For as much as Karen wanted to believe this was true, her heart still ached. Logan's determination to stay single smothered any feelings he'd allowed for her. He was still the bachelor, careless that his choices were beginning to determine the course of her life too. Karen would miss Logan during these four days on the farm in his absence, but unless he wanted her as a part of his life, she'd spend the rest of her days missing him.

CHAPTER TWENTY-EIGHT

*L*ogan stepped off the train and took hold of Mama's hand while she took the last step onto the platform. "Careful, Mama."

"Thank you, dear." She wobbled a bit and leaned on him for balance.

A lamp glowed in the broad window of the depot. Logan led Mama toward the light inside.

"Pastor Logan!"

Logan would know that voice anywhere. He scanned the waiting room, looking for its owner. In the corner near the stove, Paul Ellenbroek waved.

Mama leaned in and whispered, "Who is that man?"

"Mayor of Oswell City. He's here to give us a ride to the parsonage." Logan had written to Paul to tell him of the travel plans. Pleased to have his good friend officiate his daughter's wedding, Paul had written back to insist on chauffeuring both Logan and his guest on the day of arrival.

"Good to see you." Logan shook Paul's hand enthusiastically. "Please meet my mother, Mrs. Sandy De Witt."

"Welcome to Oswell City, Mrs. De Witt." With a smile at her,

Paul shook Mama's hand. "I've got the Ford parked out back along the street ready to load up."

Mama's breath caught. "Do you mean a car?" She looked at Paul and then at Logan with round eyes. "We get to ride in a car?"

Logan chuckled. "Yes, Mama, that's exactly what it means." He slapped Paul on the arm of his tweed wool coat. "Paul drives the newest and the best."

Now Paul laughed. "Thanks to good deals from Oswell City Auto. Couldn't afford them otherwise." He held the ornate wooden door open. "It's good for business, you know, to have the mayor puttering around in the latest model."

On the snow-packed street, Logan helped Mama into the passenger seat next to Paul. Logan settled in the back with the suitcase for company. One of the satchels blocked his view out the windshield. He dragged it onto his lap so he wouldn't miss a thing.

Paul motored through downtown where swags of greenery decorated lamp posts along both sides of the street. Wreaths with bright red bows hung on several shop doors, including the county bank. Maybe the answer to his problems in Silver Grove lay right here in Oswell City. The deficit in his farm account book still weighed on his mind. Once he returned to Silver Grove, he had one week to cough up the total.

All of the money made from milk sales, Karen's boarding payment, and preaching still didn't meet Eldon's demand. His banker had been right. Logan needed another plan. He settled against the seat as a new plan formulated in his mind.

When Paul turned left at the Oswell Community Church onto Fifth Street, he slowed the car to a stop in front of a square, one-story brick house.

Logan lost his fight with the grin that stretched all the way across his face. Boy, it was good to be home again.

Paul gathered up the satchels while Logan took the suitcase. "Lorraine is still planning on the ten-thirty meeting in the morning." Shifting his load, Paul pulled a key from his coat pocket that he used to open the door.

"So am I." Logan followed Mama into the house.

Paul set both the satchels on the floor of the small foyer. "It's good to have you back, even if only for a few days." He shook Logan's hand once more before returning to his idling Model T.

Logan hastened to light the lamp on the table, then he hung up Mama's coat.

She wandered farther into the house. "You have a lovely home, dear." Her gaze took in the navy blue rug on the dining room floor, the ivory seat cushions on the straight back chairs, the writing desk in the corner, and the carved furniture in the adjacent parlor.

"Thanks, Mama. Come this way. I'll show you your room." Logan brought Mama down the short hall to the spare room. He placed the suitcase on the bed. "Go ahead and unpack. There's a closet behind the door."

"Oh, closets, too." Mama spoke with awe. She went to the closet, opened it, and looked inside. "So different from the farm."

Logan smiled. Mama probably didn't realize she'd spoken the thought. Yes, his snug parsonage in town was worlds different from farm living. "I'm going to take a look at that stack of mail I see on the table." He stepped closer to kiss her cheek. "It's wonderful to have you here with me, Mama. Enjoy your stay."

AFTER HIS MEETING WITH LORRAINE, Logan discovered delicious smells when he opened the door to his home. He followed his nose to the dining room where he found a table set with his dishes. Mama stood in the kitchen, wrapped in an apron.

"You cooked lunch." He couldn't decide whether to thank her or offer a rebuke.

"Well, of course." Mama waved the spatula she used to turn

meat in a skillet. "What else am I to do with myself while you run around to meetings?"

"You're supposed to be on vacation." He moved to the table to study the food steaming in serving bowls. Mashed potatoes. Peas. "What will Tillie say if I return you to the farm worn out and sick of the kitchen?"

"You exaggerate." Mama transferred cuts of meat to a platter. "Sit down before the food gets cold. You promised to take me Christmas shopping this afternoon. We need to eat so that we have enough time."

Mama opened the conversation as soon as Logan had food on his plate. "There's something I want to talk to you about. This seems like a good time since the girls aren't around."

"What is it?"

"I think Karen should move out."

He dropped his fork. It clattered onto his plate, sending splatters of gravy over the edge onto the table as well as onto his tie. "Why?"

"For Tillie's sake."

"I don't follow." Hands shaking, he picked up his napkin. The silly thing refused to unfold.

"The girls don't get along. That's not any news to you. I'm concerned about Tillie. I want her to go to church again. Enjoy life. Act like the Tillie I know. In a way, I feel like I've lost both John and Tillie. I can't do anything about losing your father, but maybe I can still do something about Tillie. It makes sense to me to stop expecting her to live with, and, if I can say it, put up with someone she's been at odds with since the first day. Plus, I'm tired. Life at home would be so much easier if I didn't need to referee fighting matches whenever the two of them are together."

The napkin finally cooperated. He swiped at his tie, but instead of clearing it of gravy, his clumsy fingers made the mess worse.

"Could Karen board with another family?"

Logan sucked in some air. He'd stayed on the farm with the

express goal of easing Mama's burden, but surely that didn't mean forcing Karen out. "All of our neighbors have large families. We are the only ones with extra space."

"What about the Bettens? They have a spare bedroom. Maybe Karen could use it."

Logan didn't want Karen living with Pete and Anna. He wanted her living with him. "The church is farther away from the school than our farm. She'd have a long walk."

"But wouldn't you rather see Tillie happy? Karen's extended walk to school is a small price for her to pay."

He wanted Tillie to be happy, but he wanted to keep Karen too. If she moved to Pete's, he'd only see her at church. Plus, Eldon would have the advantage of Logan's absence. He surrendered the napkin. It fell to the table beside his plate. He could only deal with one problem at a time.

"You don't like the idea."

"No, I don't. I'd lose—"

"The room and board income. Of course. I didn't think of that."

He'd been ready to say he'd lose the benefit of seeing her every day, of talking things over with her, of laughing together about the daily happenings at school. Everything would change if Karen went to live with Pete and Anna.

"Still, I'd rather have my daughter back as well as my own peace of mind than ample flour or sugar on hand. We'd get by."

"How do you know Karen's move out of our household would improve the situation?"

Mama shrugged. "I don't, but it seems like the right thing to do. Tillie needs our help, and I can't sit back doing nothing any longer."

Yes, Tillie did need help and something should get done, but did it have to come at such a high expense? Not the loss of cash, but of Karen herself?

Enough talk about this unpleasant subject. "How about I help you with the dishes so that we can get to that Christmas shopping?"

Mama gazed at him, distress still present in her eyes.

He went to the kitchen and began filling the sink with water. Within an hour, they had the small kitchen clean, their coats buttoned, and Mama's mind off her troubles and onto her Christmas list.

Walking down Main Street, Logan introduced her to people he knew. The whole parish of the Oswell City Community Church had the same idea as he and Mama. Everyone walked the street, shopping for gifts. Each person expressed delight in meeting Reverend De Witt's mother. Mama appeared quite flattered by the attention and the handshakes.

As the afternoon progressed, Mama and Logan found gifts for Tillie, Pete, and Anna. Logan found his gift for Mama, and Mama found a gift for Karen. When they passed the store that supplied books and sheet music, she tugged on his hand. "I want to stop in here a moment. Will you wait for me?"

"Sure. I'll wander down the street a bit."

She smiled and went inside.

Mama had no one else left on her list, only him. Logan moved away from the store window in order to give her some privacy. He still had some shopping to do anyway. One name remained on his list too. Karen's.

He'd searched all afternoon for the perfect gift. He didn't know what in the world a man should buy for a young woman like Karen. A hat? Clothing? He couldn't get her candy or flowers. No way. Those gifts signaled courtship. He and Karen weren't courting. Certainly not.

Maybe he should have followed Mama into the bookstore and looked at music. Karen liked to sing. But that sort of gift didn't seem right either. He'd have the luck of giving her something she already owned or heaven forbid, having to choose from a whole array of love songs. He'd been in the Oswell City bookstore often enough to know about the types of music kept in supply.

No appropriate ideas coming to mind, Logan strolled along the street. Stalling a little longer, he meandered to the end of the block. He turned around, meeting up with Mama just as she left the store.

"I found it," she announced on the walk home. "You'll love it."

"Can't wait to open it."

Mama smiled at him with a conspiratorial look in her eye.

When they arrived at his house, Mama raided the closet in her room for wrapping paper. "Don't you have more?" She held up the lone roll of holiday paper from his collection.

Logan shrugged. "Be glad you found that one."

Mama wrinkled her nose at him. "I should have bought some this afternoon."

He left for Lorraine's rehearsal, wishing his gift-giving troubles were no more serious than the paper to wrap them in.

CHAPTER TWENTY-NINE

*B*lack robe in place over his suit, Logan stood at the front of the church. Wedding guests filled the pews. Soft music wafted from the organ. Flames flickered from the candles on the sills of the stained-glass windows.

Brandt entered. He came to stand at Logan's side.

One look in his eyes told Logan the groom could use a little encouragement. "Nervous?"

"Very." Brandt's voice jittered.

He shook Brandt's hand. "You'll do just fine." Logan may have found reasons to envy Brandt in the past, but he didn't envy him now. He counted his blessings he was the preacher and not the groom standing around waiting for the bride to appear.

Brandt's nerves eased for a few seconds but were back in his eyes again when one of Lorraine's cousins, wearing a dark green dress, walked the aisle. The young woman moved off to Logan's right. Another young woman, Brandt's sister, followed.

Two groomsmen emerged from the door leading to Logan's study. They, too, were nervous. Each one gave Brandt a tight smile.

The music changed. Mrs. Ellenbroek stood and looked to the

rear of the church. The other guests followed her lead. On her father's arm, Lorraine slowly walked the aisle. Paul was so proud escorting his daughter to meet the young lawyer. Brandt and Lorraine made a good match, better than he first thought. A song from last Sunday's service pressed against Logan's lips. He hummed a brief phrase of the *Doxology* on behalf of this new couple.

Logan's gaze slid off of Paul and onto Lorraine. The sight of the bride in the flowing white gown transported him back to the farm, bringing the past months into painful focus. Recollections of summer storms, Sunday afternoons, and that startling kiss flooded his senses. Logan forced his eyes shut. If he blinded himself to the bride inching toward him, maybe he could somehow stop the image forming in his mind.

But he still saw it as clearly as the sun on a cloudless day. Karen took shape in his vision, dressed not for a summer Sunday or a holiday party in town, but for her own wedding.

His eyes popped open. Maybe if he focused again on his surroundings, the vivid image in his mind would fade.

It didn't work. The stunning picture stayed with him. His pulse swung so far out of rhythm, Logan's heart would never be the same.

Lorraine and her father halted before him.

He'd stood in this place dozens of times, watching a bride walk the aisle. Each one waited, as Lorraine did now, for him to say the words that united her to someone else.

What if that changed, just once? What would it be like to have the vision materialize and come to him, not as the preacher but as the groom?

Logan's breathing slowed. A deep, sweet ache enveloped his heart, his world, his whole life. He found the courage to face the truth that he'd tried so hard to stuff below the surface of his own grief. He needed Karen. She belonged here with him, sharing his life. Not as his boarder or even as his friend. Oh, goodness no. He desired her love.

A cold sweat broke out under the layers of his robe, his suit coat, and his white shirt. The shirt Karen had given him. If only he could sneak off to his study. Then he could be alone to absorb this new revelation.

But he couldn't. The organ stopped and Lorraine waited.

Logan blinked, licked his dry lips, and cleared his throat. "Dearly Beloved, we are gathered here in the sight of God and these witnesses." No stutters. Thank goodness. He'd pull through if he kept his mind on the script created in the meeting yesterday instead of the one getting written this very minute in his heart.

As the wedding progressed, Logan guided the couple through the vows and the exchange of rings. The wedding ended with Brandt kissing his bride. Logan announced the new Mr. and Mrs. Brandt Koelman. The organ played a march as the bride and groom left, followed by their attendants.

While guests filed out of the sanctuary, Logan finally got the chance to slip away. In his study, he removed his robe and hung it up. He replaced his Bible on the shelf and came to rest before the window. Gazing out on the town in the twilight, Logan willed his pulse to quit pounding through his veins.

He was in love. Deeply and irreversibly in love with Karen. Had been for months. Ever since her first night in town when he carried her up the hill, muddy skirts and all, he'd traveled a straight path destined for today's revelation.

Saturday morning, Tillie awoke with a pain in her head that almost outdid the pain in her heart. When would Mama and Logan come home? The calendar told her they'd return tomorrow, but it seemed so far away. Yesterday had dragged at such an excruciating pace that Tillie was exhausted. Even though she stayed in her room for hours on end and slept for most of them, fatigue still drained her. Life had to get easier when Mama and Logan came home again. Her survival depended on it.

She dragged herself to a seated position. Her head ached. Probably from the crying she'd done in the night. A Christmas without Dad. The tears threatened again. If only the release of tears would ease the pain, but each tear seemed to squeeze her heart tighter and tighter. She'd never live through the endless days stretching before her. Dad was gone. Andrew had deserted her. Logan and Mama were both out of town. The one person left in Tillie's life was Karen.

Tillie pushed to her feet. Karen. The pampered, rich girl who invaded Tillie's life. Karen had nothing to give her. Nothing. All Karen did was take. She took time to teach how to cook, and she took space at the table for mealtimes. She took over Tillie's place in the buggy. But worst of all, she took Logan's attention.

He used to look after only Tillie. Once school started and the teacher moved in, Logan no longer thought her special. A little sister was just a bother. Another person for him to provide for, like a horse or cow in need of feed. She witnessed his embrace of Karen before he left on Monday. Tillie used to be the only one he hugged like that. Now she must share him.

She hiccuped and moved to the dresser. She pulled open the drawer where she kept her three work dresses. Empty. All her dresses were in the laundry. Tillie groaned. If she wanted clean clothes, she'd have to get busy. She couldn't depend on Karen to do the wash. Oh, no. Karen would refuse to get her hands dirty in water used to wash farm clothes. Tillie wrinkled her nose like Karen probably would at the sight of a laundry tub. Then she laughed as she pulled one of her old dresses from a shelf. Too short and faded, the dress clung to Tillie's skinny frame. She gave it a tug. Good thing the worn fabric hadn't ripped anywhere.

Karen stood at the stove. One of Tillie's aprons covered her fancy blouse and dark blue skirt. Eggs sizzled in the cast-iron skillet. Water steamed in the copper boiler.

"Good morning, Tillie," she said pleasantly. "I thought I might work on the laundry this morning. Your mother shouldn't come home to all that extra work. You may help me, if you wish."

Tillie snorted on her way to the table. Of course she'd help. The little priss wasn't going to show her up. No way.

Karen brought the eggs to the table. "I only have toast to go with the eggs. I'm afraid I'm still not very good at frying pancakes without burning them." She made another trip between stove and table with a plate of toast. "I guess I'll be the one to pray for us this morning." Karen bowed her head.

Tillie sniffed. Karen made a sorry substitute. If Logan was here, he'd solve the problem. He'd do a good job of it too.

The meal started, quiet and subdued. Not much spiced up life when the person who shared your table turned out to be a proper, high-class, city girl.

"You know what I think we should do today?" Karen's eyes brightened.

Tillie almost opened her mouth in reply, so abrupt was Karen's question. She quickly closed it though. Karen still deserved the silent treatment.

Her silence did little to dampen Karen's spirits, for she went on talking without an answer. "We should get some decorations out. Your mother set a large box in the hall when she searched for the suitcase in the attic. Wouldn't it be fun to surprise your mother and Logan? They'd arrive home to a house ready for Christmas."

Tillie shrugged. She wanted to forget the whole season. If the calendar skipped from December 23 to 26, Tillie wouldn't complain.

"Of course, we still need the tree, but your mother said we'd decorate it together on Christmas Eve. That doesn't mean we can't get a head start. Will you help me?"

Decorating the house for Christmas had been such fun. Dad

would cut down a tree and bring it to the house. In the midst of much banter and teasing, Dad, Mama, and Tillie would set the tree up in the parlor and hang ornaments on it. Sometimes Logan would arrive by train that night and walk to the farm. He would burst into the kitchen, sprinkled with snow, red-cheeked, and eyes twinkling. She'd run to hug him. He'd join the rest of them for their Christmas celebration, staying two, maybe even three days.

"Oh, I'm sorry. I didn't mean to make you cry." Karen reached out to touch her arm.

Had she been crying? The memories assaulted her with more strength than she expected.

"It would cheer us up, though, to start decorating. We'd have something to work on as well as a change of scenery."

She could use a change of something, but decorating the house with Karen? She'd rather freeze in the snow.

"Let's get those cookies baked your mother told us about. Wouldn't it be nice for her and Logan to come home to a collection of decorated cookies?" Karen downed the rest of her meal and rushed through washing the dishes.

When the kitchen was put in order, Tillie followed Karen upstairs to help carry the large box of decorations.

With Karen so enamored by the Christmas decorations, she'd miss Tillie's aversion to them. Tillie located Mama's cut-out sugar cookie recipe, brought ingredients from the pantry, and mixed up a batch of dough.

While Karen lifted trinkets from the decoration box, Tillie rolled the dough and cut shapes. Cookies resembling stars, angels, and bells covered the baking tins. When two of the tins were full, Tillie slipped them into the oven. She mixed up two batches of frosting, one red and one green. The familiar work distracted her from her bleeding heart. She worked silently and methodically.

"Oh, how adorable!" Karen's voice cut through Tillie's rhythm.

She turned. Karen held high an ornament in the shape of a

wreath. Small silver jingle bells decorated the wreath. Karen shook it.

"They ring. How darling is that." She shook it again. "Look, Tillie. Isn't this just the cutest ornament you've ever seen?"

Tillie had to admit that it was. She'd given it to Dad as a gift during her second grade year. That was before Logan left for college. Back when they were all happy, healthy, and together.

The ringing bells drew closer until stopping next to her ear. She gritted her teeth against the memories of years gone by and a father never to return.

"Come on, Tillie. Tell me what you think. Doesn't this cheer you up?" Karen jingled the wreath over and over while smiling right in Tillie's face.

Deep down a band of tension broke. "Shut up," Tillie snapped at Karen's goofy smile. The girl acted too happy. If she didn't quit ringing those irritating bells, Tillie would end the misery herself once and for all. "I said, 'shut up.'" Tillie turned to Karen and slapped her. The act left a satisfying smear of gooey dough on Karen's otherwise flawless cheek.

The bell jingling ceased. Karen gasped and backed away. Her hip hit the counter and sent a dish of red frosting flying at Tillie.

The frosting splattered Tillie's hair and dress. Tillie may not have as fine of clothing as Miss-perfect-who-stole-the-show, but she didn't need to make it obvious by smearing globs of hideous red frosting all over Tillie's outgrown dress. "How dare you," Tillie ground out from between gritted teeth.

"You know what I think?" When no words left Karen's gaping mouth, she continued. "I think you've been trying to ruin my life from the moment you walked in this house. If you'd never come here so helpless with no idea how to find your way around a kitchen, I wouldn't be the laughingstock of the town. I'd still have Andrew. Logan wouldn't spend every Sunday morning with you instead of me, and I wouldn't be left alone with a pampered, spoiled lily." She spat the last word into the air.

Karen's face turned red, and her hands went to her hips. "You want to know what I think? I'm sick of your unreasonable accusations." She shook her finger at Tillie like a stuck-up school teacher. "I've said nothing about your unfairness, but I'll say something now. You are a beast. You've been nothing but a selfish child since the day I came. I try to be a friend, learn from you, encourage you. Nothing works. I give up."

"You're the selfish child. Not me." Tillie rushed at Karen, ready to slap her again, but her foot slipped on a glob of slimy frosting. She caught hold of Karen's apron in an attempt to steady herself, but ended up pulling Karen down on top of her. "Get off of me." Tillie struggled to get out from under Karen, but the tangle of skirts on a floor made slippery by frosting worked against her. Her blood coursed hot through every vein of her body.

KAREN ROLLED over sending Tillie sprawling against the legs of a chair. She could only imagine the condition of the kitchen. She sat up and scanned the damage. Ornaments covered the table. Flour and butter littered the counter. Dirty utensils scattered the cupboard. Red frosting smeared the floor, their shoes, and dresses. Karen touched her crown and grimaced at the slime that coated her fingers. She and Tillie had some work ahead of them to get this all cleaned up before Sandy came home.

"Let me help you up. We need to talk." Karen struggled to her feet and tugged on Tillie's arm.

"I lost my father just like you did. My mother was left without a cent to her name when my father died. He'd been sick a long time. I watched him worsen day after day. We had nowhere to go after he died. I didn't have any brothers, so my uncle took us in. Still, the Lord cared for us. I look back on those days and remember how it felt." Even though her father had made some serious mistakes in his lifetime, his death still left his family devastated. Karen reached for one of Tillie's hands. "You'll get through this, Tillie. I promise. But it's hard. And it takes time."

Tillie made no acknowledgement of Karen's words, but beads of moisture gathered in the corners of her eyes.

CHAPTER THIRTY

S aturday morning, the suitcase lay open in the parlor, ready to receive stacks of clothing. Logan rushed about the parsonage collecting various items to take back to Silver Grove with him. His assortment included stationery, two more ties, and a tin of his favorite coffee grounds. He arranged the items in the suitcase and went in search of Mama. He didn't need to look far. She stood at the stove frying ham for their breakfast. "I'm running over to the church for books I want to take back to the farm with me."

She waved. "Fine, dear."

Snow had fallen in the night. His footsteps broke a new trail across the lawn. While he walked, his thoughts turned to yesterday afternoon. All his amazing feelings for Karen left him with a large problem. God called Logan to singleness. As a minister, he must put the Lord first in his life. Love for a young lady interfered in the worst possible way. Logan's steps dragged as he entered the church. He'd have to live in disobedience to God's will in order to pursue Karen. Or he must pursue God and forget about Karen. Either choice brought him pain. He wanted both. But past experience taught him that he must choose.

Logan took the hall to his study, fished in his pocket for the key, and let himself in. *"I'm trusting God to meet me in his time and his way. Maybe you should too."* Karen's words replayed in his thoughts. Of course he was trusting God. He couldn't imagine why Karen would think he needed to hear those words.

He pulled several commentaries from his shelf that he planned to use in sermon preparation for the Meadow Creek folks after the first of the year. *"I'm willing to follow the Lord wherever He might choose to lead."* More of Karen's words. He flipped one of the books open. Karen shouldn't feel the need to tell him that. He'd always be willing to follow the Lord wherever He led. In fact, she'd heard him say that several times whenever he felt she needed the reminder. He crossed the room to his desk. On the corner, pages of his message from yesterday's wedding lay stacked. Funny he didn't put them away. Given his state of mind in the moments following the wedding, it didn't surprise him. Logan grasped the page lying on top. He'd read from Genesis to open the service. The passage caught his attention, *"it is not good that the man should be alone; I will make him a helper as his partner."*

He dropped the paper as if it burned his fingers. All the way down the steps and during his search of a downstairs closet, memories of those Sunday afternoons with Karen as his helper refused to leave him alone.

Returning to his study with a sufficient box, Logan ventured over to his desk again. The second page of his notes lay exposed. He reached to pick it up. The essence of his message rushed back into his memory as he scanned the words on the page. *"faithful support of each other . . . bear each other's burdens . . . share each other's joys."* He'd preached the truth for Brandt and Lorraine as they began their life together. Experience had given him the words to say. This experience came from his relationship with Karen.

His heart thundered deep in his chest. He and Karen supported each other, partnered together in so many ventures, and shared joys as well as sorrows. Even more, along the way she'd become the prayer support he'd thought forever gone from his life after the loss of Dad. He stared at the pages in his hands, attempting to read them. His mind spun. In all of Logan's efforts to stay focused on God, God had actually dropped right into Logan's life the perfect woman for him.

He sank into his chair. His heart still pounded. Karen. The beautiful young woman with a compassionate heart, more talent than he'd thought possible for one voice, and not to mention the most appealing figure he'd ever allowed himself a second look at, may be God's choice for him.

Rubbing his eyes, Logan thought back to that evening with Lorraine. Her rejection convinced him courtship had been impossible because God didn't have a woman picked out for him. That meant God wanted Logan to serve undistracted and offering better service than if he was married, according to the apostle Paul. He knew the passage from First Corinthians well. He'd staked his future on those words.

But now God spoke an opposing word to Logan's heart.

He stood and reached for the stack of books on his desk. One by one, he placed them in the box. He didn't know what to believe. God couldn't contradict himself. He couldn't lead Logan down two paths, especially ones headed in opposite directions.

Releasing a deep breath, Logan pulled his bank book from his pocket. He may not know where to go with his love for Karen, but he knew what he needed to do about his deadline with Eldon. Nine days. He had that much time to pay off the interest at the bank. If his plan worked, he'd beat the deadline with time to spare.

Logan studied the figures. In order to satisfy his father's account, he'd need to drain his own. If his modest savings would have made a difference in Mama's finances, he'd have used it months ago. His savings helped him now because he'd managed to make payments on time before any more interest piled up. Ready to leave his sermons notes and the conflict they stirred, Logan abandoned his study and walked downtown to the bank.

"Good morning, Reverend De Witt. How may I help you?" A

teller with his spectacles settled far down on his nose extended a greeting.

"I'd like to make a withdrawal, please." Logan retrieved his bank book.

"Of course. For how much?"

"All of it."

The man peered at Logan over the top of his glasses. "You're closing your account?"

"Yes."

"Are you moving away?" The teller flipped the pages in Logan's book.

"I'll be back in town next spring."

The man wrote in Logan's book and went to the safe. When he returned, he counted out a stack of bills into Logan's hand. "That closes your account. Thank you for all the years you banked with us."

The man looked like he could use a smile, so Logan gave him one. He took his money to a small table near the wall and counted out the bills he'd need to pay Eldon. A small stack of bills remained, but one count through them assured Logan he had enough to finish up his Christmas shopping.

He'd planned to buy Karen's gift with money from his own account, but he didn't expect to have so much to work with. *Lord, I've prayed about this for days. Please show me what I should get Karen for Christmas.* He left the bank and paused on the sidewalk while his gaze traveled over the various shops downtown.

Mr. Goud stepped onto the street in front of his store. He lifted his arm in a wave. "Good morning, Reverend De Witt. Nice to have you back in town."

Logan returned the wave and headed in Mr. Goud's direction. "It's good to be home. How's business these days?"

"Lots of sales with the holidays next week." Mr. Goud leaned on the broom he used to sweep fresh snow off of his front step. "Stop in today if you're still looking for that perfect gift."

Logan grinned at the older man. "I still have a name on my list. Maybe I'll come by this afternoon."

A large smile on his face, Mr. Goud nodded and resumed his sweeping.

Chuckling, Logan turned toward the parsonage. He'd need a sale in order to swing a purchase from Mr. Goud. The little man, along with his wife and family, operated Oswell City's only jewelry store.

KAREN SAT at the table reading. The wind rattled the windows, sending flurries of snow skidding against the glass. Her gaze left the pages and moved to the darkness beyond the glowing lamp in the warm kitchen. Logan and Sandy should hurry if they planned to reach the farm ahead of the storm.

She bent over her book once more, but the faint howl at the eaves drew her attention away from Tennyson's poetry.

The lamp flickered. Two low chimes rang from the grandfather clock in the parlor announcing the time, nine-fifteen.

Karen continued to read. She covered two more pages before Pete's horse and sleigh drew up to the picket fence. Sandy's voice carried on the wind, followed by the men's voices. Through the window, she watched Logan keep a steady arm around his mother as she walked at his side against the wind and swirling snow.

Karen's insides quivered when their footsteps thudded on the porch's wooden floorboards. Logan was home. She'd waited for this moment when she might see him again. Maybe even hear him declare his love and ask her to share his life.

The door pushed open.

Flipping her book shut, Karen took a deep breath.

"Watch your step, Mama. Some snow blew in. It might make the floor slick." Logan's arm left her waist.

Karen stood and smoothed her skirt.

"I'm fine, dear." Sandy removed the woolen scarf from her head. She draped it over a chair and looked at Karen. "We made it home. Glad to see you." Sandy approached and hugged her.

"I'm happy to see you too." Karen returned the embrace. Seeing this woman again impressed on Karen a new respect for her. Logan had a special mother. Karen had missed her. She tightened her hug. Sandy had given her so much. She thought back to the days of her cooking lessons. She must have tried Sandy's patience terribly. Thank goodness Sandy hadn't given up on her. She owed this woman much for the changes in her life. Karen prayed she had somehow given back in ways that eased Sandy's burden of keeping up with the kitchen tasks or brought light to places darkened with grief.

Logan removed his coat and hung it up. His gaze landed on her. A thoughtful look entered his eyes and softened them as he watched her embrace his mother.

Sandy drew back from Karen's arms. "Where's Tillie?"

"In bed. She's had a rough couple of days and needed her sleep." Tillie still struggled, but Karen believed healing had begun to take place in her life.

"Oh." Concern shadowed Sandy's eyes.

"She was sorry to miss your homecoming but wanted to rest up for tomorrow. You'll see her in the morning."

Sandy moved to the stairs with heavy steps. "Well, it's wonderful to come home again. Train travel wears me out. I'm headed for my own bed." The steps creaked under her feet.

Karen's gaze ventured in Logan's direction. "How was the train ride?"

"Fine. Couldn't have asked for better." He unpacked a few items from one of the satchels.

"You'll have to tell me all about your week in Oswell City sometime."

He embraced her. "I'd love to. Good to see you again, Karen." He held her a moment before releasing her. "I missed you."

Logan actions gave no indication of the state of his heart. This fact left an ache in the back of her throat.

After he'd taken the stairs, Karen turned to the table to gather up her poetry book. A small, blue book lay on the top of the pile Logan had removed from the satchel. Logan's name and Oswell City address were written on the cover.

She bent over to read the smaller print below Logan's name. Oswell City Savings Bank. Her breath caught. The temptation to read the dollar figures listed in the book proved too great. She flipped open the cover and tilted her head until the script came into focus. Logan's banking history reflected a predictable pattern of deposits with occasional withdrawals until she noticed the last number. It was a zero.

Nausea rolled through her. Logan had lost all of his money. Memories of her father's crimes overwhelmed her. Maybe someone had demanded all Logan's funds from him. Or maybe he'd fallen into dishonesty and was cheating others when he really had nothing. Perhaps he gambled. Karen covered her mouth. She really shouldn't go snooping around in a man's bank book. If only she could forget what she'd seen. But the damage had been done.

He was hiding something.

Tears gathered in her eyes. Her world crumbled. A man she loved had mishandled money. Uncle Henry had been right to maintain a low view of preachers. Logan was no different.

Karen's insides trembled. She should confess to him that she'd stolen a peek at his bank book. But then Logan might try to defend himself. She'd never be able to handle the truth. Karen turned around and ran upstairs to her room.

TILLIE MIXED another spoonful of powdered sugar into her bowl of frosting. It was red frosting to replace the batch spilled during her tussle with Karen.

"Ladies, I'm going to the barn for a moment. I need to talk to Logan." Mama removed her apron and draped it over a chair.

The kitchen empty of everyone except Karen, Tillie took a deep breath. "You said yesterday that you lost your father."

"Yes."

"How did you stand it? Didn't you feel like your heart had gotten ripped out of your chest?"

"All the time."

"How did you get over it?"

"My father made some bad decisions during his life, but he was still my father and I had to grieve my loss of him. My whole life changed when he died. My mother and I moved in with Uncle Henry and Aunt Fran. My sister got married."

Tillie heard the pain in Karen's voice. The death of her father meant that her whole family broke up. Karen also had to move to a different home. Maybe even in a place among strangers. She shuddered.

"At least you have Logan." Karen spoke as she frosted the top of a star-shaped cookie. "He gave up his career to stay on the farm with you and your mother so you could keep your home. You should feel very thankful for that."

Her words pricked Tillie in a tender place. She loved Logan and wanted him to stay here with them. "I do, but I miss Dad. I was special to him as his only daughter. Now that he's gone I feel deserted and forgotten."

Karen laid her knife down. "Logan loves you. Your mother loves you. No one has forgotten about you."

"Then why do I feel so alone? I wish things would go back to the way they were. I was happy then. I have this terrible pain that won't go away. Mama seems so calm and at peace with everything that's happened, but I find each day harder than the day before." Tillie sank into a chair. "How can I go on like this? How can I stand a whole lifetime stretching before me without him? The loneliness will kill me. Oh, Dad, why did you have to die and leave me like this?" Tillie sank her head onto her arms and sobbed.

Karen laid her hand on Tillie's arm. "Tillie, listen to me. This may be hard for you to hear, but I'm going to tell you the truth. You have to let God back into your life."

Tillie shook her head. "No. He took my father. God hurt me so much. The only way I can keep it from getting worse is to stay away from Him."

"That's not how God works. God didn't take your father. Everyone dies. At some point all of us come to the end of our lives. God gives your father life, not death. He provided a place in Heaven for him to continue living. It may not be here with you, but you can trust that your father is alive. He'll never die again. If you believe God gives eternal life, then you'll live forever, too, Tillie. You'll see your father again. You'll get to enjoy each other. Forever. Don't you want that?"

The words trickled way down into a tiny crevice of Tillie's heart. Everything Karen talked about Tillie wanted. How marvelous if she could see Dad again without any fear of another separation. Her sobs eased. An occasional hiccup jerked at her throat.

Karen continued in a soft voice, "God loves you, Tillie. Come back to him."

She'd heard those same words from her brother. If Karen believed this, too, then maybe those words really held truth. What a relief it would be if Tillie could know God as a loving father like Logan did. Memories of that visit he paid to her in her room flooded her mind. "Now you sound like Logan." The table muffled Tillie's voice.

"Then that must mean I know a little of what I'm talking about."

Tillie sat up and rubbed her eyes. "If I come back to the Lord, how do I know He won't hurt me again?"

"You have to trust Him, Tillie. That doesn't mean hard things won't enter your life, but it does mean that you know He's faithful and capable of taking care of you. People die and cause our lives to change, but God will never leave you."

The crevice in her heart widened, allowing more of Karen's words to flow in. "I want that. I want to know I'll always be taken care of, but I don't know if I can trust God to be the one to do it."

"Maybe you must try to forgive Him. Let God off the hook for the wrong He never did to you."

Those words hurt. "I can't."

"Then start by forgiving the people God uses to display his love to you. You know who they are."

Yes, she did. Those names came to mind easily. "Mama. Logan. You."

Karen smiled. "What about Andrew?"

She drew in a deep breath. "He wants a wife of faith." Two hiccups jerked her throat again. "I want to be that for him someday. If he comes back."

"Maybe the person you need to forgive most of all is you."

Those words hurt even more. Tillie shook her head. "I don't deserve it."

"Why?"

Tillie's throat thickened, making breathing difficult. She gulped in more air. "I left the barn. Dad asked me to take some milk to Mama at the house." Tillie wiped her face. "It was Sunday morning. We needed to rush so we could get to church on time. He died alone. I should've stayed in the barn. He'd still be here if I never left him." Tillie covered her face with her hands.

After many minutes passed, Karen's soft voice caught her attention "Tillie."

She looked up, the tears still blurring her vision.

"God knows all about your father. God had his life planned out even before he was born. You father would've gone to Heaven on that summer day regardless of who was around or what had been happening. You can rest in God's plan."

All those places that had been growing hard and sharp over the past months started to soften. Maybe God really could take care of her. If He did, she'd never be alone. It might be worth a try. "I need help."

Karen moved around the table and sat next to Tillie with an arm around her. "Are you willing to pray?"

"I think so." She released a deep breath. "This is hard."

"It'll get easier with time."

"A lot of time." The climb out of her despair was a long one.

"Logan, your mother, and I will help you."

Tillie nodded.

"Ready?" Karen held her hands out, palms up as an invitation.

"Yes." Her hands tingling, Tillie stretched them along the table's surface until Karen held them.

CHAPTER THIRTY-ONE

*L*ogan's focus left the strip of leather between his oily fingers when the barn door opened.

Mama entered, picking her way across the dirt floor. "You probably noticed the changes in Tillie."

"Yeah." While decorating the tree this morning, Tillie had given Karen a treasured ornament. It was the wreath with the small bells that Tillie made sure found a place on the tree every year.

"She and Karen seem to have worked things out."

"Appears that way." The girls had become friends. He slicked thick oil along a new section of harness.

"We don't need to ask Karen to move out any longer. The problem is solved."

Drips of oil landed on the packed earth at his feet. He watched the darkened spots grow as the liquid soaked into the barn floor. Relief should fill him at Mama's words. Disappointment took its place, soaking into all the little pores of his heart, darkening his hopes. He exhaled a heavy breath.

"Aren't you happy?" Mama asked.

He met her gaze. "Are you?"

A smile grew over her mouth. "Yes, I suppose I am. I like

Karen. She's a special young lady. I'm quite proud of her. She turned out to be a rather good cook. I'd be perfectly content to keep her in our home."

Her words pricked Logan's conscience. No way could Karen stay in his home. He loved her with a passion that frightened him. His hand shook, sending the can of oil on a crash course to the floor. He bent to set it up right before too much spilled out.

"But, I've noticed Eldon Kent paying her a considerable amount of attention lately. A move to the parsonage may speed a courtship along since it's closer to town."

He'd thought of that. Eldon would move fast if Karen ever left Logan's household.

"What do you think we should do, dear?"

Boy, he hated impossible decisions. Whatever choice he made would be a bad one. If Karen moved out, Eldon could court her unhindered. If she stayed, Tillie gained the friend he'd wanted her to have, but he'd lose his grip on his own honor.

His throat went dry. "We need to stick to our plan, Mama. Karen should move out."

"I didn't realize you felt so strongly. I expected you to want her to stay. That's what you said when we discussed this on our trip."

"Yes, but that was before." Biting his lip, he laid the oiled strip of leather on the straw and leaned to pick up a new one.

"Before what, dear?"

Logan held his breath. He had too much conflict to put into words. "Before I uh, realized you were right about getting by with a few less groceries, since we'd lose the room and board payment."

"Oh, yes. Karen seems so much like a family member that I keep forgetting about the boarding arrangement."

He needed reminded once in a while too.

"When should we tell her?"

"Tonight, I guess. Let's discuss it after the Christmas Eve service." And after that, when he had the parlor all to himself, he'd tell Karen the real reason why he wanted her to move out of his home. Then he'd give her the gift he'd found for her in Oswell City and hope with all his heart she liked it.

"Fine."

"I'll catch Pete at church and ask him." His buddy would take all the credit for this new development. Logan hid a grin.

"Thank you, dear." Mama bent to kiss his forehead. "You do so much for us." She left the barn.

Yeah, he might do a lot for them, but it was never enough. His banker and that insatiable account book gave him constant reminders. One more payment for the year awaited deposit. When he returned to the house, he sat at his desk and counted every bill in the stack of cash he'd accumulated. Logan's chest tightened. He still fell short. How could that happen? He counted it all again with the same results. Logan stood and rubbed his forehead, his mind reviewing all his sources of income. Karen's room and board. He'd put that in the bank last week before he left town. Milk sales. Yes, he'd made that deposit the week before. The payment from Meadow Creek. Logan's heart skipped a beat. That's what he was still missing. Maybe it had come in the mail while he'd been gone.

Logan sprinted downstairs. "Mama, have you seen the mail?"

She turned from the sink. "No, dear."

Tillie straightened away from the cookies she and Karen decorated. "We didn't get the mail while you were gone."

Logan's breath caught. His payment from Meadow Creek was still in his mailbox at the post office. He didn't like the idea of money sitting around out in the open for days on end. "I'm going to town." His announcement streaming over his shoulder in his haste, Logan sprinted from the house.

At the post office, Logan waited in line while the postman handed over stacks of envelopes that must contain Christmas cards. Logan inched closer to the counter. Finally, his turn came.

"Ah, Logan. Back in town. Merry Christmas." The postman greeted him with a cheery smile.

"Thanks. My sister tells me there's still mail here for the De Witts."

"I'll check." The postman turned around and reached in a box.

A grin stretched Logan's face at the sight of the envelopes in the postman carried. Surely one of them came from Meadow Creek. He waved and left the building.

Out on the street, Logan rifled through the letters. Two cards from Mama's relatives in Bridgewater Springs. Another from Karen's mother. A feed bill. Nothing from Meadow Creek. Logan read the return addresses again. Still no payment.

He kicked at a patch of snow. So close. He just about had that interest knocked out at the bank. Well, the end of the year was still one week away. Maybe the payment would show up before then. Logan trekked off to the bank and asked to see Eldon.

DRESSED IN HIS SUIT, Logan arrived in the kitchen after supper. The horse stood in the lane hitched to the sleigh ready to transport himself, Mama, and Karen to church. Or so he thought.

A third passenger made her appearance while Logan buttoned his coat.

"Tillie!" He really shouldn't have yelled, but the sight of her in Karen's elegant holiday dress caught him completely off guard. "What are you doing?"

"I'd like to attend church with you."

All movement in the room came to a halt. Mama looked at Logan. Logan looked back at Mama. Both of them turned to Karen.

She nodded her head. "I invited her."

"Karen let me borrow her dress." Tillie grasped the skirt and held it out away from her legs. "Isn't it beautiful?"

Logan took a step closer. "You look very nice." He placed a kiss on the top of her head.

"Is there room for me in the sleigh?"

"There's always room for you."

At the church, Karen hastily removed her coat, exposing a pretty royal blue dress. The white lace trim at the neckline enhanced her fair skin. A velvet hat of the same color blue covered her hair. She glanced up at him from under the brim. "I'll see you later."

"Won't you sit with us?"

"Not this time." She hurried down the aisle to the front pew.

He trudged along with Mama and Tillie to the De Witt pew. In an effort to keep his attention off of Karen, he allowed his gaze to wander over the congregation. Meadow Creek people sat across the aisle from him. More were sprinkled among Silver Grove congregants down front.

Pete emerged from a side door. He paused to visit with Karen, pointing to a sheet of paper in her hand.

Eldon strode up to the front pew and sat down beside her.

Logan's stomach plunged. Karen didn't sit with him because she'd already made plans to meet up with Eldon! His worst fear came true. Karen welcomed Eldon's attention. Maybe he'd even come to the farm to see her this past week in Logan's absence. Memories of Lorraine's announcement of Brandt's courtship assaulted him. Surely it couldn't happen twice. Those deep places where Karen's kiss lived on began to shrivel.

Logan's eyes widened when Eldon's arm crept along the top of the pew behind Karen. They leaned close, engaged in a private conversation with their heads almost touching.

Karen never said a word about Eldon. But why would she? Logan walked away from her in a moment when he should've stayed. He couldn't have sent her a clearer message of his unwillingness to commit. She'd been left with no choice but to give her support and affection to another.

A sharp pain pushed against his throat, forcing him to call her name. Logan gulped it away. He'd missed his chance. Understanding came too late. Karen had gotten swept out of his life as abruptly as she'd entered it. By the time he finally figured out what she meant to him, she'd slipped away.

"KAREN, you understand when you need to come to the pulpit and sing?" Pete pointed to the typed page in her hand. "After this prayer, we'll sing carols. Down here after the sermon is your solo. At the end of the service, we'll sing one more carol."

Karen nodded.

"Anna and I are leaving immediately after the service so that we can catch the train. We'll spend Christmas with her family. I may not see you again tonight, so I'll tell you now. Thank you for singing. Since you've helped Logan so faithfully on Sunday afternoons, it's only fair that you assist me during a service when both congregations are invited." Pete's eyes twinkled.

Karen couldn't help but smile.

"Good evening."

Her stomach lurched when Eldon's voice reached her ears. She jerked her gaze to the side where the voice came from. Eldon stood there dressed in the dark suit and white bowtie he'd worn to the bank's social events.

"May I join you?"

Pete cleared his throat.

Karen turned. One eyebrow rose above the rim of his spectacles. She could almost hear his thoughts. There were two men in her life. One who forced himself in and one who tried his best to stay out.

Pete's gaze also seemed to ask if this was what she wanted. No. Not one bit. She knew what she wanted, but Logan had to decide he wanted it too. So far, he had not.

She was stuck with Eldon.

Pete left, and Eldon settled in at her side. That was so like him.

To wait until a time when she couldn't get away and then impose his company on her.

"I thought you said you don't go to church. What are you doing here?" Karen asked in a low voice.

Eldon leaned closer. His arm circled her shoulders from behind like a long, black snake sent to suffocate her. Too bad she couldn't swat him, but seated in the front row, she'd only make a scene.

"I always go to church during the holidays. It gives me a chance to connect with many of our bank customers."

Karen shivered as though a reptile had found its way up the back of her dress. "I never asked you to sit with me." She had to get this man away from her. The school board chairman, along with every other parent of her students, watched from their pews further back. If she allowed Eldon to stay, she'd lose her job.

"You weren't seated with the De Witts so that's how I knew to come find you."

"Please leave."

"Thanks to the brilliant work of our local paper, the town already assumes we're courting. People expect to see us together."

Something about Eldon's voice implied the article had been a set-up. His words grated on her nerves. Eldon had set a trap. He wanted her as his girl and had appealed to public opinion to bring it about.

Karen breathed deep and turned around until she could see Logan out of the corner of her eye. He stared straight ahead and ignored her. He didn't care. He really didn't care. He'd come home as determined to live his life alone as the day he left.

Karen's chest began to ache. Nothing she could do or say would change his mind. At Pete's cue, she went to the front and sang. The joyful message of the carols helped to lighten her heart as the service progressed. It may have lasted if Mr. Hinkley hadn't searched her out when church ended.

"Miss Millerson, I'd like to have a word with you, please."

Karen's middle shrank at the sound of Tom Hinkley's voice.

"I saw Eldon come over here and take a seat next to ya." Mr. Hinkley's voice and his expression turned solemn.

"I didn't encourage him. I've tried to stay away from him as I promised." At least he'd deserted his seat before the last song ended, saving her the displeasing task of spending more time with him or receiving an invitation for a ride home.

He nodded. "I aim to have a talk with Eldon's father. The Senior Kent runs the show. He's also got grandkids in school. He don't want anyone in his family causin' us trouble. If I tell him what's been goin' on, he'll keep Eldon in line."

Karen blinked. Mr. Hinkley saw Eldon as the one creating problems and not her. "How do you know Eldon will listen? He thinks he can have whatever he wants."

"Eldon is the only one in his family who doesn't send kids to school. His brother and sister will think Eldon is causin' trouble for them, too, if he keeps this up. Eldon won't wanna be on the outs with them. It could cost him his position at the bank and in the community." Mr. Hinkley nodded, totally convinced of his own words. "He should leave ya alone from now on." He turned to Karen with a handshake.

Weakness invaded Karen's arms and legs. She had a great desire to laugh. No, to giggle and tell the whole world of her new freedom. "Oh, thank you, Mr. Hinkley. This issue has concerned me for months."

He smiled. "Merry Christmas, Miss Millerson."

CHAPTER THIRTY-TWO

*L*ogan stood before his dresser, the sock drawer hanging open. Karen's gift lay in his hand. He wouldn't need it anymore. Perhaps he acted more on impulse than on faith Saturday morning in Mr. Goud's store. The pain of losing someone close to him influenced how Logan interpreted God's call on his life. Tonight it happened again.

Lorraine had rejected him. Believing he must serve as a single man became easier than accepting loss.

It was the same with Dad. His death had been another loss Logan had needed to grieve. Instead of someone he wanted to court, Dad had been family. Staying single would protect Logan from both kinds of losses.

He should still hold onto this theory. It was solid and dependable. If Eldon ended up tearing Karen out of his life, this thinking would provide a good protection against losing yet another person close to him. It might work if this sick feeling over seeing Eldon's arm around Karen would go away.

Exhaling a long, slow breath, he replaced the gift in the drawer. Turning his back on the dresser, he shuffled down the stairs.

Mama stood at the stove heating hot chocolate. "What did Pete say?"

"I didn't get a chance to talk to him. He must have left early." Logan snitched a handful of popcorn from the bowl on the table. "I'll stop in at his house sometime after Christmas." He tossed a few kernels into his mouth.

Mama poured hot chocolate into mugs, placed them on a tray, and handed the tray to him. "Carry this to the parlor, please, dear. I'll bring the popcorn."

Logan stuffed the rest of his popcorn into his mouth so his hands were free to heed Mama's request.

Tillie sat with Karen on the love seat chatting about the church service. "Didn't Karen do a wonderful job tonight?" Tillie asked.

"Very nice." Mama settled into the rocking chair. "You are quite talented, Karen."

"Thank you. I love to sing." Karen accepted a mug from the tray Logan held before her.

"What did you think?" Tillie asked him as she reached for a mug from the tray.

He'd heard her sing before. If the choice belonged to him, he'd spend the rest of his life listening to her. But he'd missed out. "You were unforgettable tonight, Karen." He claimed the last mug, settled on the settee, and chugged a mouthful before anyone could ask him any more questions.

For the next hour, conversation included stories of happenings in Silver Grove while Sandy and Logan had been away. Karen told tales of mischievous schoolboys. Tillie related articles from the newspaper.

Logan faded in and out of the conversation. His mind kept going back to the picture Karen made standing behind the pulpit singing. Something about the pleasure in her eyes and the delight in her voice pestered him. Is this how she looked every Sunday afternoon when she'd come along to help him?

He sipped more hot chocolate, his attention fixed on the dark window beyond the women gathered around. She wouldn't have needed to come with him at all. He could've handled things just fine on his own. But she'd insisted and would probably still be helping him out if he hadn't told her to stay home. He stole a glimpse of Karen's face as she related an animated story to his sister. If he'd been the one told to stay home instead of leading the Meadow Creek folks in worship, he'd protest in the worst way, putting up a fight and doing whatever he must to make sure he was on the scene to help those people draw closer to the Lord. Just the thought of getting cut off from such a pleasure drove him crazy.

Maybe she'd felt the same way. She had put up a bit of a fight. But why would she feel the need to be there, week after week?

The answer nearly caused him to spew hot chocolate onto the rug. He'd thought she'd been worried about Agnes, which did happen to be part of the truth. But what if Karen felt the same way about serving the Lord that he did? What if her love for the Lord directed her path just like it did his?

If that was the case, then he was the blindest fool who ever lived. His chest got all tight, and his throat swelled shut. No point trying to get any more hot chocolate down it. He stood up. "I'm going to the kitchen."

The women stopped chatting and watched him leave. He really should apologize for deserting them so rudely, but his heart was demanding a bit of attention at the moment.

Logan set his near-empty cup down on the counter with a thunk. Then he leaned over the sink, almost wishing he could throw up. God's directions were based on love, not the need for protection from pain. God hadn't challenged Logan with a choice after all. The path God intended for Logan to follow had only ever been one of love. Karen occupied that path. She wanted to share in ministry with him. She enjoyed it and she encouraged Logan to keep doing it. This meant that he wouldn't need to make any sacrifices in the obedience department at all if he shared his life with

Karen. It was a matter of merely welcoming her into the work God had already begun.

Logan shook his head. Boy, had he been wrong to think he could keep on living his life without her in it. All those times he resisted her help, stiffened away from her kisses, and told her she was unnecessary to him were in reality his fight against a beautiful gift.

The laughter and chatter of the women in the parlor brought with it the memory of the afternoon in that same location when he dragged himself away from her touch, her lips, and her support. To think he actually said "no" to her kisses. Twice. Any man would endure great difficulties to get a woman like Karen to even look at him. And here Logan had her in his own home, under his very nose, willing to be his friend and helper.

The pain of rejection and loss still poked at his soul. But love had proven to be stronger and was swallowing up all the old hurts and grief. All he wanted was a life with Karen. He turned away from the sink and watched her sip from one of the dainty cups in Mama's collection. He and Karen could grow something new and beautiful together. That's what he longed for more than anything. He loved the Lord and wanted to serve him. Karen wanted the same in her life. He stood at an intersection of blessing, a place he wished to remain for the rest of his days.

But Eldon stood in his way. Logan turned back to the sink. The vision of Eldon's black-sleeved arm curling around Karen's shoulders sneaked back into his memory. Logan leaned over. Now he really could throw up.

KAREN REACHED for Sandy's cup. "Let me wash those cups for you and straighten up the kitchen. You've had a long first day back from your trip and tomorrow will be busy. I'd love to help you."

"Thank you. I am quite tired. Keeping up with Logan the past few days has worn me out." Mama gathered the popcorn bowls and carried them to the kitchen.

Tillie carried the tray of empty cups.

Karen poured water into the sink and filed off strips of lye soap with a knife.

"I'd love to stick around and help, but I have a gift I need to finish." Tillie set the tray on the table.

"I'll help Karen." Logan straightened away from the counter and reached for a towel.

"All right. Good night." Tillie turned and followed Mama up the steps.

Logan's presence so near to her left side made Karen's pulse race. If her hands didn't need to stay in the water, she'd inch away from him.

She tried to think of anything to talk about except the happenings of this evening, but curiosity won out. "Did you enjoy the service?"

"Yes." Logan rubbed his towel over the exterior of a mug. "Rarely do I get the privilege to sit in the pews and receive."

"Pete hoped you'd feel that way. He said so when he invited me to sing tonight. On Sunday, he invited the Meadow Creek people to join us tonight. Did you see them there?"

"I did."

"The Harpers were there too. Even Mr. Harper. He seems to be doing well. Agnes is completely recovered. I'm glad."

"You care about that little girl."

"I do. I wish she attended my classroom."

"So that some of your beauty and sophistication might rub off on her." Logan reached for a mug she rinsed, their hands brushing.

His compliment, along with the brief contact, set off a parade of events on Karen's insides. Vibrations shimmered from her fingers, up her arms and through her chest. "I hadn't thought of it that way, but I hope I might influence her a little."

Logan moved to put the mugs away. Clinks of porcelain getting stacked together broke the silence. "You had asked for me to tell you about my time in Oswell City."

She should tell him about her moment of weakness looking at his bank book. Swallowing, Karen worked up her courage. "First, I must confess something."

A question hung in his eyes.

"Sunday night. After you returned home, I well." She forced her gaze to meet his. "I stole a peek at your bank book."

He shook his head as gravely as a doctor giving a fatal diagnosis. "You weren't supposed to see that, Karen."

"I know that now. I'm sorry. But your little book, it was lying right there in the open." The air rushed out of her lungs. "Please forgive me."

Logan smiled in his warm, I-can-see-right-into-your-heart manner. "Actually, my stories from Oswell City were about my visit to the bank."

"They were?" Karen frowned. Not only had she committed the secret act of looking at his bank book, now she apparently could read his mind.

"Yeah. I closed my account. Most of the money will go into the bank here in Silver Grove. Eldon set a deadline for the end of the year. When Dad died, he left behind a substantial debt. The interest on it must get paid by December 31." Logan put his towel down. "I haven't been making enough from my dairy sales and preaching for Meadow Creek to cover it. While I was in Oswell City, I drained my account so that I could satisfy Eldon."

"And the rest of it?"

A mischievous grin cut across his face. "Christmas shopping."

Karen felt lightheaded. He hadn't lost his money. He'd given it away to the bank for the sake of his mother and his sister. Whatever he'd kept, he spent on gifts. She didn't want to believe that his story could be his cover up. But Father had lasted in his ministry for six months before anyone saw through his tales. She had to know. "You don't owe anyone else?"

Logan shook his head. "No. Just Eldon."

"What are you going to do when the bank is paid? You won't have anything left." Karen felt her equilibrium returning.

Logan raised his hands. "Start over I guess."

"Start over?" True or false, Logan's story had a few holes in it.

He nodded. "The rest of the debt needs paid off by spring. Oswell City found a substitute for me until then. When my work is done here, I plan to return to preaching. Mama and Tillie would be able to afford hired help if they are no longer in debt."

Karen's world just got put back together. All of those crumbles from a moment ago fell into place, creating a vivid and beautiful picture. "You mean to say that you don't intend to keep farming?"

"No. Not any longer than I have to."

Heat rushed up her neck. Logan told the truth. He wouldn't include his mother and his sister in a fabricated story.

He leaned against the counter, his sensitive eyes searching her face. "Eldon came to church tonight."

Karen shivered. "I didn't expect to see him."

"Did he call on you while I was away?"

"No."

"I'm surprised. He appears serious about courting."

"He is, but Mr. Hinkley is going to put a stop to it. He understands now, thanks to your influence on him." Karen gave Logan a faint smile.

She lifted another cup from the water. "Besides, for all Eldon knows, I left a special someone behind in Chicago."

Logan pushed away from the counter. "Did you?"

"No." Karen turned away from the sink and looked into his eyes. "Unlike you, Logan, I cannot count on one hand the times I kissed someone." Karen's heart pounded at the serious look that crossed Logan's face. "I've only done it once."

His brows formed a straight line above his eyes while he searched her face. "Are you sorry your record's been broken?"

She shook her head. Her breaths shortened to shallow ripples when Logan's hands rested on her shoulders.

"You and I have some unfinished business, Miss Millerson." His eyes twinkled even though his voice stayed serious. "May I help you set a new record?" His head lowered.

"Please." She stretched up to meet him.

Their lips met. Logan's hands slid across her back, drawing her into his embrace. She surrendered to the voices within screaming at her to let him know her fears about his farming occupation and his trustworthiness had finally been laid to rest. The best she could do was hold him in her arms, cherishing the feel of his hard muscles against her softness, while her lips pressed his with a gentle fervor.

Logan cupped the side of her head. He pulled away far enough to catch a breath, but not so far his lips left hers. He whispered, "Sweetheart, we need to talk."

Karen's limbs weakened, even her tongue went limp. All she managed was a nod. She pressed his chest for support.

Logan placed a light kiss on her forehead. "Good night." He released her, turned towards the stairs, and disappeared into the darkness of the farmhouse's upper story.

He had changed. It actually happened. Men intent on avoiding marriage didn't kiss the way Logan kissed her. Neither did they toss around endearments. Karen's heart constricted. She hung up the dish towel, dumped the water from the sink, and blew out the lamp. What could Logan possibly want to discuss with her?

CHAPTER THIRTY-THREE

*K*aren stood at the end of the dining room table with a spatula in her hand. "May I serve you the first slice, Sandy?"

"Yes, thank you." Sandy pushed her china dessert plate closer to the pie pan.

"It's apple, Mama. No salt," Tillie informed her mother with a laugh. "I watched her mix it up."

"Then I'm sure it will taste delicious." Sandy accepted the plate of apple pie that Karen handed to her.

"And you, Logan?" Karen's voice shook when she said his name.

"The largest one you have." He grinned, lifting his coffee cup in the air as a sort of toast.

She set to work scooping out for him precisely one-sixth of her flaky crusted pie.

Karen cut the next slice for Tillie and the last one for herself. The persistent tightness in her stomach challenged her enjoyment of the delicious pie. She'd struggled enough to eat a decent amount of Sandy's tasty Christmas dinner. After four bites, Karen gave up, tired of the effort.

"Don't you like it?" Tillie studied her.

"I do, but I ate too much already." Karen smiled. If only the reason was really that simple.

"I think it turned out really well." Sandy laid her fork down on her plate. "Nice job, Karen. You have developed into a good cook. I'm proud of you."

The praise produced tears in the corners of her eyes. "Thank you. I wanted to learn how so that I could fit in better with all of you."

"I'd say you accomplished your goal." Sandy beamed a smile at her, bringing a flush to Karen's face.

Silence fell as they finished the meal. Tillie bounced out of her seat. "Mine's gone. Let's open gifts."

Logan chuckled. "Hang on a minute. Give Mama a chance to catch her breath. She's still recuperating from her trip. Don't go tire her out again."

Tillie wrinkled her nose at him. "We should do the dishes later. That will save some work."

"And time." Sandy pushed back from the table. "You've got the right idea, Tillie. Let's move to the parlor."

Karen claimed a spot on the love seat, the tears from Sandy's praise filling her eyes. She'd done well through the tree decorating, the Christmas Eve service, and the large meal. But now homesickness settled over her. How she missed Mother, Uncle Henry, and Aunt Fran. If she were home with them today, she'd sit in their large, beautifully decorated parlor exchanging gifts.

She drew in a deep breath. If only she could go home to see them. But she wasn't allowed to leave until the school year ended. That May day seemed worlds away from now.

"Karen?" Tillie approached. "What's wrong?"

"Just missing my family. It didn't hit me until I saw all of the gifts under your tree." She wanted nothing more than to retreat to her room.

"I know how you feel. I've been missing Dad today. This is our first Christmas without him." Tillie settled onto the love seat next to Karen.

Karen reached over and gave Tillie a hug. "I know it hurts. I miss my father every year."

Sandy approached the tree. "Here, Karen. This may cheer you up a bit." She handed Karen a large box. "Pete gave it to us at church last night. He said it came through the mail last week while Logan and I were gone."

Karen accepted the package. It possessed a Chicago return address. "Oh! It's from Mother." She worked at opening the flaps on the top.

The first item in the box was a letter. Karen unfolded it and scanned it, thrilled at the news including stories of Julia's new baby. Next were three wrapped packages with names on them. "These are for you from my family." She handed them to Tillie, Logan, and Sandy.

Sandy opened hers first. Mother had sent her a beautiful glass vase. "This is lovely. Your mother is very thoughtful. Thank you, Karen."

Karen went to her and hugged her. Sandy's return hug eased Karen's longing for her own mother.

Tillie opened hers next. She pulled a collection of lace doilies from her package.

Logan went last. A grin crossed his face as the contents of his gift appeared. He held up a set of three books by Charles Spurgeon.

"Do you already have those?"

"I don't. I can certainly use them. Thanks, Karen."

More items rested in the bottom of the box. Karen pulled out sheets of music, monogrammed stationery, hatpins, and a set of lace handkerchiefs.

"Those are pretty," Tillie said, leaning over Karen's shoulder.

"Would you like one?" Karen reached the top handkerchief out to her.

Tillie accepted it. "Thanks."

The gifts exchange continued with Logan opening a small ordinary-looking box.

"Mr. Harper from Meadow Creek sneaked that to me at church last night. He said it came from everyone in their congregation." Sandy watched him rip the paper and lift the lid.

Logan took out a slip of paper and read. In an instant, the sober expression disappeared from his face. He erupted out of his chair with a hearty laugh.

"Goodness, dear. What on earth was in that box?" Sandy asked as Logan pulled her out of her rocking chair and spun around with her once.

"Meadow Creek gave me a cash gift for being their pastor this fall." He brought Sandy to a stop. "This means I'll be able to pay off the bank!"

"Really? Oh, that's wonderful!" Sandy clasped her hands and a smile broke out on her face. "I'm so proud of you, dear. You've been working so hard."

Tillie joined the celebration. She hugged Logan and then her mother.

Karen's eyes grew moist. Logan really was who he appeared to be. Honest, compassionate, and kind. She was proud of him too.

When Logan settled down, the gift exchange continued. Tillie and Sandy gave gifts to Karen. Tillie's was a hand-knit shawl of delicate white yarn. Sandy gave her recipe cards. For as much as Karen appreciated their thoughtfulness, the empty floor beneath the tree sent her one message. Logan didn't get her anything. There was no gift under the tree for her from him.

That fact shouldn't distress her so much. After all, she was his boarder. His family didn't have to include her in their Christmas celebration. She had no connection to them other than the money she paid every month for her room.

Pain squeezed her heart. Karen gathered up her collection of gifts as well as her shredded dignity. "I'm going to my room." She climbed the stairs and added her new possessions to her already overcrowded apartment. She sat on the edge of her bed and stared out the window at the white world. This was the worst Christmas she'd ever known.

"IS SOMETHING WRONG?" Tillie watched Karen leave the parlor.

"Maybe she's still homesick," Logan suggested with a shrug.

"You're probably right." Tillie picked up one of the doilies from Karen and studied it. Karen had helped her so much in the past few days. She would've never endured today without Dad if she hadn't talked with Karen first.

Logan stood. "I'm going to start the milking," he said on his way out of the room.

A knock came at the kitchen door.

"I'll get it." Mama left her rocking chair. She returned. "Tillie, Andrew is here."

Her heart pounded. "Why?"

"You'll have to ask him."

Tillie forced herself off the love seat. With heavy steps, her feet carried her through the dining room and into the kitchen.

Andrew stood there with his cap in his hand. "Merry Christmas, Tillie."

Her mouth hung open. She must say something. "It's good to see you."

"I saw you in church with your family last night." He licked his lips. "Does this mean you're planning to attend again?"

Tillie nodded. "I'm going to try. I may not make it every week, but I want to come back."

A smile stretched across Andrew's face. "May I call Friday night?"

"You'd be most welcome."

Andrew pulled a small gift from his coat pocket. "Here. This is for you."

Tillie took it and unwrapped it. Opening the box, she discovered a delicate bracelet. "This is beautiful." She held it up. "Thank you."

Andrew stepped closer. He took the jewelry and fastened it around Tillie's wrist. "When it came in at the store, I couldn't resist. I bought it, hoping you'd accept it from me."

"It's the best."

"Glad you like it." Andrew returned his hat to his head. "See you Friday."

Tillie nodded, pressing the door shut behind him. She stood at the window and watched him gallop his horse down the lane. When he reached the road, she turned her attention to the new gold chain on her wrist. It glimmered in the afternoon sun. A quiet joy entered her heart. The first joy she'd felt since that terrible Sunday morning when Dad left them. She may have lost him, but now she had Andrew. He wouldn't walk out of her life again. Not unless she told him to. They'd spent enough time together over the past two years for her to know he was serious this time. Someday Tillie would be living in town as Mrs. Carter. A smile crossed her face.

But before that time came, she still had one giant she must deal with. The barn. Logan was right. She needed to face her losses. The assurance of a future with Andrew made this task a little easier.

Tillie put on her coat. She left the house and trudged across the snowy yard. In the lane, she paused and stared at the hip roof, the red siding, the long row of windows. *Oh, Dad, I still miss you. I wish you were here to see my new bracelet. You'd be so happy for me.*

Logan flashed in a window. Tillie willed her shaky legs to carry her to the barn's entrance. Her fingers went cold as she tugged on the large, metal ring and eased the door open. The hummed melody of *Silent Night* floated on the air. Fighting the longing to hide, she followed the melody to the last stanchion on the left side of the barn.

Bent over on the stool, Logan rhythmically squeezed milk into the pail nestled in the straw.

She waited.

The humming ended. Logan stood, grabbed the pail and the stool, and turned to the aisle. "Tillie!" He bumped into her.

"You were right."

His brow furrowed. "Right about what?"

"Moving on." She pulled her hands from her pockets.

Logan nodded. Moisture made his eyes shine.

Tillie swallowed away her own tears.

"It's been a hard day, hasn't it?" Logan asked, his voice low.

She nodded. "I still miss him."

"So do I." Logan set the pail and the stool down. He opened his arms to her.

Tillie leaned on him, soaking in comfort. "Karen and I were talking on Monday. She reminded me how special you are." Tillie pulled back and glanced up at him. "You gave up everything to come home and take care of Mama and me."

Logan blinked. A drop of moisture rested between his blond eyelashes. Fine lines appeared at the corners of his mouth.

"I just want to say thanks. I haven't been very easy to live with, but I think it'll be better now." She clutched his coat sleeves.

He didn't say anything, only continued to gaze at her out of tear-dampened eyes.

"Did you see Andrew?" she asked him.

"I did."

"He gave me this." She pulled back her sleeve.

Logan examined the bracelet. A smile tugged at a corner of his mouth. "Beautiful. We'll have to see what the future holds for you. Stay until I finish. I'll walk you to the house."

CHAPTER THIRTY-FOUR

*K*aren rose from her bed refreshed from a nap. She caught a glimpse of the barnyard below her window. Tillie and Logan exited the barn. He carried a pail of milk. Tillie smiled. They appeared to be sharing an entertaining conversation. Karen shook her head while a smile stretched her lips. Tillie had made strides over the past few days. She no longer harbored bitterness. Karen delighted in watching Tillie's whole character freed from the burden she'd carried for so long.

She straightened her skirt and re-pinned her hair. The evening meal would arrive soon. She should appear at the table without wrinkles in her dress or strands of hair hanging loose. This might be a farm, but propriety and decorum still applied.

Her hair arranged satisfactorily, Karen took the stairs to the kitchen.

Sandy set the table with a platter of ham, thick slices of bread, and slabs of cheese. A dish of cooked apples sat near Logan's end of the table. He and Tillie took turns at the wash basin. Karen claimed her chair at the table and waited for the others to join her.

After Logan said the prayer and the meal had started, Sandy turned to Tillie. "I'm dying of curiosity. What happened around here while Logan and I were gone? Why are you girls suddenly getting along now?"

Tillie smiled at Karen across the table. "Do you want to tell her?"

Karen shook her head. "I think you should."

"We got in a fight." Tillie announced matter-of-fact while she laid a slice of ham on her bread.

"Really. Anyone get hurt?"

"No. Some frosting got smeared on the floor, but we cleaned that up." Tillie reached for a piece of cheese.

"Why did you fight?"

"I've been so jealous of Karen. She has beautiful clothes and she comes from the city. But I discovered a true friend in her while we stayed home together."

Sandy's gaze met Logan's, a hint of relief present in her eyes.

"Mama, did you know that Karen lost her father too?"

"I didn't."

"She told me all about it. We have so much in common now." Tillie spooned apples onto her plate. "Karen, you should tell Mama and Logan the things you told me."

Karen swallowed the bite of food in her mouth and set her sandwich down. "My father died after I graduated from high school. He'd been sick for a long time. He worked as a salesman for Uncle Henry's steel company. After my father's death, my sister got married, but Mother and I didn't know where we would go or how we were going to live. That's when my mother's brother asked us to come live with him." Karen gulped as memory after painful memory rolled over her. "Father had been a pastor when Julia and I were little."

"What happened?" Sandy's concerned voice poked a hole in the dam shoring up the past. Venturing into deep waters she hadn't even shared with Tillie, Karen allowed everything to gush.

"Father got arrested for embezzlement. The offering had to wait until Mondays to be deposited and the leader of a local gang attempted to rob the church, but Father caught him in time to prevent it. The police came, but the gang leader got away. After this, the gang grew more dangerous in their attempts to get the church's money. Father didn't want to put his wife and two small daughters in danger, so he never brought the money home with him. He gave in when threats were made on his life and offered to give the gang a certain percentage each week if they would leave him and the church building alone.

"But he'd kept some money for himself. The local gang hadn't received all of the funds Father took from the offering. He started gambling. He finally got caught when someone he owed visited our house. Father couldn't pay so the man had him investigated." Karen pushed the food around on her plate recalling the day the police came to their house.

"Did he go to jail?" Tillie asked.

"Yes, but Uncle Henry paid the bail. Then he offered Father a job as a salesman. To give him a chance to earn a living and receive a steady income, but I think it was more to keep an eye on him." She could still see the notice in the paper where all of their names had been listed. Mother had longed to move away wishing to put the past behind her as much as Karen did. Julia's marriage to an upstanding lawyer helped. Taking Uncle Henry's surname and changing all of her and Mother's legal documents had completed the break with scandal. To the outside world, Karen's relationship to her notorious father no longer existed. But on the inside, Karen had carried those horrible memories for years.

"I'm grateful for the way the Lord protected you." Sandy reached over and patted her arm. "He'll never stop loving you and caring for you."

The truth of those words drained the shame from Karen's heart that she'd felt over her father's misdeeds for so long. Sandy gave her a wonderful gift. This Christmas might turn out better than she thought.

KAREN RECLINED on the love seat with one of Logan's new books. He sat in the rocking chair nearby with another one. Tillie focused on needlework in her place on the couch near the lamp. Sandy sat in the chair near the fireplace, a quilt covering her lap. The glowing fire Logan built after supper still radiated warmth.

Her gaze swung over to Logan where he sat reading. The bib overalls had stayed in the drawer today. He'd actually dressed up, wearing a pair of brown trousers and the white shirt Karen had given him after she so disgracefully ruined his other one. The memory brought with it a wave of guilt followed by a desire to laugh. She chuckled under her breath.

Logan looked up. "What's so funny?"

"I was thinking about your dress shirt I ruined this fall when I was learning how to do housework."

He laid his open book over one knee, stretched out both arms, and grinned at her. "Two cuffs."

Karen laughed harder. "You were a good sport to wear that mud-stained shirt to church the next week. And then when I burned the sleeve, you still didn't get mad at me."

Logan picked up his book again, a solemn expression in his eyes. "I never felt like getting mad at you."

If he hadn't felt anger, then Karen wished he would've at least felt like giving her a Christmas gift. The empty space beneath the tree still mystified her.

Sandy roused. She shifted her position to look at them. "Can't an old person get any rest around here?" She smiled at her son and then at Karen.

"Sorry, Mama." Logan grinned at her not looking very sorry.

"It's late anyway. I'm headed upstairs. Probably should've done that instead of sleeping by the fire." Sandy stood and folded up the quilt. She walked over to Logan. "Good night, dear. I had a good day."

He kissed her cheek. "I'm glad. I did too."

Logan returned to his book. Karen wished to do the same, but she abandoned the love seat for the chair near the warm fire.

The flames diminished to glowing embers.

"It's getting too dark to see my stitches," Tillie said. "I think I'll go to bed too." She put her embroidery cloth away in a bag near the couch and crossed the room to Karen. She gave her a hug and then went to Logan.

Her footsteps thumped on the hard wood floor of the dining room. The stairs creaked. A door shut somewhere above Karen's head.

Logan came over to the fireplace. Instead of dousing it with water to extinguish the flames, he threw on another log, large enough to provide several hours of light.

Sparks flew away from the chunk of wood when it crashed on top of the others. Karen watched the flames lick up around it until a blaze ignited.

Still Logan stood near.

Her gaze ventured off of the flames and onto his face. "Planning to stay up late?"

"I'll stay up as long as I need to." The solicitous tone in his voice sent tingles over her shoulders. "Come with me." He grasped her hands, drew her out of the chair, and led her to the settee on the other side of the fireplace.

Karen settled in at the end nearest the fire.

"Remember me saying we needed to talk?" Logan sat down next to her.

"I do."

"Something happened to me while I was gone." He picked up one of her hands and held it. "Friday afternoon when I stood before the congregation at that wedding, I realized how deeply I love you."

The parlor tilted off to the side.

Logan looked into her eyes. "Karen, I don't want to try anymore to live my life without you in it. I need you."

The room needed to go back to the way it should be. She was getting dizzy.

"I want to ask you to forgive me for the things I've said and the ways I've hurt you. I'm sorry." His thumb rubbed a small circle on the top of her hand. "You probably noticed that you had no gift from me under the tree this afternoon."

"I did notice. It hurt me."

Logan reached into his shirt pocket. "I got you a gift, but it's been in my pocket. Not under the tree."

She frowned at him, struggling to pick up his meaning.

He let go of her hand, turned it over, and laid a smooth object in her palm.

Her gaze landed on the small piece of metal, gold and shiny in the firelight. A ring, studded with one large diamond and two smaller ones lay in her hand. "An engagement ring?" Her gaze flew to his face.

He nodded.

She studied it as the diamonds flickered bits of light from the flames. "Oh, Logan. It's beautiful. I never dreamed. I mean, when you left here, you were determined to stay single. You told me so yourself."

"I know."

"And now you give me this. I don't know what to say."

"Let me help you." Logan left the couch and knelt before her. "Karen, I've come to realize how much you mean to me. I believe making you a part of my life and my ministry would make the Lord very happy." He picked up her free hand. "Would you agree to become my wife?"

Karen nodded. She would have spoken, but tears rolled down her face, and more clogged her voice. "Yes, Logan. You know I will."

Logan joined her on the couch. After slipping the band onto her finger, he cupped her chin and sealed her answer with his kiss.

The swirling room came to a halt, but a traumatic idea came to mind. The tilt of the room and the dizziness in her head grew worse than the first time. "Logan, we have a problem."

"What is it?"

"Can't you see it?" This man was a preacher, for pity's sake.

He shook his head.

Karen lowered her voice to a whisper as though she were a school girl who didn't want the teacher to discover her misbehaving. "I can't wear your ring if I live in your house."

Laughter rolled from his mouth.

"Shh!" If she didn't quiet him, he'd wake his mother and sister. She certainly did not want them in on this discussion.

"I have a plan." He announced it with absolute confidence.

"Why didn't you say so?"

"I got too busy kissing." A smirk covered his face in spite of the red staining his cheeks.

Karen shoved him.

"Seriously. I've thought this through. Later this week, when the Bettens return home, I'm going to visit with Pete and see if you can move in with them for the second semester. What do you think?"

"I like it."

"Good." Logan grinned. "Pete may take all the credit for how this turned out, but I'll let him believe it."

Karen laughed, although quietly.

"I'll have the opportunity to properly court you, and you'll get some experience living in a parsonage." Logan winked at her. "The perfect arrangement."

Karen slid the ring off her finger. "Until then, I'll just keep this in my room. I won't wear it until I am settled at the Bettens and have been for some time." She held the ring up between them.

"Whatever you say. I'm just glad you accepted it. And next

spring, when I have Dad's name cleared with the bank, I'm returning to Oswell City." He gave her a knowing look. "I'd be honored to have you there with me, and not as my Sunday assistant or as my boarder."

Karen's heart couldn't decide if it should burst with happiness or race with excitement. In that moment, it threatened to do both.

"Do you know how many gifts you've given to me and my family, Karen?" Logan stood, drawing Karen up with him.

She shook her head, not entirely sure what he was talking about.

"You got through to Tillie when Mama and I could not. She's a new creature, thanks to you."

Her gaze faltered at the praise. "It's God's doing."

"And the wonders you've worked in my heart, when I thought my desolate fate had already been decided." Logan shook his head like a drowning man who'd been thrown a lifeline. "I'm forever grateful."

"Again, it's God's work, not mine."

"Then perhaps you are the gift." Logan's expression turned serious. His eyes darkened.

She knew what was coming.

He helped her set another record. Four times. Kissed.

ALSO FROM MANTLE ROCK PUBLISHING

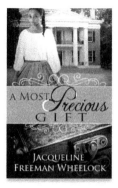
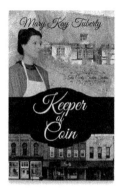
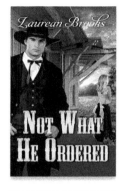

If you enjoy historical romance, Mantle Rock Publishing has many titles
waiting for your enjoyment.

CPSIA information can be obtained
at www.ICGtesting.com
Printed in the USA
FFHW02n0757251018
48966615-53219FF